A Book Of

BUSINESS STATISTICS

For B. Com. – II : Semester – III
As Per Solapur University's Revised Syllabus
Effective from June 2014

Prof. P. G. DIXIT

M.Sc., M.Phil. (Stats.)
Head of Statistics Department,
Modern College, Pune - 5.

NIRALI ™
PRAKASHAN
ADVANCEMENT OF KNOWLEDGE

N0485

(B.Com. II) Sem. – III : BUSINESS STATISTICS   **ISBN 978-93-5164-178-0**

First Edition   :   July 2014

©   :   **Authors**

Published By :

NIRALI PRAKASHAN
Abhyudaya Pragati, 1312, Shivaji Nagar,
Off J.M. Road, PUNE – 411005
Tel - (020) 25512336/37/39, Fax - (020) 25511379
Email : niralipune@pragationline.com

DISTRIBUTION CENTRES
PUNE

Nirali Prakashan
119, Budhwar Peth, Jogeshwari Mandir Lane
Pune 411002, Maharashtra
Tel : (020) 2445 2044, 66022708, Fax : (020) 2445 1538
Email : bookorder@pragationline.com

Nirali Prakashan
S. No. 28/27, Dhyari,
Near Pari Company, Pune 411041
Tel : (022) 24690371
Email : dhyari@pragationline.com
bookorder@pragationline.com

MUMBAI
Nirali Prakashan
385, S.V.P. Road, Rasdhara Co-op. Hsg. Society Ltd.,
Girgaum, Mumbai 400004, Maharashtra
Tel : (022) 2385 6339 / 2386 9976, Fax : (022) 2386 9976
Email : niralimumbai@pragationline.com

DISTRIBUTION BRANCHES

NAGPUR
Pratibha Book Distributors
Above Maratha Mandir, Shop No. 3, First Floor,
Rani Jhanshi Square, Sitabuldi, Nagpur 440012,
Maharashtra, Tel : (0712) 254 7129

JALGAON
Nirali Prakashan
34, V. V. Golani Market, Navi Peth, Jalgaon 425001,
Maharashtra, Tel : (0257) 222 0395
Mob : 94234 91860

BENGALURU
Pragati Book House
House No. 1, Sanjeevappa Lane, Avenue Road Cross,
Opp. Rice Church, Bengaluru – 560002.
Tel : (080) 64513344, 64513355,
Mob : 9880582331, 9845021552
Email:bharatsavla@yahoo.com

KOLHAPUR
Nirali Prakashan
New Mahadvar Road,
Kedar Plaza, 1st Floor Opp. IDBI Bank
Kolhapur 416 012, Maharashtra. Mob : 9850046155

CHENNAI
Pragati Books
9/1, Montieth Road, Behind Taas Mahal, Egmore,
Chennai 600008 Tamil Nadu, Tel : (044) 6518 3535,
Mob : 94440 01782 / 98450 21552 / 98805 82331, Email : bharatsavla@yahoo.com

RETAIL OUTLETS
PUNE

Pragati Book Centre
157, Budhwar Peth, Opp. Ratan Talkies,
Pune 411002, Maharashtra
Tel : (020) 2445 8887 / 6602 2707, Fax : (020) 2445 8887

Pragati Book Centre
Amber Chamber, 28/A, Budhwar Peth,
Appa Balwant Chowk, Pune : 411002, Maharashtra,
Tel : (020) 20240335 / 66281669
Email : pbcpune@pragationline.com

Pragati Book Centre
676/B, Budhwar Peth, Opp. Jogeshwari Mandir,
Pune 411002, Maharashtra
Tel : (020) 6601 7784 / 6602 0855

PBC Book Sellers & Stationers
152, Budhwar Peth, Pune 411002, Maharashtra
Tel : (020) 2445 2254 / 6609 2463

MUMBAI
Pragati Book Corner
Indira Niwas, 111 - A, Bhavani Shankar Road, Dadar (W), Mumbai 400028, Maharashtra
Tel : (022) 2422 3526 / 6662 5254, Email : pbcmumbai@pragationline.com

www.pragationline.com   info@pragationline.com

Statistical Thinking will one
day be necessary for effective
citizenship as the ability to
read and write

- H.G. Wells

Preface ...

I am very happy to place this book is in the hands of B.Com. – II : Semester - III students and professors of Solapur University. The overwhelming response for last 24 years due to the readers has encoureged us every time. This book is written according to new syllabus which comes in force from the academic year 2014. Although it is a first book for Solapur University. Author has published 65 text books for various classes.

This book will also partly serve the purpose of students preparing for preliminary and intermediate examinations of C.A. and I.C.W.A. While writing the book we have borne in mind that majority of the students have not offered mathematics at XI and XII commerce, so that they are studying mathematics after a break of two years.

Simplicity is a strength of the book, so readers will be interested in studying.

In the present edition, we have simplified the numerical problems and further classified them subtopicwise. It will help all sorts of students from beginers to expert.

We are extremely thankful to our publisher Shri. D. K. Furia, Shri. Jignesh Furia, and staff of Nirali Prakashan especially Mr. Santosh Bare, Mrs. Anagha Kaware, Mrs. Anjali Mulye for bringing out this book.

Suggestions for further improvement of the book will be appreciated and thankfully acknowledged. I whish with this book students will perform well.

Authors

Syllabus ...

1. INTRODUCTION TO STATISTICS (20)

Introduction : Meaning and Scope, Stages of statistical investigation, Methods of data collection, Census and Sampling methods, advantages of sampling methods, Concepts of simple random sampling and Stratified random sampling.

Analysis of Uni-variate Data : Concept of classification and Tabulation, Construction of frequency distribution, Relative and Cumulative frequency distribution.

Graphical and Diagrammatic Representation : Construction of histogram, Frequency polygon, Ogive curves, Pie chart and pyramids.

2. MEASURES OF CENTRAL TENDENCY (15)

Concept of central tendency and Requirements of good measures of central tendency, Mean, Median, Mode and their comparison. Quartiles, Properties of arithmetic mean (without proof). Numerical examples.

3. MEASURES OF DISPERSION (15)

Concept of Dispersion, Requirements of good measures of dispersion, Absolute and Relative measures of dispersion. Range, Quartile deviation, Standard deviation, Mean deviation about mean and their relative measures. Variance, Coefficient of variation, Properties of standard deviation (without proof). Numerical examples.

4. CORRELATION AND REGRESSION (10)

Correlation : Concept, Types of correlation, Scatter diagram, Measures of correlation : (i) Karl Pearson's correlation coefficient (Ungrouped data). Interpretation of $r = +1$, $r = -1$ and $r = 0$. (ii) Spearman's rank correlation coefficient.

Regression : Meaning, Linear regression, Equations of regression lines. Least square method (Linear equation). Relation between correlation coefficient and regression coefficients. Numerical examples.

Contents ...

•••

Chapter 1 ...

Population and Sample

Contents ...

Key Words :

Uses of statistics, Scope of Statistics, Limitations of Statistics, Sample, Population, SRSWOR, SRSWR, Stratified Sampling, Random Sampling.

Objectives :

In this chapter the various aspects of statistics, uses, scope and applications in various fields are discussed. The concept of statistical population and sample is also introduced. Random sample and methods of drawing sample are introduced.

1.1 Introduction

It is believed that Statistics is in use from the time when man began to count and measure. In ancient days kings used to maintain records of land, agricultural yield, wealth, taxes, live stock, soldiers, weapons, deaths and births etc. There are references that Hebrews conducted population census. In ancient days Maurya kings, King Ashoka, Gupta kings had collected Statistics. Kautilya's Arthashastra mentions that the statistics of population, land etc. were collected from time to time. Emperor Akbar gave details of population, land, agriculture etc. in his publication Ain-i-Akbari.

It is considered that the word Statistics seems to be derived from the Italian word 'statista' or the Greek word 'statistika'. Both the words have the same meaning 'political states'.

The word statistics carries several meanings. Many times statistics is considered as statistical data, which contains numerical information of a characteristic under study. *For example :* Statistics of a batsman, population statistics etc.

Statistics or statistical methods is treated as a branch of science which deals with **(i) collection, (ii) presentation, (iii) analysis and (iv) interpretation of data.**

Wherever data are generated, the use of statistics becomes inevitable. Statistics performs number of functions such as (i) presentation of facts and figures. This enables to get an overall idea about the phenomenon. (ii) forecasting, (iii) planning, (iv) controlling, (v) exploring etc.

Statistics plays a role in every walk of life, right from simple situation such as finding average marks in examination to a very complex phenomenon such as rainfall prediction or measuring changes in prices.

Statistics helps in decision-making whenever phenomenon contains uncertainities. LIC, banks, defence department, government agencies, industries, business, trade etc. make use of statistics in planning, forecasting, controlling, decision-making. Index numbers are widely used in almost all fields such as economics industry business, import, export etc. Now-a-days ISO 9000 makes use of statistical tools for standardising the quality of industrial production.

1.2 Definition

Statistics can be defined as the science of collection, presentation, analysis and interpretation of data.

Number of statisticians had made an attempt to define statistics. They used statistics for different purpose, with a different view-point. Accordingly they defined statistics emphasizing their view point. Two definitions are given below.

(a) Webster's Definition : Webster defines statistics as "the classified facts representing the conditions of people in the state, especially those facts which can be stated in a table or tables of numbers or in any tabular or classified arrangement."

The above definition gives importance to presentation of facts and figures. Remaining aspects of statistics are not considered in this definition.

(b) Horace Secrist's Definition : Secrist defines statistics as follows : 'By statistics we mean aggregates of facts affected to a marked extent by multiplicity of causes numerically expressed, enumerated or estimated according to resonable standards of accuracy, collected in a systematic manner for a predetermined purpose and placed in relation to each other.

The above definition takes into account almost all functions and aspects of statistics. It covers the fair important aspects viz. (i) collection, (ii) presentation, (iii) analysis and (iv) interpretation of data.

1.3 Importance of Statistics

We know that many phenomena in nature and activities, experiments are subject to measurements, moreover variation in different types of characteristics is inevitable. For example, income of a family, height of a person, sales of a company, electricity consumption of a city etc. This produces voluminous data. It becomes difficult to comprehend. This forces the use of statistical methods. Thus statistics is important from the following view points.

(i)   Statistical methods enable to condense the data. It facilitates several functions apart from summerisation.

(ii)   Statistical methods give tools of comparison.

(iii)   Estimation, prediction is also possible using statistical tools.

(iv)   We can get idea about the shape, spread, symmetry of the data.

(v)   Inter-relation between two or more variables can be measured using statistical techniques.

(iv)   Statistical methods help in planning, controlling, decision-making etc.

(vii)   The use of statistical methods is important because considerable amount of time, money, manpower can be saved.

(viii) Uncertainities can be reduced to get reliable results.

(ix)   Statistical methods give systematic methods of data collection and investigation.

Thus statistics reveals several aspects of phenomena.

H. G. Wells expresses the importance and need of statistics in the following words.

"Statistical thinking will one day be necessary for effective citizenship as the ability to read and write".

1.4 Steps in Statistical Investigation

(a)   Defining a problem : The aim of the project is to study the situation, collect the data, analyse and draw conclusions. Make the predictions. Any problem to be studied using statistical methods has to be formulated first. For example, whether India is progressing is to be studied. First of all we need decide which type of progress is expected viz. agriculture, industry, transport, education, import export, trade, mineral production, IT sector, health, defence, research, tourism, foreign investments, space research.

If we decide to study whether the health conditions in India are improving are not. We need to decide the indicators of health, for example : Average life expectancy, infant mortality rate, availability of doctors and medical facilities in proportion to population. Control over epidemics, immunisation programs.

If the problem is defined clearly one can decide which type of data are required to be collected.

(b)   Collection of data : Data to be collected is related to the problem of study. For example, health and hygiene survey, socio-economic survey, computations of GDP, computations of rate of inflation. Data are to be collected using different methods

(i)   designing a questionnaire or schedule

(ii)   investigation taking interviews of relevant authorities

(iii)   using secondary sources of data.

Data validation : It is always required to scan the collected data for validation. The errors if any are corrected. For example, the number of students passed in examination should be less than those are appeared.

(c) Presenting or organising data : We classify and tabulate data collected. We use graphical tools to present the data to get an idea about the interrelation between different factors.

(d) Analysis of data : Using different statistical methods, analysis is carried out. Now-a-days there are several statistical softwares available as per requirement.

Forecasting, projection, interpolation, testing of hypotheses, analysis of variance are some popularly used statistical tools.

(e) Interpretation and Reports : Based on the analysis, the findings, conclusions are reported to the concerned party. The limitations of survey are also mentioned. Further scope, sources of information, bibliography would also be supplimented with the report if needed.

1.5 Scope and Applications of Statistics

The tools and techniques given by statistical methods are used in almost all fields at several phases. Because of diversified applications of statistics, an exhaustive list of fields is difficult to prepare. However, some of them are stated below. We find use of statistics indispensable in the agriculture, business, commerce, demography, economics, education, government agencies, industries, social sciences, biological sciences, medical sciences, management sciences etc. We discuss briefly the scope of statistics in some of the above stated fields.

(a) Statistics in industry : Industry makes use of statistics at several places such as administration, planning, production, growth and development. In many industries 'Statistical Quality Control' division is separately operating. Mainly, whether manufactured goods possess a desirable standard or not is examined using various control charts. These inspections are done at the time of production. On-line process capability study is conducted to set-up the machines to give desired standards. Moreover purchased goods or semifinished goods are inspected using acceptance sampling plans of various types. Now-a-days, ISO 9000 makes use of Statistics to a large extent. Apart from this in some industries the technique known as designs of experiment is also used. Newly installed machinery is tested for its performance using statistical methods. Sampling is required to be used because of its several advantages. Multiple regression planes are used for forecasting, when several factors are interlinked. Efficiency measurement, index number of production, work sampling etc. are very much useful for administration and planning department.

(b) Statistics and Economics : In the field of economics, huge amount of data are needed to be processed and interpreted. Statistics is very much helpful in this field. In order to collect data, various statistical methods of investigations are used. Many a times questionnaires are drafted. A proper representative of a group is selected using sampling methods. Statistical methods are used in this activity to get reliable results. Estimation of national income, per capita income, poverty line, industrial production etc. is done using statistical techniques. Probability distribution of income can be useful in various economic activities. A tool known as index number developed in Statistics is used every now and then in economics. It performs number of functions. It measures average increase in prices, production, income, volume of import, export etc. Index numbers are called as economic barrometers. Index numbers are used in determining real income, deflation, cost of living index numbers. To measure the changes in prices of shares in stock market index number provides the best tool. Several interlinked activities in economics can be studied. For example, (i) the relation between prices and supply (ii) the relation between demand and prices (iii) the relation between sales and profit.

Demand analysis, time series analysis techniques are mainly developed to study economics. Those are the gifts given by statistics.

Richard Lipsey says " The role of statistical analysis is two fold. First, we wish to use observations from the real world to test our theories. Second, we wish to use such observations to give us measures of the quantitative relations between economic variables.

(c) Statistics and Management Sciences : Most of the managerial functions make use of statistics. For efficient working of various sections of management such as sales, production, marketing statistical method are used. Different statistical tools such as forecasting, tests of significance, index numbers, time series analysis, statistical quality control, estimation play vital role in management activities. Apart from this, various optimisation techniques known as linear programming, transportation techniques, job assignment problems, sequencing, CPM and PERT, replacement problems, inventory control are also useful.

Portfolio management makes use of regression analysis. The regression coefficient called beta index in portfolio is used in decision-making. Risk measurement is done using standard deviations, covariance. Various statistical techniques are used in decision-making.

(d) Statistics and Social Sciences : Bowley says "Statistics is the science of measurement of social organism, regarded as a whole in all its manifestation". Research in social sciences need questionnaire. Further analysis is required to be done using statistical tools. In social sciences we need to test association between two variables such as (i) education and criminality (ii) education and marriage adjustment score (iii) sex and education (iv) richness and criminality etc.

1.6 Population and Sample

In order to study a group of large number of items we require to draw sample. We use technique of sampling several times in every day life. *For example,* while purchasing food grains we inspect only handful of grains and draw conclusion about the whole sack. Similarly while examining blood of an individual, few drops are enough for diagnosis. Quality of milk is tested with the help of a small quantity of milk taken out of can, instead of entire milk in the can. Sampling is a well accepted means of collecting information. Moreover it is believed to be scientific and objective procedure of selecting items. Sampling plays very important role in statistical inference.

Population : In the technical language of statistics the word population is used in somewhat a wider sense. It does not mean only a human population. For example, (i) In the study of industrial development, all the industries under consideration is the population. (ii) In the study of socio-economic conditions of a particular village, all families or houses in the village will be a population. (iii) In the study of agricultural yield, all the cultivated farms together will be a population. (iv) In titration experiment solution in beaker is a population. Thus population may be a group of employees, collection of books, total industrial production, a group of persons suffering from a particular disease, collection of explosives, group of students etc.

We give a specific definition below :

Definition : An aggregate of objects or individuals under study is called *population or universe.*

Population may contain finite or infinite elements. Accordingly, it is called as *finite* or *infinite* population.

Statistical Population : We have defined population as an aggregate of objects or individuals; however, many a times we record some quantitative or qualitative characteristic of each member in the population. These observations (or data) are collectively called as *statistical population.* Thus in the further study we will be interested in 'statistical population'.

In order to study the population, one of the ways is to collect information about each and every element in the population. This method is called as *census* or *complete enumeration.*

After every ten years 'population census' of India is conducted. In this census, information regarding every individual is collected.

Limitations of census method : (1) Census method provides reliable results; but due to voluminous work, it is expensive and time consuming. It requires a large amount of manpower.

(2) There are some situations where census is possible but impracticable. For example, testing blood of an individual. In this case, entire blood cannot be tested. Thus census cannot be used here. Similarly in testing explosives, testing of average life of bulb produced in a lot, testing strength of construction material, census method cannot be used.

(3) If the population is infinite, census cannot be used.

Sampling : In order to overcome the limitations of census, sampling is used. In this case, some representative items are selected from the population, so that all important characteristics of population are covered in the items of this group. Such a group is called a sample and the method of selecting such a group is called as sampling method.

Definition : Any part of population under study is called a *sample*.

Illustrations : (i) While purchasing food grains, we inspect only a handful of grains and draw conclusions about the quality of the whole lot. In this case, handful of grains is a sample and the whole lot is a population.

(ii) While examining blood of an individual, a few drops are taken out of human body for diagnosis. These drops form a sample whereas entire blood in the body is a population. In this case, conclusions based on sample are accepted for population without any doubt as far as the method is concerned. In this case, census is impracticable. Sampling method is appealing in such situations.

(iii) For testing quality of milk, a small quantity of milk is tested instead of entire bulk.

(iv) A housewife confirms whether the food is properly cooked or not with the help of few particles taken out of the container. Clearly, the food in the container is a population, whereas food taken out of container for inspection is a sample.

Note that (a) Sampling is a well accepted means of collecting information. (b) It is believed to be scientific and objective procedure of selecting items. Thus, sampling plays important role in further statistical analysis.

As the sampling methods are used to study population, the samples should be chosen carefully. A natural requirement would be that the sample should be representative of concerned population. There are several methods of sampling in practice. We shall deal with some of these in later sections.

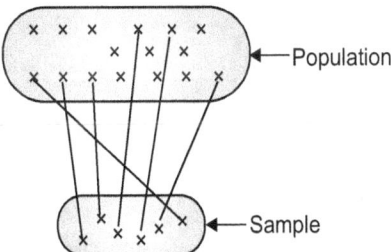

Fig. 1.1 : Nature of Sample

Advantages of Sampling Over Census :

1. **Reduced Time :** As compared to census, sample consists of a less number of elements. Hence there is a considerable reduction in processing time. The results can be obtained quickly due to time saved in data collection and further analysis.

2. **Reduced Cost :** There is reduction in cost, both in terms of time and manpower. In sampling, only a part of population is under consideration. Therefore expenses incurred in collection of data and its analysis are always less than those in census. Thus sampling is economical.

3.   Greater Accuracy : As compared to census, only limited number of elements are to be processed. Therefore, sophisticated machinery, well-trained staff can be used and accuracy can be increased. Due to the reduced volume of work, it can be completed efficiently and without fatigue. Moreover, elements will be free from non-sampling errors such as incompleteness of returns, biases due to interviews, inaccurate returns etc.

4.   Greater Scope : (a) If population is infinite or too large or cost per unit is too high, census is impracticable. (b) If testing is destructive i.e. element gets destroyed in the analysis, sampling is the only alternative available to us; for example, testing the life of a bulb, testing strength of building construction material, testing fat percentage of milk, testing human blood etc. (c) Suppose a company manufactures a remedial medicine for a certain disease. All the patients suffering from the particular disease may not be ready to try the newly manufactured medicine. In this case sampling has larger scope than census.

Sampling Unit : Members or elements of population are called sampling units. In the sampling process, population is divided into small units which are called the sampling units. For example, in a socio-economic survey, a family is a sampling unit; whereas in a health survey, an individual will be a sampling unit. Sampling units must be distinct and unambiguous in nature. Sampling units together must cover the entire population. In other words, sampling unit is the smallest part of the population which cannot be further subdivided for the said purpose.

Sampling Frame : It is an exhaustive list of all members or elements of population. Sampling frame gives guidelines to cover the entire population. The frame should be up-do-date and suitable for the purpose of survey or enquiry. In a socio-economic survey, frame may be determined from the records at grampanchayat or ration cards. To prepare a good frame is a difficult job. Defective frame does affect the result of the survey.

Samples can be selected in two ways :

(i)   Deliberate selection of items or non-random sampling : In this method investigator selects elements in any manner which is suitable to him. For example, he may select elements on first come first served basis.

This method is unscientific. It may produce unreliable results. There is a likelihood of a partial view in this method. The figures collected in this way do not obey statistical laws or laws of probability. Hence, such data will not be useful for further analysis and interpretation. To avoid such problems, another method is used.

(ii)   Random Sampling : In this method, the selection of units in sample is done impartially. Personal or any kind of bias in selection is avoided in random sampling.

Further, it each unit has an equal chance of selection, the sample is called as **simple random sampling.**

Discussion regarding need of randomness and how to achieve it is included in later part.

1. Sample is selected with a view to study the concerned population. Therefore, sample should be so selected that it will represent all important characteristics of the population. This may be achieved if elements in sample are selected at random.

    Thus, sample is a miniature of population.

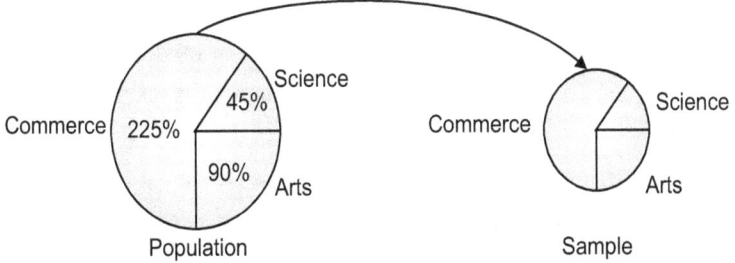

Fig. 1.2

    In sample the components of population should be in more or less same proportion.

2. Sampling units should be independent.

3. Sample should be evenly spread over the population. It can be achieved by dividing population in homogeneous sub-groups and selecting a random sample from each sub-group.

Randomness and its need : It is really required to decide the way in which sampling units are selected. In order to draw a sample of suitable size (which is pre-determined) we need to select the elements from the population one by one. Which element should be chosen ? If we select elements according to our convenience or wish, then personal bias is likely to creep in. Some elements may be deliberately selected in sample. This may result in getting unreliable conclusions.

In a random selection, equal chance of selection is given to each sampling unit. This avoids biased selection, or purposive selection. Moreover, random selection is objective.

Methods of Achieving Randomness :

It is noted above that randomness is quite essential while selecting a sample. It can be achieved by the following two ways :

(a) Lottery method : In this method, we serially number the elements from 1 to N. If possible we put all the elements together or put N different slips bearing numbers 1 to N together. Slips are made of the same size and shape. Thus, the slips represent the elements in population. All these elements or slips are kept in a drum with a handle for proper mixing. With the help of the handle, slips are thoroughly mixed and n elements or slips are drawn one by one.

The 'n' elements corresponding to the numbers on the selected slips will form a sample.

(b) Use of 'random numbers' : Instead of lottery method, use of random numbers is made for selecting a sample just for operational convenience. There are several random number tables available for this purpose. Random number tables are so prepared that each of the digits 0, 1, ..., 9, will have same frequency or chance. The digits are arranged in rows and columns. For selecting two digit numbers, two columns are considered together so that we get numbers from 00 to 99. Similarly for 3 digit numbers, 3 columns are read together which give rise to numbers from 000 to 999.

In order to draw a random sample by this method, we select any page of random numbers and choose the numbers serially in row or column selected at random. If the number selected in this manner is between 1 and N, the corresponding element is taken in the sample. Thus n elements are chosen.

(c) Random Numbers Generated by Computer : Now-a-days random numbers within a required range can be generated on computers. These numbers satisfy the properties of the random numbers, however, they are generated by using some formula, hence those random numbers are called as pseudo random numbers. In most of the computer languages and software packages there are inbuilt functions which generate pseudo random numbers.

1.7 Types of Sampling

A success of sampling method mainly depends upon proper selection of sampling method. Different sampling methods are used in practice. A sampling method which suits to the purpose is selected. Sampling methods are mainly classified into two classes viz. (i) non-random sampling and (ii) random sampling (or probability sampling). In the earlier discussion we have studied the importance of random sampling. We discuss two popularly used random sampling methods. (1) Simple random sampling (2) Stratified random sampling.

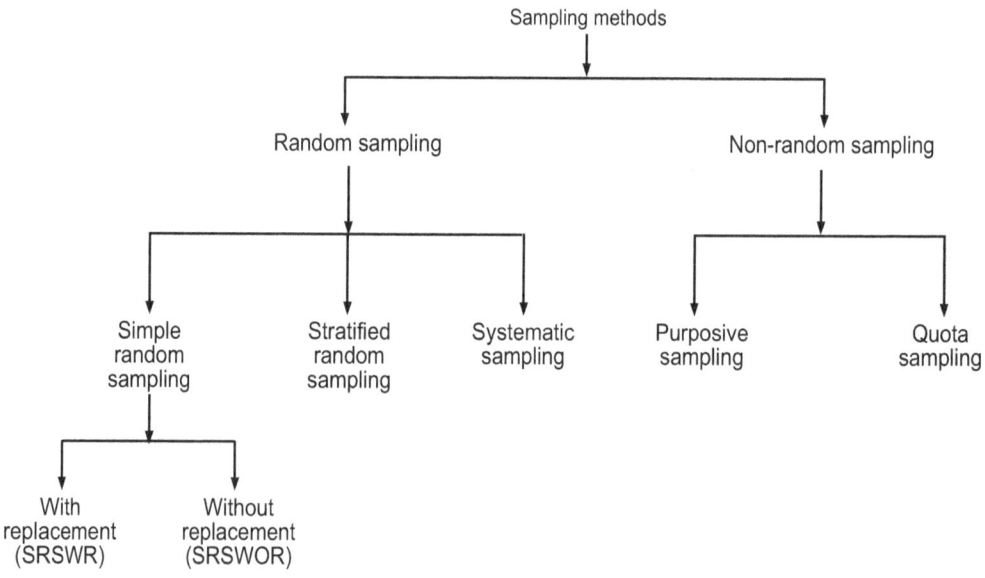

1. Simple Random Sampling (SRS) : It is the easiest and most commonly used method of sampling. In this method each element of population is given same chance of getting selected in the sample. If population consists of N elements then probability of selecting any element at any draw is $\frac{1}{N}$.

Further, there are two types of simple random sampling due to slight difference in procedure of selecting the elements.

(a) Simple Random Sampling with Replacement. (SRSWR) : In this method, first element is selected at random from the population. It is recorded or studied completely and then replaced back in the population. Afterwards second element is selected similarly. This process is continued till a sample of required size is selected. In this method population size remains the same at every draw. This method of sampling is called as *simple random sampling with replacement.*

One of the serious drawbacks of this method is that, the same element may be selected more than once in the sample.

(b) Simple Random Sampling Without Replacement (SRSWOR) : There is another procedure of selecting elements in which, elements are selected at random but those are not replaced back in the population. This method of selecting sample is called as simple random sampling without replacement. In this method population size goes on decreasing at each draw. The drawback of getting the same element selected more than once is overcome in SRSWOR.

Illustrations of Simple Random Sampling :

(i)   Suppose a lot of 500 articles is submitted for inspection to determine the proportion of defective articles one can use SRSWOR.

(ii) In order to conduct a socio-economic survey of certain village we can take SRSWOR and find per capita income of a village.

(iii) In order to test average petrol consumption of a lot of scooter manufactured SRSWOR or SRSWR can be used.

(iv) To find diameter of a rod, generally we take reading at few points on a rod and then find the average of readings. These readings form SRSWOR. This is practised for physical measurements of articles.

(v)   Testing human blood by taking few drops out an individual's body is a SRSWOR.

(vi) In order to find average life of a bulb we take SRSWOR from a manufactured lot.

Simple random sampling is widely used due to its simplicity and convenience. However, it suffers from some drawbacks such as, it may not be proper representative when population is heterogeneous, widely spread etc. Some part of population may not be represented in simple random sample at all. In order to avoid these problems some other sampling methods are in use.

2.   Stratified Random Sampling : If population is not homogeneous, SRS is not very effective. Therefore the entire population is divided into several homogeneous groups called as strata (singular stratum). A simple random sample of a suitable size is selected from each stratum and then combining these sampled observations we can form a sample. The sample thus formed is called as a *stratified random sample*.

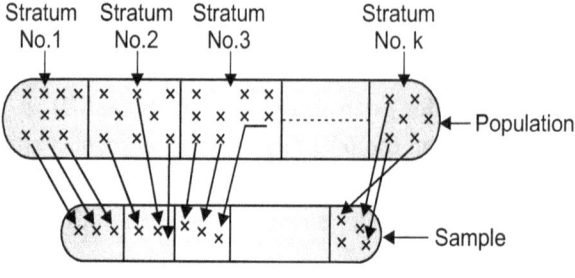

Fig. 1.3

A properly designed stratified random sampling gives better results than simple random sampling. Moreover this method is more suitable from administrative point of view.

Illustrations of Stratified Random Sampling :

(i)   To estimate annual income per family we divide the population into homogeneous groups such as families with yearly income below ₹ 20,000; between ₹ 20,000 - ₹ 50,000; between ₹ 50,000 - ₹ 1 lakh and above ₹ 1 lakh. Afterwards we use stratified random sampling taking above groups as strata.

(ii) Suppose the proportion of defective articles is to be estimated in a manufacturing process. Then we can use stratified random sampling by taking strata as production in the different shifts.

(iii) In order to estimate crop yield we can divide the field under cultivation in plots, which are equally fertile considered as strata.

(iv) To conduct health survey in a college we can use stratified random sampling by considering strata as the faculties or classes or sex etc.

In the above discussion we have seen how stratified random sampling is better than simple random sampling. However, in practice an another simple procedure is adopted which we discuss below :

Case Study

A manager on a highway mall observed that, customers demand for tea and coffee was increasing and it should to be served at the earliest. He was thinking of installing automatic tea and coffee machine. He decided to take customers' opinion. Whether the customer would like the test of tea, coffee prepared on machine. He gathered opinion of customers for a week by using simple random sampling and installed the machine due to favarable opinion about machine made tea and coffee. He also took review for a month by asking the customers at random whether they were satisfied with the tea and coffee. It saved time and gained customers' satisfaction also.

Points to Remember

1. Advantages of sampling are (i) reduction in time, cost, manpower, (iii) increases accuracy, (iii) greater scope.

2. Random sample is preferred to non-random sample because it is proper representative. The result based on random sample are statistically valid. It is unbiased selection procedure.

3. Stratified sampling is used if population is heterogeneous.

Exercise 1.1

A. Theory Questions :

1. Define 'statistics'.

2. Explain the importance of statistics or statistical methods.

3. Describe the scope and utility of statistics in the field of (i) industry, (ii) economics, (iii) management sciences, (iv) social sciences.

4. Mention the application of statistics in the following fields :

   (i) industry, (ii) economics, (iii) management sciences, (iv) social sciences.

5. Explain the terms with illustration : Population, sample, sampling unit, sampling frame.

6. Describe the steps in statistical investigations.

7. Describe the limitations of sampling over census.

8. Describe the advantages of sampling over census.

9. What are the requirements of a good sample ?

10. Explain what is a random sample. Why random sample is preferable ? Explain the various methods of achieving randomness.

11. Explain the procedure of drawing

    (a) SRSWR

    (b) SRSWOR

    (c) Stratified random sample.

12. State the advantages of simple random sampling and drawbacks of the same. Also explain how these drawbacks can be overcome.

13. (a) State the advantages and limitations of stratified sampling.

    (b) State the limitations of stratified sampling.

14. How does SRSWR differ from SRSWOR ?

15. Make critical comparison between

    (a) Sampling and census.

    (b) Stratified random sampling and sample random sampling.

    (c) SRSWR and SRSWOR

    (d) Random sampling and non-random sampling.

16. Give illustrations of each of the following sampling methods :

    (a) SRSWR (b) SRSWOR (c) Stratified sampling.

17. Explain the situation where sampling has larger scope as compared to census.

18. Explain with illustration the terms (i) finite population (ii) infinite population.

Exercise 1.2

B. Numerical Problems :

1. In a population of size N = 6, the observations were 3, 4, 7, 9, 11, 14. Draw all possible SRSWOR of size 2.

2. In a population of size N = 8, the observations were 2, 4, 7, 9, 11, 0, 25, 14. Draw all possible SRSWOR of size 5.

3. If a population consists of 50 items then how many :

    (a) SRSWOR each of size 10 can be selected.

    (b) SRSWR each of size 10 can be selected.

4. Suggest appropriate sampling methods, giving reason, in each of the following situations.

    (a) To estimate the average price of books in a library a sample of 500 books is to be selected from 10,000 books having accession numbers.

    (b) In order to estimate average pocket money spent by the students in a certain college having 3000 students, a sample of 400 students is to be selected.

(c) A market surveyer wants to select a sample of 1000 persons using telephone directory.

(d) To find the daily total requirement of electricity consumption in township containing 3000 houses, 500 offices, 600 shops, 100 factories; a sample of 1000 units is to be selected.

(e) To find the daily total requirement of petrol for two wheelers in a certain city a sample of 5% of two wheelers using RTO registers is to be selected.

(f) In a socio-ecnomic survey a sample of 1000 families is to be selected from a certain village.

(g) To find the average house tax paid by citizens a sample of 500 families is to be selected using municipal corporation records.

(h) To find the average income of employee, in a certain factory employing various categories such as managers, supervisors, clerks, workers.

(i) In an industrial survey a sample of size 50 is to be selected. The area under consideration includes 100 small scale, 200 medium scale and 50 large scale industries.

5. Identify the sampling scheme used in the following situations :

(a) For a exhibition, 5 students are to be selected from each class to work as volunteers.

(b) A teacher distributed hand-outs to the students in the first row only.

(c) An examination question paper contains 10 questions of which any 5 are to be attempted. Ramesh selected questions bearing even serial numbers.

(d) Salesman contactd the first 100 customers visiting the shop for survey.

(e) Suppose there are 10 divisions of F.Y.B.Com. named as A, B, ... J in a certain college. A sample of 10 students from each division is chosen for managing sports activity.

Answers 1.2

1. (3, 4); (3, 7); (3, 9); (3, 11); (3, 14); (4, 7); (4, 9); (4, 11); (4, 14); (7, 9); (7, 11); (7, 14); (9, 11); (9, 14); (11, 14).

2. In all 56 samples are possible.

3. (a) $^{50}C_{10}$ (b) 50^{10}

4.　(a)　stratified　　　　　　　　(b)　stratified

　　(c)　stratified　　　　　　　　(d)　stratified

　　(e)　stratified　　　　　　　　(e)　SRSWOR, stratified

　　(g)　stratified, SRSWOR　　　(h)　stratified

　　(i)　stratified.

5.　(a)　stratified　(b) non-random　(c) stratified

　　(d)　non-random　(e) stratified.

❑❑❑

Chapter 2...

Frequency Distribution & Graphical Presentation and Tabulation

Contents ...

Key Words :

Variable, Attributes, Discrete Variable, Continuous Variable, Raw Data, Primary Data, Secondary Data, Classification, Frequency, Inclusive and Exclusive Method of Classification, Class Limits, Class Boundaries, Class Mark, Open End Class, Relative Frequency, Cumulative Frequency, Histogram, Frequency Polygon, Frequency Curve, Ogive Curves, Pie Diagram, Tabulation.

Objectives :

This chapter explains the first two aspects of statistics viz. collection and presentation of data. Classification is a tool of data condensation. It becomes easier to analyse the data after classification. Graphical representation has several advantages.

2.1 Variables and Attributes

While studying any phenomenon we come across two types of characteristics : (i) constant and (ii) variable. The characteristic which does not change its value (or nature) is considered as **constant**.

For example : Height of a person after 25 years of age, altitude of a certain place from sea level etc. On the other hand there are many characteristics which are qualitative or quantitative in nature and change their values (or nature). *For example :* Examination result of a candidate can be recorded as pass or fail which is a qualitative variable characteristics, whereas we can express a candidate's performance as percentage of marks which is a quantitative variable.

Statistics involves the study of variable characteristics. Hence, we include the related and necessary definitions.

Attribute (April 2009) : A qualitative characteristic like sex, nationality, religion, grade in examination, blood group, beauty, defectiveness of an article produced by a machine is called as *attribute*.

Variable (April 2009) : A quantitative characteristic (which changes its value) like weight of person, examination marks, population of a country, profit of a salesman, is called as *variable*.

It can be clearly noticed that variables can be measured by numbers.

Further the variables can be divided into two categories : (i) discrete and (ii) continuous.

Discrete variable : A variable taking only particular values or isolated values is called as *discrete variable*.   **(Oct. 2006)**

For example : Number of students in a class, number of articles produced by a machine, population of a country, number of workers in a factory etc. are discrete variables. Most of the discrete variables have integral values.

Continuous variable : A variable taking all possible values in a certain range is called as *continuous variable*.   **(Oct. 2006)**

For example : Weight of a person, length of a screw produced by a machine, temperature at a certain place, agricultural production, electricity consumption of a family, speed of a vehicle are the examples of continuous variable.

It is observed that many continuous variables such as marks, income, weight of a person etc. look like discrete variables after the measurement. This is mainly due to the limitations of the measuring instruments. Using better instruments one can have accurate measurement and overcome this difficulty.

The following diagram summarizes the various types of data :

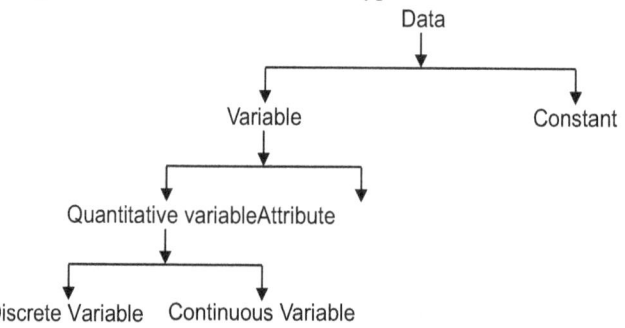

2.2 Classification

In order to study a characteristic or a group of characteristics of any type, the first phase is to collect the data.

Raw data : The unprocessed data in terms of individual observations are called as raw data.

For the sake of further statistical analysis, the data items are arranged in increasing (or decreasing) order. However, if there is a huge amount of observations, merely ordered arrangement is not enough. It does not furnish much useful information nor does it reduce the bulk of data. Data in this form are difficult to comprehend, analyse and interpret.

For example : Income of 5000 individuals is given for analysis.

It becomes quite essential to condense the data in a suitable form. Classification can be used as a tool to condense the data.

Classification : The entire process of making homogeneous and non-overlapping groups of observations according to similarities is called as *classification.*

The groups so formed are called as **class intervals or classes**.

Objectives of Classification : The objectives of classification can be summarised as follows :

1. It condenses the data.

2. It omits unnecessary details.

3. It facilitates the comparison with other data.

For example : In case of classification of income of 5000 individuals, one can find the number of individuals below poverty line or income distribution of two countries can be compared.

4. It reveals prominent features of the data.

For example : We can find the income group in which majority of families lie.

5. It enables further analysis like computation of averages, dispersion etc.

2.3 Frequency Distribution

We proceed to study how the observations are classified and a frequency distribution is formed.

Frequency distribution of continuous variable :

The procedure of classification of continuous variable differs slightly from that of a discrete variable.

Procedure :

1. Find the smallest and the largest observation. Calculate the difference between them. This difference is called as the *range.*

2. Decide the classes, by dividing the range into several intervals. The number of classes be preferably between 7 to 20.

3. Prepare first column of table by entering the class intervals.

4. Classify the observations one by one in the appropriate class by putting tally marks in the second column against the corresponding class. Cross the observation from the original data to avoid double counting.

5. Count the tally marks and enter the number in the third column.

Illustration 1 : *The following are the scores in intelligence test conducted for 80 candidates of a certain class.*

112	77	115	91	137	88	89	71
100	93	64	116	95	95	106	92
84	86	97	124	84	117	97	80
103	114	83	77	94	114	63	61
120	126	98	98	116	108	94	105
108	99	87	96	88	95	73	92
91	129	108	81	82	102	86	111
119	90	109	101	107	75	123	104
106	84	75	99	72	128	114	93
83	82	124	114	130	81	101	91

Prepare the frequency distribution of the data by taking suitable class intervals.

Solution : In the given problem we note that the highest and the lowest observations are respectively 137 and 61. Hence, the range is 137 – 61 = 76. In this case it is suitable to make 8 classes each of width 10. Since the lowest observation is 61, it is convenient to choose the first class as 60 to 69, the next as 70 to 79 and so on. The last class will be 130 to 139. According to the procedure described above, we classify the observations and prepare a table of three columns. First column includes classes, seconds includes tally marks and the third includes frequencies. The first observation is 112, it lies between 110-119, therefore, we put a tally mark to include the observation in this class. Likewise all the observations are classified and the process gives the following table 2.1.

Table 2.1 : Frequency Distribution of Scores of 80 Candidates

Class Intervals	Tally Marks	Frequency
60 – 69	|||	3
70 – 79	ℕ ||	7
80 – 89	ℕ ℕ ℕ		16
90 – 99	ℕ ℕ ℕ ℕ	20
100 – 109	ℕ ℕ ||||	14
110 – 119	ℕ ℕ		11
120 – 129	ℕ ||	7
130 – 139	||	2
Total	–	80

Frequency : The number of observations in a class is called as *frequency* or *class frequency.*

Frequency Distribution : A table containing class intervals along with frequencies is called as *frequency distribution.*

2.4 Methods of Classification

There are two methods of classification : (I) inclusive method (II) exclusive method. We bring out the difference between the two methods.

I. Inclusive Method (April 2011) : In this method the observation equal to upper limit is included in the same class. Therefore, the method is called as *inclusive method.* It can be observed that the upper limit of class is not the same as the lower limit of succeeding class. Therefore, a discontinuity is observed between the classes. *For example,*

Table 2.2

Daily Sales in ₹
2000 – 2999
3000 – 3999
4000 – 4999

II. Exclusive Method : In this method the observation equal to upper limit does not belong to the same class. It is included in the next class. Therefore, the method is called as *exclusive method.* For example, the observation 4000 is included in 4000 – 5000. In other words, the observation equal to upper limit is excluded from the same class.

For example,

Table 2.3

Daily Sales in ₹
2000 – 3000
3000 – 4000
4000 – 5000

In this case upper limit of one class is the lower limit of subsequent class. The classes are observed to be continuous without any gap in between them.

We explain below few more terms related to the frequency distribution.

Class-limits : The two numbers designating the class-interval are called as *class limits.* With reference to table 2.1, the first class interval is 60–69, in this case 60 and 69 are the class limits. The smallest possible observation that can be included in the class is *lower limit* and the largest possible observation that can be included in the class is the *upper limit.* In the above example 60 and 69 are lower and upper limits of the class interval 60–69.

Class boundaries : The class boundaries are the numbers upto which the actual magnitude of observation in the class can extend. The class boundaries are also called as actual limits or extended limits. For the sake of clarity, let us consider the frequency distribution with classes 10–19, 20–29, ... etc. In this case an observation 19.2 will be rounded-off to 19 and placed in 10–19, whereas the observation 19.6 will be rounded-off to 20 and will be placed in 20–29. Therefore, the actual magnitude of the observation in the class 20–29 will be between 19.5–29.5.

Note : If the classes are not continuous then, we need to determine class boundaries. If d is the gap between two classes then

$$\text{lower boundary} = \text{lower limit} - \frac{d}{2}$$

$$\text{upper boundary} = \text{lower limit} + \frac{d}{2}$$

The illustration below will make out the difference between class limits and class boundaries.

Illustration 2 : *Convert the class limits 10-19, 20-29, 30-39 into class boundaries.*

Class limits	Class boundaries
10 – 19	9.5 – 19.5
20 – 29	19.5 – 29.5
30 – 39	29.5 – 39.5

Solution : Note that the gap between the first and second class interval is

$$d = 20 - 19 = 1$$

$$\therefore \quad \text{lower boundary} = \text{lower limit} - \frac{d}{2} = 20 - \frac{1}{2} = 19.5$$

$$\text{upper boundary} = \text{upper limit} + \frac{d}{2} = 29 + \frac{1}{2} = 29.5$$

It can be clearly seen that in case of exclusive method of classification, class limits and class boundaries are same.

Using class-boundaries the classes are made continuous however original frequency associated do not alter.

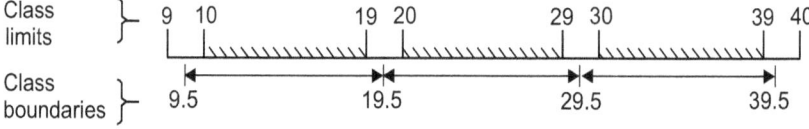

Fig. 2.1

Class-mark or Mid-values : It is the mid-point of class interval and the same can be obtained as follows :

$$\text{Mid-value} = \frac{\text{Upper limit} + \text{Lower limit}}{2}$$

$$= \frac{\text{Upper boundary} + \text{Lower boundary}}{2}$$

Class-width : It is the actual length of the class interval. We can find class width as follows :

$$\text{Class width} = \text{Upper boundary} - \text{Lower boundary}$$

$$= \begin{pmatrix} \text{Lower limit of the} \\ \text{succeeding class} \end{pmatrix} - \begin{pmatrix} \text{Lower limit of the} \\ \text{class under} \\ \text{consideration} \end{pmatrix}$$

$$= \begin{pmatrix} \text{Upper limit of the} \\ \text{class under} \\ \text{consideration} \end{pmatrix} - \begin{pmatrix} \text{Upper limit of the} \\ \text{preceding class} \end{pmatrix}$$

Open end class : A class in which one of the limits is not specified is called an open end class.

For example, in the following frequency distribution there are two open end classes.

Table 2.4

Daily Sales in ₹
below 2000
2000 – 3000
3000 – 4000
4000 and above

→ Open end classes

The class 'below 2000' has no lower limit and the class '4000 and above' has no upper limit. Therefore, these classes are open end classes. Whenever the extreme observations are widely spread, open end classes are used. In case of income distribution or the classification of sales of a company, open end classes may be required. Open end classes create some problems in further analysis, therefore, as far as possible the open end classes should be avoided.

Ilustration 3 : Find the mid-point and width of each class given the classes below 10, 10-20, 20-40, 40-60, 60-70, above 70.

Illustration 4 : Given the classes 0-9, 10-19, 20-29, 30-39 find the mid-point and width of each class.

Solution :

Class	Mid-point	Width
below 10	Not defined for open end class	
10 – 20	$\frac{10+20}{2} = 15$	10
20 – 40	30	20
40 – 60	50	20
60 – 70	65	10
above 70	Not defined for open end class	

Solution :

Class	Mid point	Width
0 – 9	$\frac{0+9}{2} = 4.5$	10
10 – 19	14.5	10
20 – 29	24.5	10
30 – 39	34.5	10

Note : Width = Difference between two successive lower limits.

2.5 Cumulative Frequencies

In many situations it is required to find the number of observations below or above a certain value. *For example* : In case of a frequency distribution of income, the number of persons below poverty line or in case of frequency distribution of examination marks, number of candidates above 60 etc. is required to be found. In this case cumulative frequencies are much useful. There are two types of cumulative frequencies : (i) less than type cumulative frequency (ii) more than type cumulative frequency.

Less than type cumulative frequency of a class is the number of observations less than or equal to the upper limit of the corresponding class. Similarly more than type cumulative frequency is the number of observations more than or equal to the lower limit of the corresponding class.

It is clear from the above explanation that the less than type cumulative frequencies can be obtained by computing cumulative sum of frequencies from the lowest class to highest class. We illustrate the procedure of computing the less than type and more than type cumulative frequencies.

Illustration 5 : *For the following frequency distribution find (i) less than cumulative frequencies (ii) more than cumulative frequencies.*

Marks	0-10	10-20	20-30	30-40	40-50
Frequency	5	12	15	4	4

Solution :

Marks	Frequency	Less than cumulative frequency	More than cumulative frequency
0 – 10	5	5	4 + 4 + 15 + 12 + 5 = 40
10 – 20	12	5 + 12 = 17	4 + 4 + 15 + 12 = 35
20 – 30	15	5 + 12 + 15 = 32	4 + 4 + 15 = 23
30 – 40	4	5 + 12 + 15 + 4 = 36	4 + 4 = 8
40 – 50	4	5 + 12 + 15 + 4 + 4 = 40	4
Total	40	–	–

It can be noted that the less than cumulative frequency is increasing in nature. Less than cumulative frequency of the lowest class is same as the usual frequency and the less than type cumulative frequency of highest class is the total number of observations. In case of more than cumulative frequencies exactly reverse observations will be seen.

A table containing upper limits along with less than type cumulative frequency or lower limits along with more than type cumulative frequency is called as *cumulative frequency distribution.*

2.6 Relative Frequencies

Two different frequency distributions may not have the same total frequency, hence for the purpose of comparison and interpretation, sometimes it is better to express the frequency of a class in terms of proportion (or percentage) of the total number of observations. The proportion of number of observations in a class is the *relative frequency*. Therefore,

$$\text{Relative frequency} = \frac{\text{Class frequency}}{\text{Total frequency}}$$

It can be noted that the relative frequency maintains the same pattern which is observed in class frequencies. The total of relative frequencies is 1.

Relative frequencies are widely used in economics, commerce etc. We illustrate how the relative frequency helps comparison.

Illustration 6 : *The following table gives the frequency distribution of marks in accountancy out of 60. Find the relation frequencies.*

Marks	0-10	10-20	20-30	30-40	40-50	50-60
No. of students	5	25	27	32	6	5

Solution :

Marks	Frequency	Relative Frequency
0–10	5	0.05
10–20	25	0.25
20–30	27	0.27
30–40	32	0.32
40–50	6	0.06
50–60	5	0.05
Total	**100**	**1.00**

2.7 Guidelines for the Choice of Classes

Classification of data is a sort of compromise, therefore, it becomes important to choose appropriate number of classes. The classes should be chosen, so that it will condense the data and it will also maintain the patterns in the original data.

(1) The number of classes should not be too large, otherwise it will not serve the purpose of condensation.

(2) The number of classes should not be too small. If the number of classes is too small it will not reveal the pattern in the original data. Moreover, due to the small number of classes, each class will be too wide. For further computations it is assumed that the observations in a class are situated at the centre of the class. The assumption will not remain valid for wider classes.

The number of classes should be between 7 to 20. However, according to the needs and requirements of the situation appropriate number of classes is chosen.

If the number of observations is large, naturally the number of classes will be large.

(3) As far as possible, classes should be of uniform width.

Sturge's Rule : If N is the total number of observations to be classified, then according to sturge's rule, the number of classes is approximately $1 + 3.222 \log N$. By the other approach as a thumb rule, the number of classes is approximately $\sqrt{N}$.

(4) As far as possible, open end classes should be avoided.

(5) The class width should be preferably 5 or multiple of 5.

(6) The lower limit of the starting class be preferably multiple of 5.

For example : The classes may be of the type 0–9, 10–19... or 11-20, 21-30 ... etc.

2.8 Graphs

Here we discuss the various graphs associated with frequency distribution. Generally graphs are used to represent mathematical relationship between two variables, otherwise diagrams are used.

(i) Histogram : It is one of the popularly used graphs for the representation of frequency distribution. It is a series of adjacent rectangles erected on X-axis with class interval as base, hence width of rectangle is equal to class width. Height of rectangle is taken as proportional to class frequency. In case of inclusive method of classification, extended class interval is used as base, where extended class interval is an interval designated by class boundaries.

Note :

1. A serious drawback of histogram is that, it cannot be drawn for a frequency distribution with open end class.

2. In case of discrete variable, histogram need not contain adjacent rectangles, those may be separated like bar diagram.

3. Histograms are useful to find mode, which is discussed in the next chapter.

Illustration 7 : *Draw a histogram to represent the following frequency distribution :*

Size of farm in hectares	1–20	21–40	41–60	61–80	81–100	101–120
No. of farms	12	38	16	5	3	1

Solution :

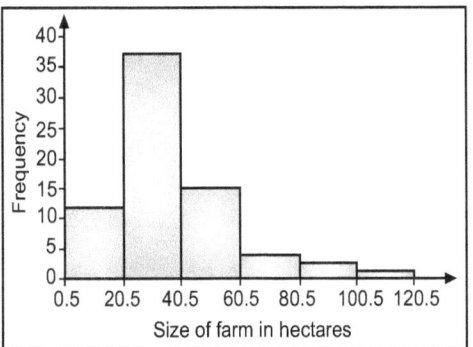

Scale :
X-axis : 1 unit = 20 Hectors
Y-axis : 1 unit = 5 Farms

Fig. 2.2 : Histogram

Histogram and ISO 9000 : Now-a-days manufacturing units and industries have to maintain quality of their product as per norms laid down by Indian Standards (IS) or International Standards Organisation (ISO). To achieve quality standards several statistical tools are used. Such tools are known as Quality Control (QC) or Process Control (PC) tools. Histogram is an important tool. It has three fold purpose (i) It displays the pattern of variation, (ii) It gives idea about process behaviour, (iii) It helps to decide where to focus the efforts for improvement. Some interpretations based on histogram are illustrated below :

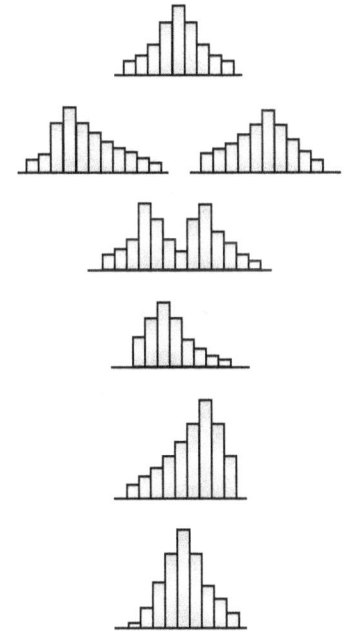

Symmetric distribution.

Non-symmetric distribution

Bimodal (having two centres) distribution. It is a mixture of two distributions.

Lower extreme values are not recorded separately.
Left end is not tapered.

Upper extreme values are not recorded separately.
Right end is not tapered.

Narrow spread distribution.

Widely spread distribution.

Fig. 2.3

(ii) Frequency Polygon : Generally a graph is expected to be in the form of a smooth curve. Histogram does not fulfil this requirement. Therefore, another important way of presentation of frequency distribution is frequency polygon or frequency curve. This type of graph enables us to understand the pattern in the data more clearly. Mid-values are taken on X-axis and frequencies on Y-axis to draw the graph. Successive points are joined by the line segments. Further, to complete polygon we obtain closed figure by taking two more classes. One preceding to first class and the other succeeding to last class. Frequency of each class is taken to be zero. Mid-points of these classes are used to get closed figure. The figure so obtained is called as frequency polygon.

Note :

1. We can draw frequency polygon using histogram. In this case we join the mid-points of upper sides of all the rectangles by line segments. Further to get closed figure we join the mid-values of preceeding class and succeeding class to the frequency distribution.

2. Histogram gives rough idea about the nature of frequency distribution. The border of histogram represents the frequency distribution. the boarder is zigzag, so we need to make it more smooth. Using frequency polygon and frequency curve it is possible to do so. The following figures will demonstrate how to make the border smooth by reducing the class width.

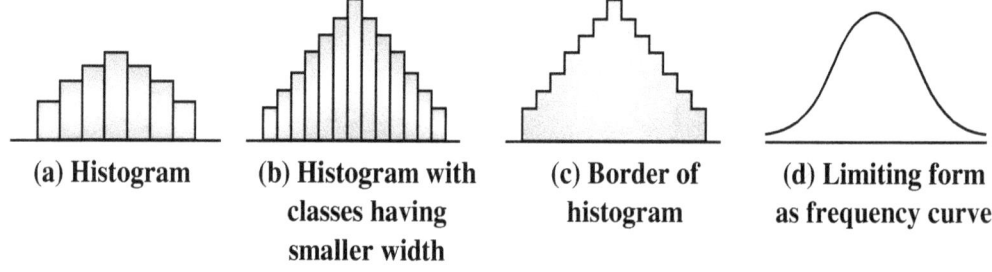

| (a) Histogram | (b) Histogram with classes having smaller width | (c) Border of histogram | (d) Limiting form as frequency curve |

Fig. 2.4

(iii) Frequency Curve : There is little difference in frequency polygon and frequency curve. If the points (or vertices of frequency polygon) are joined by a smooth curves instead of straight lines we get a closed figure called as *frequency curve*. While drawing frequency curve we should take care that the area under the curve is same as that of frequency polygon.

It can also be noticed that, we can draw frequency curve using histogram by the similar procedure which is used in case of frequency polygon.

Illustration 8 : *Draw a frequency polygon and a frequency curve for the following data :*

Monthly house rent	100-300	300-500	500-700	700-900	900-1100	1100-1300
No. of families	6	16	24	20	10	4

Solution : Mid-values of classes are taken on X-axis and frequency is taken on Y-axis. First point we need to plot is (200, 6), second point will be (400, 16) and so on. The last point will be (1200, 4). To get a closed figure we take two more points (0, 0) and (1400, 0). Joining these points by line segments (or smooth curve) we get frequency polygon (or frequency curve).

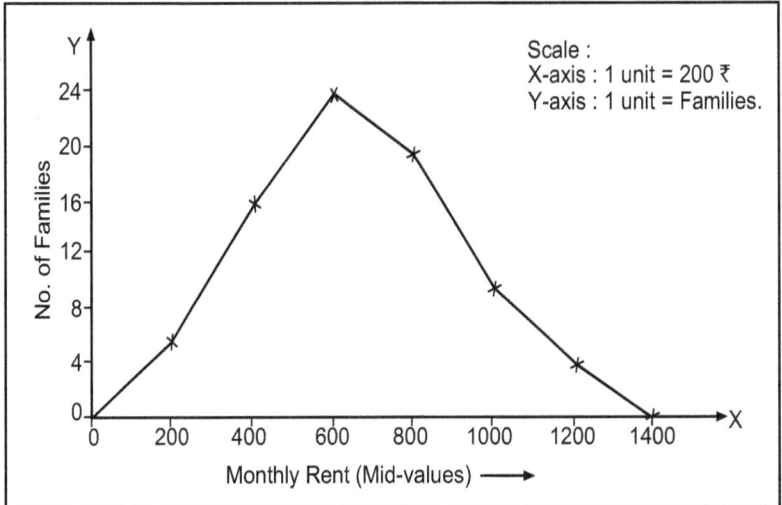

Fig. 2.5 : Frequency Polygon

(iv) Cumulative Frequency Curve or Ogive : Cumulative frequency distribution is represented by cumulative frequency curve (or ogive). There are two types of cumulative frequencies, hence, there are two types of cumulative frequency curves. For less than type cumulative curve upper boundaries of classes are taken on X-axis and less than cumulative frequencies on Y-axis. A preceding class before first class is also taken into consideration for drawing this curve. Cumulative frequency of this class is taken to be zero. Similarly, to draw more than type cumulative frequency curve lower boundaries are taken on X-axis and more than cumulative frequencies on Y-axis. In this case a succeeding class to the last class is taken with cumulative frequency zero. Those points are joined by smooth curve to get the cumulative frequency curve.

This type of curve is useful in finding median which is discussed in the subsequent chapter.

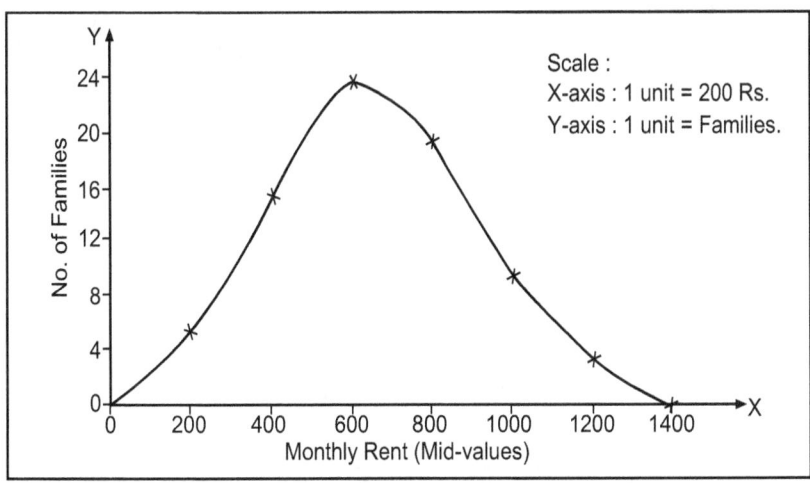

Fig. 2.6 : Frequency Curve

Illustration 9 : *Draw less than cumulative frequency curve and more than cumulative frequency curve for the following frequency distribution :*

Marks	0–10	10–20	20–30	30–40	40–50
No. of students	5	12	43	32	8

Solution : To draw less than type cumulative frequency curve we find out the required cumulative frequencies. In this problem class limits and class boundaries are same.

Upper limits	0	10	20	30	40	50
Cumulative frequencies	0	5	17	60	92	100

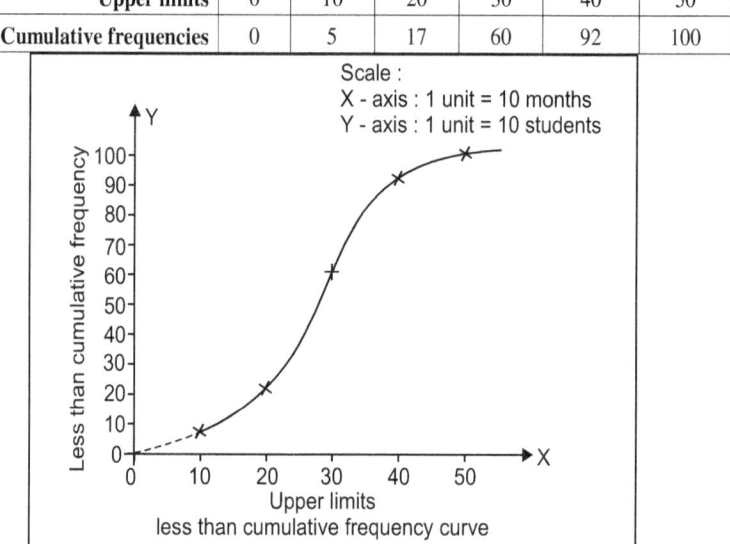

Fig. 2.7 : Less than Cumulative Frequency Curve

In order to draw more than cumulative frequency curve we obtain more than cumulative frequencies.

Lower limits	0	10	20	30	40	50
Cumulative frequencies	100	95	83	40	8	0

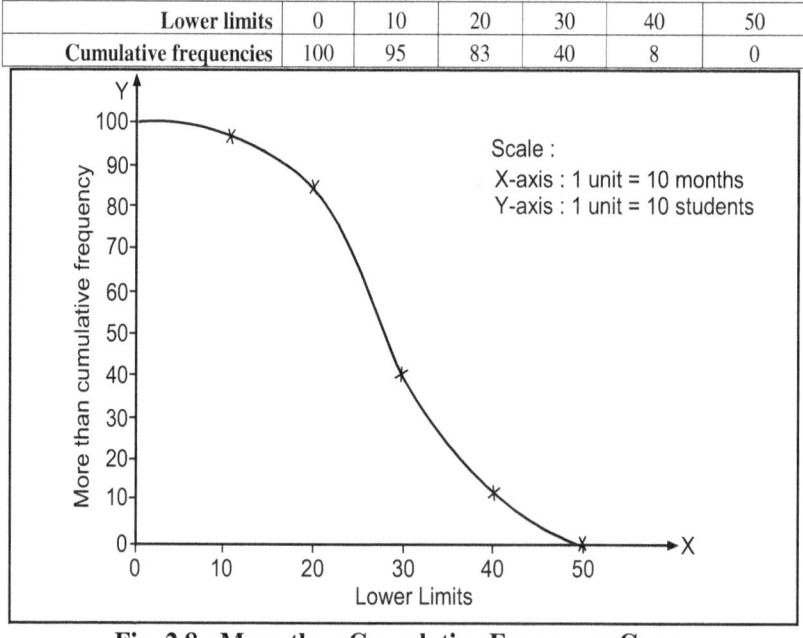

Fig. 2.8 : More than Cumulative Frequency Curve

2.9 Advantages and Limitations of Graphs

Advantages :
1. Information is presented in condensed form.
2. Facts are presented in more effective and impressive manner as compared to tables.
3. Easy to understand for a layman.
4. Create effect which lasts for longer time.
5. Facilitate the comparison.
6. Help in revealing patterns.

Limitations :
1. Using graphs we find the values approximately, while, tables give exact values.
2. Graphs give only a general idea about the phenomenon, which is not sufficient for further satistical analysis.

2.10 General Rules for Construction of Graphs

Following are the general rules which should be observed while constructing diagrams.
1. Height and width of bars in histogram should be properly chosen, so that graph looks attractive.
2. A suitable scale should be chosen to occupy the available space properly.
3. Index should be provided, if essential.
4. Graphs should be neat and clean.
5. Scale should be mentioned.

Case Study : (1) The manager of a departmental store would like assign different work at different period of time to salesmen during the day. Particularly salesman required during peak hour is more, where as during slack period, how many will be made free for other work such as to main inventory, attach price bar code, packaging, sorting removing the spoiled material etc. He obtained frequency distribution of customers during every hour. He could make available proportionate and adequate number of salesmen as well he could open the additional counters. He had prepared work shedule based upon the frequency distribution of customer.

(2) The owner of the perfect shoes manufacturing company wants to prepare production schedule according to the various sizes of shoes.

He prepared the sales frequency distribution according to size of shoes. It helped him a lot to prepare the manufacturing schedule.

Illustrative Examples

Example 2.1 : *Find more than cumulative distribution for the following frequency distribution :*

Class	11-15	16-20	21-25	26-30	31-35
Frequency	8	12	15	10	5

Solution :

Class	11-15	16-20	21-25	26-30	31-35
More than cummulative frequency	50	42	30	15	5

Example 2.2 : *The frequency distribution of daily expenditure of 100 college students is given below :*

Daily Expenditure (₹)	50-59	60-69	70-79	80-89	90-99	100-109	110-119	120-129
Number of Students	3	10	18	25	24	10	6	4

Obtain :

(i) *Class Boundaries of fourth class.*

(ii) *Class Width of any class.*

(iii) *Modal class.*

(iv) *Class Mark of last class.*

(v) *Number of students having expenditure less than ₹89.*

Solution :

(i)   Class boundaries of 4th class = Class boundaries of $(80-89)$: $(79.5-89.5)$

(ii)   Class width = Upper limit of class under consideration

                                             – Upper limit of preceeding class

                                            = 10

All classes are of equal width 10.

(iii) Modal class   : Class with maximum frequency

                                            : $80-89$

(iv) Class mark of last class   = Mid-point of $(120-129)$

                                            = 124.5

(v) Number of students having expenditure

                        less than ₹ 89 = Less than cumulative frequency of class (80-89)

                                        = $3+10+18+25 = 56$

Example 2.3 : *Draw histogram for the following frequency distribution.*

Marks	*0-10*	*10-20*	*20-30*	*30-40*	*40-50*	*50-60*
Number of Students	*15*	*25*	*60*	*40*	*35*	*25*

Solution :

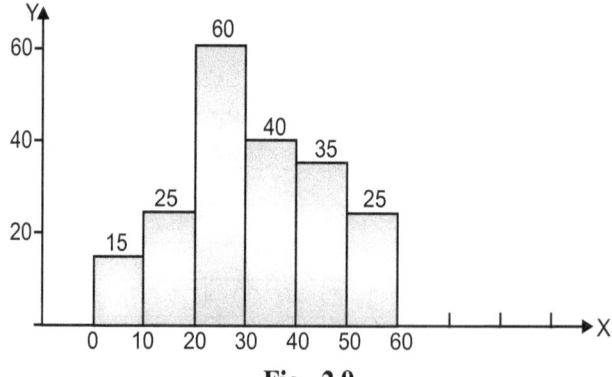

Fig. 2.9

2.11 Pie Diagram

When a variable is expressed as a sum of several components we use a *subdivided bar diagram.* Such data can also be represented by pie diagram. In this diagram, a circle is divided into several sectors as shown in illustration (by radial lines). Sectors occupy area proportional to the value of the component. Clearly, the number of sectors is the same as the number of components.

In order to draw a pie diagram, we express the data componentwise in terms of percentage of total. We take angle of 3.6° for 1%. Thus, we obtain angle for each sector and divide the corresponding circle into several sectors. The angle associated with each sector is the percentage multiplied by 3.6°. Hence, we get area of sector proportional to the value of component.

We illustrate the procedure with the help of following example.

Illustration 10 : Draw a pie diagram to represent the following data :

Group of items	Food	Clothing	House rent	Fuel and lighting	Other
Monthly expenditure (in ₹)	1080	648	720	252	900

Solution : Here the total of expenses is 3600. We express the values of components in terms of angle. Then we obtain angle for each by formula

$$\text{Angle} = \frac{\text{Value of component}}{\text{Total of components}} \times 360$$

Item	Monthly expenditure	Angle
Food	1080	$\frac{1080}{3600} \times 360 = 108°$
Clothing	648	$\frac{648}{3600} \times 360 = 65°$
House rent	720	$\frac{720}{3600} \times 360 = 72°$
Fuel	252	$\frac{252}{3600} \times 360 = 25°$
Others	900	$\frac{900}{3600} \times 360 = 90°$
Total	**3600**	**360°**

Note :
1. If there are more number of components, a pie diagram is preferable to subdivided bar diagram. However, both the diagrams serve the same purpose.
2. In order to compare two phenomenon using pie diagram, we draw two separate pie diagrams in such a way that their rail are proportional to the square root of the total value.

Choice of Diagram : We discuss below general guidelines for the choice of a suitable diagram :
1. When there is only one variable under consideration and we study the changes in the total value of the corresponding variable, bar diagram is used.

2. When we study the changes in totals for several variables together, multiple bar diagram is used.

3. When we study the changes in the components and changes in totals, subdivided bar diagram or percentage bar diagram or pie diagram is used.

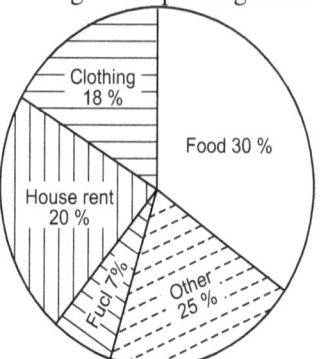

Fig. 2.10 : Pie diagram

We can draw Pie diagram using MS-EXCEL.

Consider the example on 12. Enter the group items in column a and monthly expenditure in column B as shown below.

	A	B
1	Group of	Monthly
2	Items	Expenditure
3		(in Rs)
4	Food	1080
5	Clothing	648
6	House Rent	720
7	Fuel & Lightin	252
8	Others	900

Fig. 2.11

Select the data B3:B8 by using the mouse then go to INSET command on main menu. INSERT, CHART.Then following windows will appear on screen one-by-one.

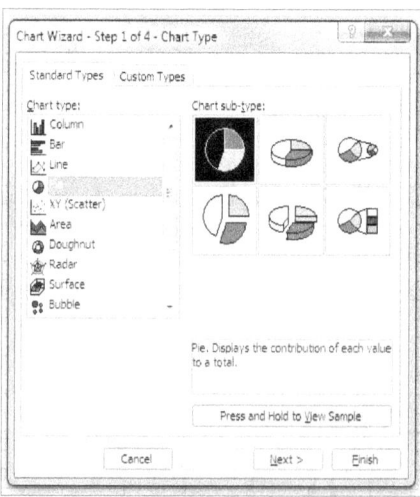

Fig. 2.12

Select the chart type (PIE) and click next.

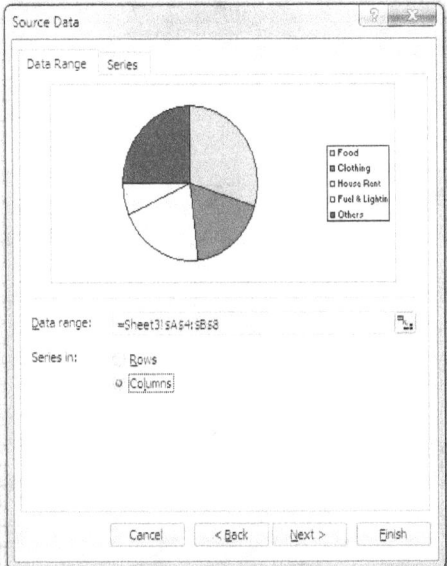

Fig. 2.13

Then click on finish and pie diagram will appear on screen.

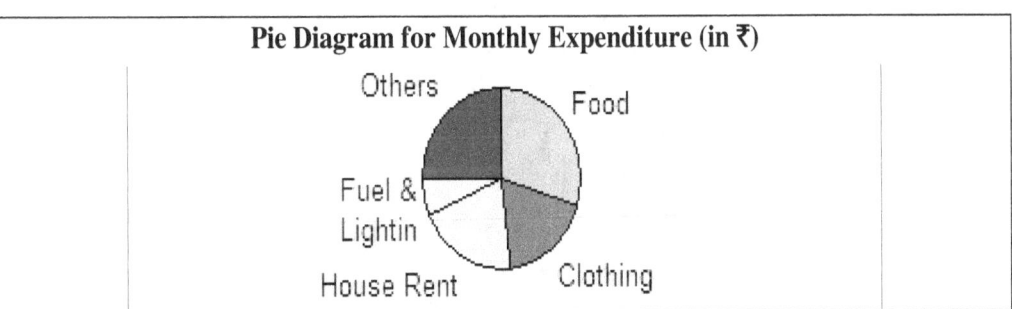

Fig. 2.14

2.12 Population Pyramid Diagrams

In the study of population dynamics, we study agewise and sexwise structure of human population. We especially use the diagram known as pyramid diagram. It is nothing but the two bar diagrams drawn together for male and female on a common base but the bars are raised opposite to each other. It resebles a picture like pyramid. Hence it is referred as pyramid diagram.

Procedure of construction : We take Y-axis at the centre. To the right side of Y-axis we errect the bars parallel to X-axis representing female population according to different age groups. Where as to left side of Y-axis we errect bars parallel to X-axis with a common base for the same age group of male. The bars go in opposite direction with a common base.

We illustrate the procedure of drawing pyramid diagram as follows :

Example 2.4 : Construct a pyramid diagram for the following data on India census 2001.

Age group	0-9	10-19	20-29	30-39	40-49	50-59	59-69	70 and above
Female population (%)	23.7	21.3	17.1	14.2	9.9	6.5	4.7	2.6
Male population (%)	23.8	22.2	16.7	13.7	10.4	6.5	4.3	2.4

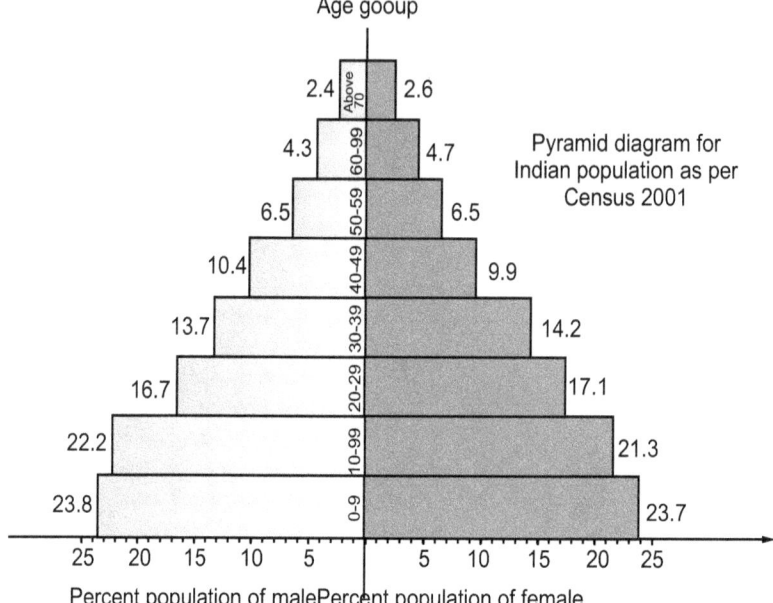

Fig. 2.15

Population pyramid diagram gives an idea of population dynamics, whether the population is (a) Expansive, (b) Stable or stationary, (c) Constrictive. Every country passes through these phases.

(a) Expansive Pyramid (Stage 1) : Population growth is high, birth rate is high, so bottom of pyramid is wide. Death rate is high for advancing ages, so there is sudden drop for next age groups. Life expectancy is short.

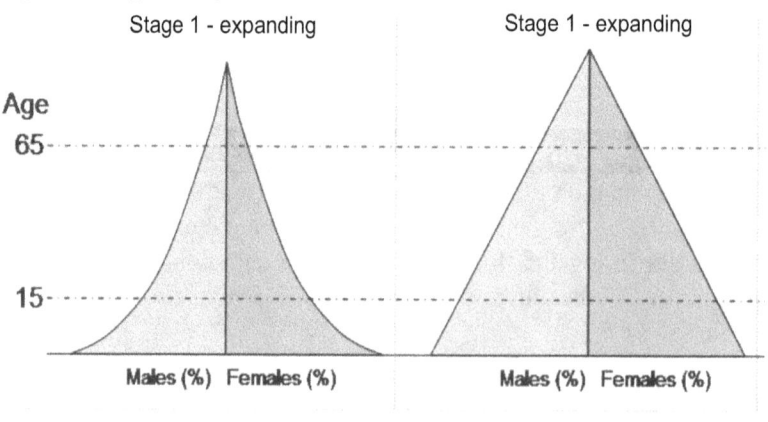

Fig. 2.16   Fig. 2.17

Third world countries fall in this category. Indian population observe pyramid close to Fig. 2.17. Where death rate reduced. Birth rate is high, life expectancy slightly longer. Young population is large, old age population small.

(b) Stable or Stationary Pyramid (Stage 2) : Population growth is moderate Birth rate declining, low death rates or unchanging patterns of birth rates and death rats. Population almost same for all the age groups declining slowly at old age. Life expectancy is long. Some countries from Europe, Scandinavia fall in this category.

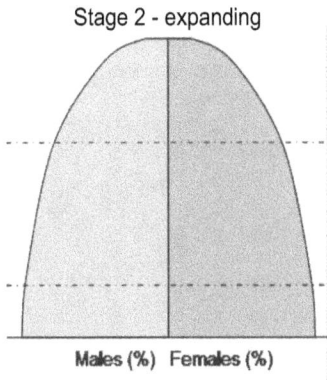

Fig. 2.18

(c) Constrictive Pyramid (Stage 3) : Population has low birth rate and low death rate. Growth it is rate is almost zero, sometimes negative. Base starts reducing to narrow, indicating children population is declining. Life expectancy is long. Dependency ratio is high. United States fall in this category.

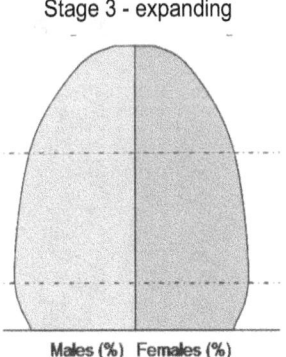

Fig. 2.19

Apart from population dynamics, pyramid diagram is used in exhibiting some phenomenon where initial values are large and later on there is sharp decline. Food chain pyramid, diet component pyramid, employees in organisation are the examples of pyramid with a pinnacle at the top. In some cases exactly reverse picture is seen.

To draw pyramid diagram we arrange components so that largest is at the bottom, next second largest and so on, smallest at the top.

Population pyramids of various countries.

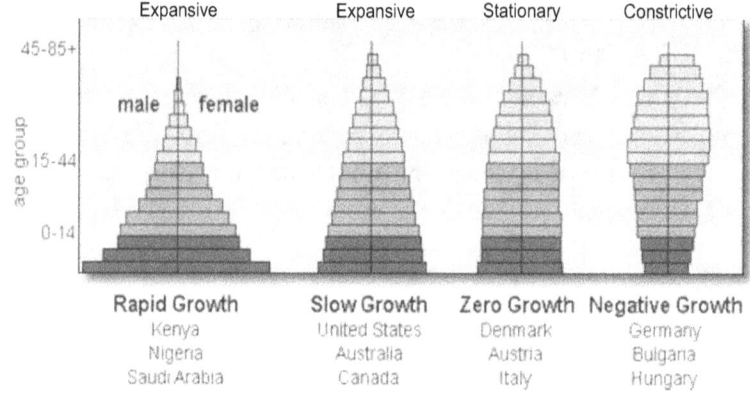

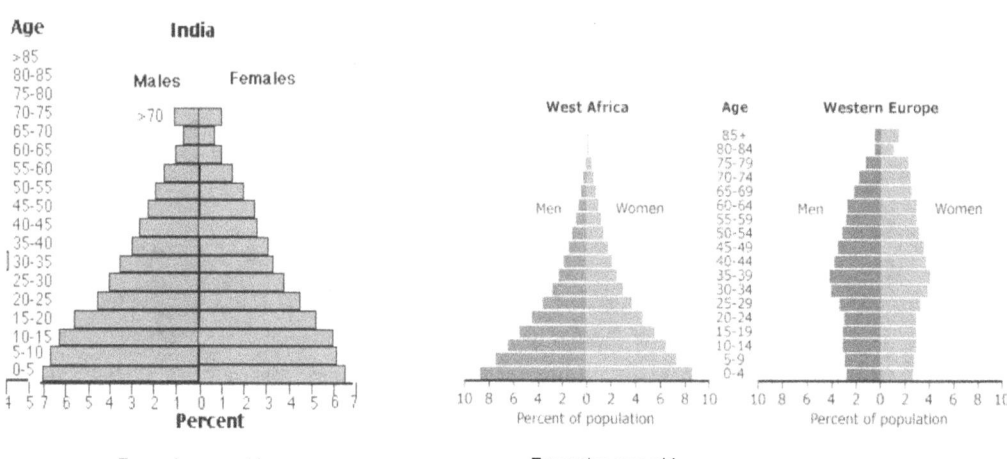

Expansive pyramid   Expansive pyramid   Constirctive pyramid

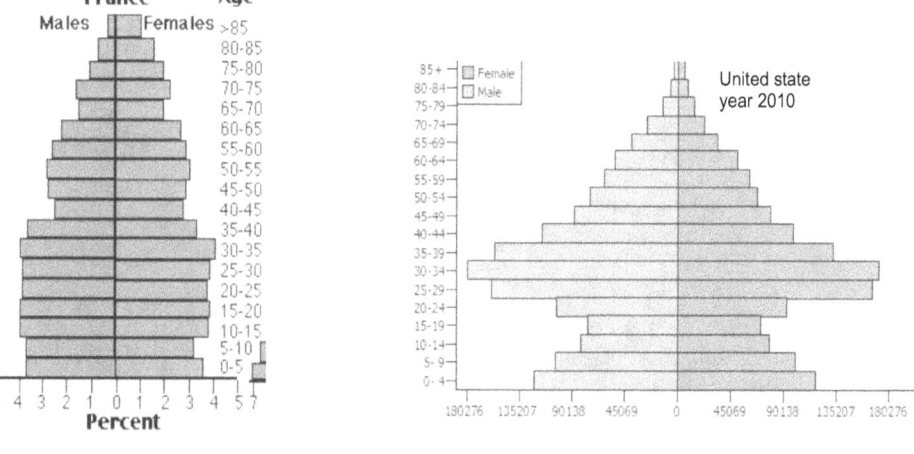

Stationary or stable pyramid   Constirctive pyramid

Fig. 2.20

Procedure to construct pyramid diagram :

Note that the volume of pyramid $= \frac{1}{3}$ area of base $\times$ height.

For simplicity we construct a pyramid with same length (h) and width of base and same height. So we get, volume $= \frac{h^3}{3}$. Thus the volume is proportional to h^3 or height is proportional to the (volume)$^{1/3}$ i.e. cube root of volumes component.

Cumulative volume in %	20	40	50	80	100
Height of pyramid	0.58 h	0.74 h	0.84 h	0.93 h	h

Example 2.5 : A factory employees 60% workers, 20% engineers. 15% marketing staff, 5% executives. Represent it by pyramid diagram.

Solution : Let us take worker section at the base, then engineers, then marketing staff and the executive at the top. Suppose we take height of pyramid 5 units.

Component	Executive	Marketing staff	Engineers	Workers
Percentage	5%	15%	20%	60%
Cumulative percentage	5%	20%	40%	100%
Height	$(0.05)^{1/3} \times 5$ $= 1.84$	$(0.2)^{1/3} \times 5$ $= 2.92$	$(0.4)^{1/3} \times 5$ $= 3.68$	5

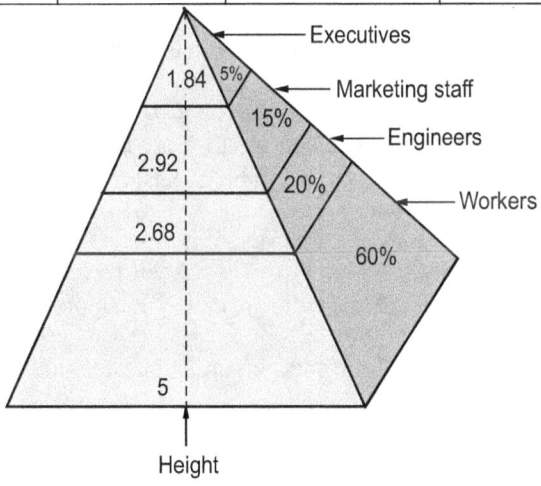

Fig. 2.21

2.13 Tabular Representation

(a) Introduction :

In earlier we have studied classification of data. Tabulation can be considered as the next operation to classification. We use in day-to-day life various types of tables e.g. marklist, electricity bill, balance sheet, time-table of a class, railway time-table. Presenting the information in tabular form has many advantages. Statistical table gives an orderly arrangement of data in columns and rows. Tabulation is one of the simplest way of summarizing data. It is an important way to convey the information in a meaningful fashion. Statistical table helps in many respects like locating desired information, getting overall view of the phenomenon under study. Tabulation is found to be widely useful in several fields.

(b) Classification and Tabulation :

Definition : A statistical table is the logical listing of quantitative data in various rows and columns with self explanatory title, row headings, column headings and notes regarding source of data, context etc.

Tabulation is a classification of qualitative characteristic. *For example :* Sex of 100 students is recorded, which is divided into two groups viz. boys and girls and frequency is placed against the respective group. One can easily notice that classification and tabulation serve the same purpose of presenting data in neat and compact form. Both the processes simplify the complexities and facilitate comparison. Whenever there are two qualitative characteristics, two way table is used; which is discussed later in the same chapter.

(c) Parts of Table :

We discuss below the different parts of a table.

1. Table number : At the top of every table, a number should be mentioned for ready reference. *For example :* Socio-economic condition of a certain city is given in table 31.

2. Title : A table should have suitable, brief and self-explanatory title. It should give an idea about the contents of the table, when the data are collected and to which it relates. Preferably title is placed at the top of the table in bold face type lettering.

3. Stub : Row titles in a table are referred as stub.

4. Caption : Column headings in a table are called as caption.

5. Body : This is the main and most important part of a table. This includes numerical information.

6. Head note : Usually the units of numerical data are specified in the head note. Similarly, it gives information which is not covered in the title, stub or caption. It is placed just below the title.

7. Foot note : It includes the information regarding numerical data such as explanation of symbols, signs, abbreviations etc. The rounding off rules those are used in the formation of a table are also mentioned here. It is placed directly below the table.

8. Source note : It is observed just below foot note. It gives particulars of the source data such as publication, page number, table number etc.

The following diagram is a sketch of a table showing its various parts.

Table No.			
Title :			
Head Note			
		Caption	Total
	Stub	**BODY**	
Foot Note :			
Source Note :			

(d) Objective of Tabulation :

The objectives of classification and tabulation are more or less same. We list below the objectives of tabulation :

1. It simplifies the complex data.

2. It omits unnecessary details.

3. It facilitates comparison with the other data.

4. It reveals prominent features and the patterns present within the data.

5. It helps in further analysis and interpretation.

(e) Requisites of a Good Table :

In order to make a table effective, attractive and intelligible some general guidelines are given below.

1. A table should bear a number for ready reference.

2. Each table should have a brief and self-explanatory title.

3. Stub and caption should be clear enough.

4. The use of short forms in stub and caption should be avoided except those which are very commonly used like Rs., cm., cc. etc.

5. To distinguish main classes, thick lines should be used and to distinguish sub-classes, thin lines should be used.

6. Use of dash (–) instead of zero should be avoided. No entry to be kept blank.

7. Use of ditto marks (") should be avoided, because there is a possibility of taking it to be 11.

8. Explanation regarding signs, symbols, abbreviations, rounding off rules etc. should be mentioned in foot note.

9. Sub-totals should be obtained as and when required.

10. Units should be mentioned in head note.

11. Columns (or rows) to be compared should be placed adjacent to each other.

12. Larger figures should be abbreviated. *For example,* if all values are of the type 16000, 20000, ... then those could be written as 16, 20 ...... However, it should be mentioned in the foot note that the figures are in thousands.

Types of Tables :

Tables are classified on the basis of number of characteristics involved in it. We discuss the following types of tables.

1. One way table : This is a simple type of table which considers single characteristics. Stub or caption is subdivided to include the group of characteristics under study.

Illustration 11 :

Table 2.5

Classwise distribution of number of students in a college ABC

Class	Number of students
F.Y.	
S.Y.	
T.Y.	
Total	

The above table uses only one characteristic viz. class. In this case stub is subdivided into three groups to include the three classes viz. F.Y., S.Y., T.Y.

2. Two-way table :   In this type of table two characteristics are considered simultaneously. Stub and caption are subdivided to include the two characteristics under consideration. One characteristic is taken in stub and the other in caption.

Illustration 12 :

Table 2.6

Classwise and sexwise distribution of number of students in a college ABC

Class \ Sex	Male	Female	Total
F.Y.			
S.Y.			
T.Y.			
Total			

The above table uses two characteristics viz. class and sex.

3. Three-way table : Such a table considers three characteristics simultaneously. In the construction of such tables an order of precedence among the characteristics should be first fixed on the basis of their importance.

Illustration 13 :

Table 2.7

Classwise, facultywise and sexwise distribution of no. of students in a college ABC.

Class	Faculty									Total		
	Arts			Science			Commerce					
	M	F	T	M	F	T	M	F	T	M	F	T
F.Y.												
S.Y.												
T.Y.												
Total												

Foot Note : M = Male, F = Female, T = Total

The above table includes three characteristics viz. class, faculty, sex.

4. Higher order or manifold table : This type of table contains more than three characteristics. However, as the number of characteristics increases, table becomes large, complicated and confusing. In such cases it is advisable to construct several two-way or three-way tables.

Illustration 14 : Information obtained from a college register is described below. Represent the same in a form of neat table.

"The number of students in a college in the year 1961 was 1100, of those 980 were boys and rest girls.

In 1971, the number of boys increased by 100% and that of girls increased by 300% as compared to their strength in 1961. In 1981 the total number of students in a college was 3600, the number of boys being double the number of girls."

From the table also determine the percent increase in

(i)   the total strength

(ii) the number of girls

(iii) the number of boys in 1981 as compared to 1961.

Solution : In the problem we can see that there are two-characteristics viz. sex and year. Hence, we have to make a two-way table.

In 1961, total strength and number of boys is given. Hence the number of girls will be 1100 – 980 = 120.

In 1971 boys are increased by 100% means, the boys increased by the same number exactly. Hence the number of boys will be 980 + 980 = 1960. The number of girls is increased by 300% means the increase will be $\frac{120}{100} \times 300 = 360$ and hence the number of girls will be 120 + 360 = 480. In the year 1981 total strength 3600 is to be divided in the ratio 2 : 1. Therefore, we get 2400 boys and 1200 girls. The table containing the above calculated entries will be as follows :

Table 2.8

Sexwise and yearwise strength of a college

Class \ Sex	Boys	Girls	Total
1961	980	120	1100
1971	1960	480	2440
1981	2400	1200	3600
Total	5340	1800	7140

Source Note : Data are taken from college records

(i) Net increase in total strength for 1981 as compared to 1961

$$= 3600 - 1100 = 2500$$

$$\text{Percent increase} = \frac{2500}{1100} \times 100 = 227.27$$

(ii) Net increase in the strength of girls for 1981 as compared to 1961

$$= 1200 - 120 = 1080$$

$$\text{Percent increase} = \frac{1080}{120} \times 100 = 900$$

(iii) Net increase in the strength of boys for 1981 as compared to 1961

$$= 2400 - 980 = 1420$$

$$\text{Percent increase} = \frac{1420}{980} \times 100 = 144.90$$

Illustration 15 : Out of the total number of 1807 women who were interviewed for employment in a textile mill at Ahmedabad, 512 were from textile areas and the rest from the non-textile areas. Amongst the married women who belonged to textile areas, 247 were experienced and 73 inexperienced, while for non-textile areas, the corresponding figures were 49 and 520. The total number of inexperienced women was 1341 of whom 111 resided in textile areas. Of the total number of women, 918 were unmarried and of these, the number of experienced women in the textile and non-textile areas was 154 and 16 respectively. Present the information in tabular form.

Also obtain the percentage of experienced women, percentage of married women amongst those who were interviewed.

Solution : The above information is regarding three characteristics : experience, residential status and marital status. Hence, we prepare three-way table. From the given figures, remaining figures can be easily obtained just by addition or subtraction of related figures.

Table 2.9

Distribution of number of women according to experience, marital status and residential status

	Textile area			Non-textile area			Total		
	E	N-E	T	E	N-E	T	E	N-E	T
Married	247	73	320	49	520	569	296	593	889
Unmarried	154	38	192	16	710	726	170	748	918
Total	401	111	512	65	1230	1295	466	1341	1807

Foot Note : E = Experienced, N - E = Non Experienced, T = Total

Source Note : ....

Percentage of experienced women amongst interviewed women

$$= \frac{466}{1807} \times 100 = 25.79$$

Percentage of married women amongst interviewed women

$$= \frac{889}{1807} \times 100 = 49.20$$

Points to Remember

1. There are two data types : variables and attributes. The attributes are qualitative where as variables are numerical quantities.

2. Inclusive classification : classification with classes which include both the limits. Exclusive classification : classification with classes which exclude the upper limits of classes.

3. Class mark is the mid-point of class internal.

4. Class frequency is the number of observations in a class.

5. To make the classes continuous, we obtain class boundaries.

6. Histogram gives the idea of symmetry, spread and central value of frequency distribution.

7. Relative frequency = class frequency ÷ Total frequency.

8. Class width = Upper limit of succeeding class – Upper limit of the class.

Exercise 2.1

A. Theory Questions :

1. Explain the need of classification.

2. Explain the different methods of classification briefly.

3. Explain the following terms with illustrations :

(i) attribute (ii) variable (iii) discrete variable (iv) continuous variable (v) raw data.

4. Explain the following terms :

(i) class limits (ii) class boundaries (iii) class width (iv) class frequency (v) less than type cumulative frequency (vi) more than type cumulative frequency (vii) relative frequency (viii) open end class.

5. Explain the general guidelines or principles of choosing the classes.

6. What do you mean by classification ?

7. Discuss the importance of classification in statistical analysis.

8. (a) State the advantages of graphical presentation of data.

(b) State the limitations of graphical presentation of data.

9. Explain the construction of the following graphs along with the rough sketches :
    (i) histogram (ii) frequency polygon (iii) frequency curve (iv) ogives.

10. What are the uses of histogram and ogives ?

11. Discuss the importance of graphs in presentation of statistical data.

Exercise 2.2

B. Frequency Distribution :

12. Heights in cm of 50 students in a class are given below :

168.9	163.1	161.5	168.0	167.1	157.5	163.9	168.9
166.7	160.8	161.3	161.5	162.0	166.3	162.6	168.0
170.1	165.8	165.2	164.5	171.3	158.0	158.7	159.6
167.4	162.1	166.7	169.0	167.0	160.3	167.7	157.7
164.9	168.3	164.0	157.6	172.5	171.1	168.2	172.6
169.3	159.2	171.7	163.7	162.3	171.9	169.7	167.7
170.2	169.0						

Classify the above data by using 'exclusive method' of classification. Take the first class interval as 157–160.

13. The marks out of 100 scored by 40 students in the subject statistics are given below :

56	78	62	37	54	39	62	60	47	41
28	82	38	72	62	44	54	42	50	52
42	55	57	65	68	47	42	56	47	48
56	56	55	66	42	52	48	48	53	68

Classify the data by using 'inclusive method' of classification. Take the starting class to be 25 - 29.

14. Following is a frequency distribution of 95 shops according to daily shops in a super market on a particular day.

Daily sales (in '000 ₹)	No. of Shops
10 – 20	12
20 – 30	23
30 – 40	47
40 – 50	*
50 – 60	3
60 and above	2

(i) Find the missing frequency.

(ii) Form the less than type cumulative frequency distribution.

(iii) Is the classification exclusive ?

(iv) How many shops have sales less than or equal to ₹ 50,000 ?

(v) Obtain the more than cumulative frequency distribution.

(vi) How many shops have sales more than ₹ 40,000 ?

(vii) Is there any open end class ? If yes, state those.

(viii) Obtain the width of class and class mark of the classes for which it is possible.

15. Following is a frequency distribution of number of students according to marks scored in a certain examination.

Marks	0-19	20-39	40-59	60-79	89-99
No. of students	8	26	24	12	5

(i) State whether the classification is inclusive.

(ii) Obtain class-boundaries of each class. Are the class boundaries and limits same ?

(iii) Find width and class-mark of each class.

(iv) Obtain the less than cumulative frequency distribution, hence obtain the number of students scoring marks less than or equal to 59.

(v) Obtain the more than cumulative frequency distribution and hence find the number of students scoring marks more than or equal to 60.

16. The following is the distribution of the height of students in a class of secondary school.

Height (in cm)	Number of students
130 – 134	5
135 – 139	15
140 – 144	28
145 – 149	24
150 – 154	17
155 – 159	10
160 – 164	1

Find : (i) class mark of 3rd class.
     (ii) class width of any class.
     (iii) class boundaries of 5th class.
     (iv) class limits of 6th class.
     (v) number of students whose height is less than 149 cm.

17. Answer the following questions for the given frequency distribution :

I.Q.	60-69	70-79	80-89	90-99	100-109	110-119	120-129
Number of students	21	37	51	49	21	13	4

  (i) State the type of classification.
  (ii) State the class mark of 4th class.
  (iii) State the class-boundaries of 5th class.
  (iv) How many students have I.Q. less than 99 ?
  (v) How many students have I.Q. more than 80 ?

18. The frequency distribution of marks obtained by 100 students in F.Y.B. Com. is given below :

Marks	0-9	10-19	20-29	30-39	40-49
No. of students	10	24	30	20	16

Answer the following questions :
  (i) State the type of classification.
  (ii) Find the class-mark of 3rd class.
  (iii) State the class boundaries of 5th class.
  (iv) Find the class width of 2nd class.
  (v) Find the number of students getting marks less than 30.

19. Answer the questions using following frequency distribution of age of 50 citizens :

Age (years)	Below 30	31-40	41-50	51-60	61-70	Above 71
Frequency	3	7	–	16	8	2

  (i) State type of classification.
  (ii) Identify open end classes and state them.
  (iii) Find missing frequency.
  (iv) Find class-mark of fifth class.
  (v) Obtain class boundaries of fourth class.

20. Following is the frequency distribution of number of students according to marks scored in a certain examination :

Marks	0-19	20-39	40-59	60-79	80-99
No. of students	8	26	24	12	5

  (i) State the type of classification.
  (ii) Obtain the class boundaries of the third class.
  (iii) Class width of the fourth class.
  (iv) Class-mark of second class.
  (v) How many students getting the marks less than 79 ?

21. Answer questions using the following frequency distribution of 100 companies :

Profit (00,000) ₹	No. of companies
0-100	09
100-200	15
200-300	18
300-400	21
400-500	–
500-600	14
600-700	05

(i) State type of classification.

(ii) Find missing frequency.

(iii) Find class-mark of fifth class.

(iv) Identify median class.

(v) Find class width of third class.

22. The frequency distribution of daily expenditure of 100 college students is given below :

Daily Expenditure (₹)	50-59	60-69	70-79	80-89	90-99	100-109	110-119	120-129
Number of Students	3	10	18	25	24	10	6	4

Obtain :

(i) Class boundaries of fourth class.

(ii) Class width of any class.

(iii) Modal class.

(iv) Class-mark of last class.

(v) Number of students having expenditure less than ₹ 89.

23. The following data relate to the income of 90 persons :

Income (₹)	500-999	1000-1499	1500-1999	2000-2499
Number of Persons	15	22	45	8

Answer the following questions :

(i) Find class-mark of 3rd class.

(ii) Find class width of 2nd class.

(iii) Find number of persons having income less than Rs. 1,500.

(iv) Find percentage of persons earning more than Rs. 1,500.

(v) State the modal class.

C. Cumulative Frequency Distribution :

24. Obtain less than cumulative frequency distribution for the following data. Also represent it graphically.

Class	100-150	150-200	200-250	250-300	300-350
Frequency	12	15	08	03	01

25. Find less than cumulative frequencies and more than cumulative frequencies for the frequency distribution given below :

Class	100-150	150-200	200-250	250-300	300-350
Frequency	12	15	30	8	2

Also draw ogive curves.

26. Find more than cumulative distribution for the following frequency distribution and represent it by suitable graph.

Class	11-15	16-20	21-25	26-30	31-35
Frequency	8	12	15	10	5

27. Can the following be a less than type cumulative frequency distribution ?

Upper limit	10	20	30	40
Less than cumulative frequency	2	18	12	50

Justify your answer.

28. Obtain the frequency distribution from the following, cumulative frequency distributions :

(a)

Marks below	Number of stuents
10	1
20	8
30	35
40	46
50	50

(b)

Age in years	No. of persons
Less than 20	15
Less than 30	35
Less than 40	72
Less than 50	108
Less than 60	120
Less than 70	124

Also find greater than cumulative frequencies.

29. Prepare the frequency distribution from the following cumulative frequency distribution :

Income more than Rs.	No. of persons
500	100
1000	96
1500	92
2000	59
2500	28
3000	2

30. Convert the following less than cumulative frequency distribution to usual frequency distribution. Also find more than cumulative frequencies.

Waiting time in minutes at octri check post	No. of vehicles
less than 1	12
less than 3	58
less than 5	206
less than 8	372
less than 12	500
less than 16	520

31. Convert the frequency distribution from the following more than cumulative frequency distribution. Also obtain the less than type cumulative frequency distribution.

Height of students	No. of students
More than 145 cm.	130
More than 150 cm.	123
More than 155 cm.	111
More than 160 cm.	89
More than 165 cm.	51
More than 170 cm.	21
More than 175 cm.	0

D. Graphical Presentation :

32. Draw the histogram, frequency polygon and ogive curves for the following frequency distribution. :

Weight in *lb*	80-89	90-99	100-109	110-119	120-129	130-139	140-149
Frequency	8	16	20	26	50	13	5

33. Draw a histogram for the following income distribution :

Monthly income	1000-2000	2000-2500	2500-3500	3500-5000
Frequency	120	125	180	150

34. Draw less than cumulative frequency curve for frequency distribution of intelligence quotient given below. Also obtain number of candidates having intelligence quotient between 105 and 125.

I.Q.	60-69	70-79	80-89	90-99	100-109	110-119	120-129
Frequency	21	37	51	49	21	13	4

35. Draw a frequency curve, frequency polygon and histogram for the following data :

Mid-values	25	35	45	55	65
Frequencies	5	12	33	13	7

36. Draw less than cumulative frequency curve and more than cumulative frequency curve for the following frequency distribution of marks in statistics :

Marks	0-20	20-40	40-60	60-80	80-100
No. of students	2	18	42	28	5

37. Draw histogram for the following data :

Weight (kg)	30 - 40	40 - 50	50 - 60	60 - 70	70 - 80
Number of Students	40	50	70	30	10

38. Draw histogram, frequency polygon and ogives for the following frequency distribution.

Class	0 – 10	10 – 20	20 – 30	30 – 40	40 – 50
Frequency	4	12	18	16	3

39. From the following frequency distribution of weights of 50 students, draw less than ogive curve :

Weight (kg)	10-15	15-20	20-25	25-30	30-35
Number of Students	5	12	15	10	8

E. Diagrams :

40. Present the following information using suitable diagram :

Mode of transport	Bus	Train	Aeroplane	Private vehicle	Own vehicle	Total
No. of passengers	1250	2250	100	600	500	5000

41. Answer the questions based on the following diagram

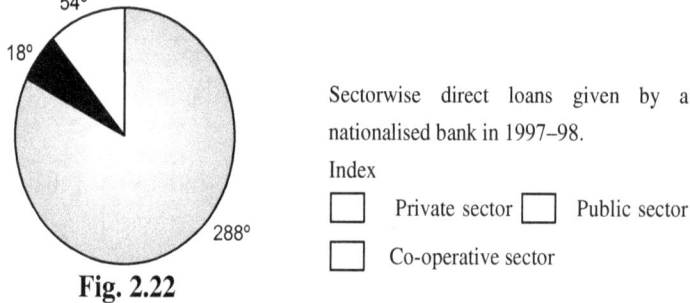

Sectorwise direct loans given by a nationalised bank in 1997–98.

Index

☐ Private sector   ☐ Public sector

☐ Co-operative sector

Fig. 2.22

(a) What is the type of diagram ?

(b) State the sector taking maximum loan amount.

(c) State the sector taking minimum loan amount among all the sectors.

42. Following diagram shows industrywise direct loans given by a industrial development bank, using the diagram answer the questions given below the diagram.

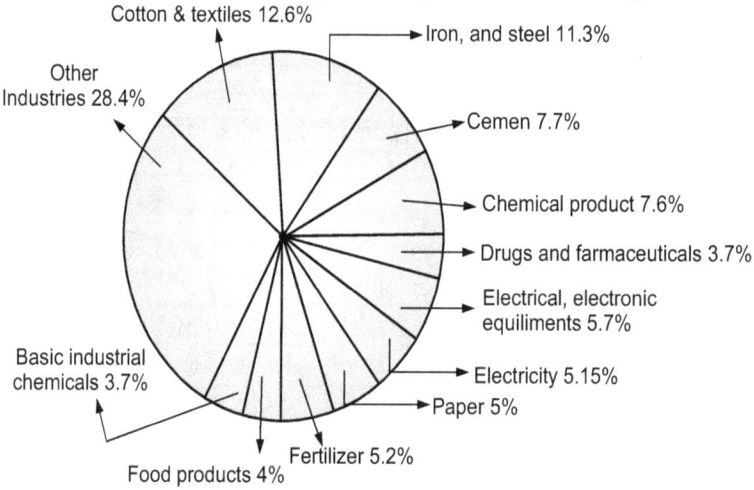

Fig. 2.23

(a) State the type of diagram.

(b) State the sector which is allotted maximum loan amount.

(c) State the industrial sectors receiving loan amount less than 5%.

43. Composition of port folio of a industrial development bank is given by the following data draw a suitable diagram.

Rupee loans : 56 %	Refinance : 6 %
Foreign currency loans : 11 %	SIDBI : 5 %
Investment in Industry : 8 %	Investment in financial institutions : 5 %
Bills finance : 7 %	Equipment leasing : 2 %

F. Tabulation :

44. Prepare a blank table giving the following information about workers in a certain industry.

(a) Sex   :   male, female
(b) Age group   :   20-30, 30-40, 40 and above
(c) Skill   :   skilled, unskilled.

45. Draw a blank table to summarise examination result of a college.

(a) Class   : F.Y. B. Com., S.Y. B.Com., T.Y. B. Com.
(b) Examination grades :
              Fail, pass, second class, first
              class, first class with distinction.
(c) Sex   : male, female.

46. Represent the following information in the tabular form giving a suitable title.

A supermarket divided into main sections viz. grocery, vegetables, medicines, textiles and novelties recorded the following sales in 1981, 1982 and 1983.

In 1981, sales in grocery, vegetables, medicines and novelties were ₹ 6,25,000, ₹ 2,20,000, ₹ 1,88,000 and ₹ 94,000 respectively. Sale of textile was 30% of the total sales during the year. In 1982, the total sales showed 10% increase, while grocery and vegetables showed respectively 8% and 10% increase over their corresponding figure in 1981. Medicine sale was dropped by 13,000 while sale of textiles was ₹ 5,36,000.

In 1983, though the total sale remained the same as in 1982, grocery fell by ₹ 22,000, vegetables by ₹ 32,000, medicine by ₹ 10,000 and novelties by ₹ 12,000.

47. Represent the following data in the tabular form :

The chairman of a group of three companies A, B and C in his annual statement, gave the following analysis of the profit for the year ending on 31st Dec. 1969, from the trading in the various parts of the world : "For company 'A', the total profit was ₹ 1,30,000 of which ₹ 1,00,000 came from U.K., ₹ 10,000 from trade with countries in Asia, ₹ 3,000 from African countries, ₹ 15,000 from countries in Europe and only ₹ 2,000 from U.S.A. As for company 'B' it made ₹ 67,000 profit from U.K., but had no trade with U.S.A., profit from countries in Asia and Africa were respectively ₹ 2,500 and ₹ 1,500 while that from European countries was ₹ 5,000 making the total profit of ₹ 76,000. Finally, company 'C' made the lowest total profit of ₹ 52,800 of which ₹ 40,000 was made in U.K., profit from countries in Asia was ₹ 5,700 compared with ₹ 2,100 from African countries and ₹ 5000 Europe.

48. Production of wheat during 1972-73 in a certain state was 1.02 million tonnes. It was considerably increased in the next year. In 1973-74 it was increased by 0.172 million tonnes. The production of rice and jowar was increased by 0.02 million tonnes and 0.123 million tonnes respectively in 1973-74. The production of pulses was 0.122 million tonnes in 1973-74, which was less by 32 thousand tonnes than the previous year. The

production of jowar was 1.79 million tonnes and that of rice was 0.83 million tonnes in 1973-74.

Tabulate the information given above.

49. Prepare a complete table from the following information :

"In the year 1980 the total strength of students of three colleges X,Y, Z in a city were in the ratio 4 : 2 : 5. The strength of the college Y was 1000. The proportion of girls and boys in all colleges was in the ratio 2 : 3. The facultywise distribution of boys and girls in Arts, Science and Commerce was in the ratio 1 : 2 : 2 in all the three colleges."

50. Present the following information in a tabular from. Obtain the quantities which are not directly supplied.

In the annual report of a XYZ Oil Company it is stated that the company drilled in all 882 and 487 wells during the year 1987 and 1988 respectively. Company constructed two types of drilling machines viz. wild cat and developmental. During the year 1987 total of wild cat wells and a total of developmental wells were 40 and 842 respectively; the corresponding figures in 1988 were 46 and 441. Wells were further divided into three categories viz. oil, gas and dry hole.

Among the wild cat wells drilled in 1987, 6 resulted in oil, 4 in gas and 30 in dry holes, whereas the corresponding figures in 1988 were 6, 4 and 36. Out of the developmental wells drilled in 1987, 660 resulted in oil, 77 in gas and 105 in dry holes, the comparable figures for 1988 were 300, 77 and 64.

51. The total number of accidents in Southern Railway in 1960 was 3500 and it decreased by 300 in 1961 and by 700 in 1962. The total number of accidents in meter gauge section showed an increase from 1960 to 1962. It was 284 in 1960, 346 in 1961 and 428 in 1962. In meter gauge section 'Not compensated' cases were 49 in 1960, 77 in 1961 and 108 in 1962. 'Compensated' cases in broad gauge section were 2867, 2587 and 2152 in these three years respectively.

Prepare a neat table from the above report.

52. Total strength of a certain college is 2000. Exactly 60% of this belong to rural areas and the rest from urban areas. The total strength of Arts faculty and Science faculty are in the ratio 4 : 1. The total number of students of Arts faculty residing in rural areas is 1000, while that of Science is 200. There are 900 male students of Arts faculty who stay in rural areas and 500 male students staying in urban areas, the corresponding figures from Science faculty are 175 and 125.

Present the information in a suitable tabular form. Obtain figures which are not directly provided.

53. Present the following information in a tabular form, by computing the figures which are not directly given.

Exactly 20% of the number of students in a university of strength 20,000 are ladies, 33 out of every 40 students are Maharashtrian, 13 out of every 16 gents are Maharashtrian, 40% other than Maharashtrain gents and 55% of Maharashtrian gents have taken Arts subjects, whereas 40% of ladies from Maharashtra and equal percentage of ladies from other states have taken Science subjects.

54. Prepare a neat table and present the following information.

In 1984, exports and imports of a certain country in crores of ₹ were 320 and 250 respectively. In 1985 export was increased by 20 crores and import by 4%. In 1986, export did not change in its value. However, import decreased by 20. In 1987, export was further decreased by 30 crores and import decreased by 15%.

55. Present the following information in a tabular form.

Company	Data
A	Prices increased, demand decreased
B	Prices increased, demand not changed
C	Prices decreased, demand decreased
D	Prices decreased, demand decreased
E	Prices not changed, demand decreased
F	Prices increased, demand not changed
G	Prices decreased, demand increased
H	Prices decreased, demand increased
I	Prices increased, demand increased
J	Prices not changed, demand decreased
K	Prices doubled, demand decreased
L	Prices increased, demand decreased
M	Prices not changed, demand not changed
N	Prices increased, demand decreased
O	Prices decreased, demand decreased
P	Prices increased, demand decreased
Q	Prices increased, demand increased
R	Prices increased, demand decreased
S	Prices increased, demand decreased
T	Prices increased, demand decreased

56. Present the following information in a tabular form. In a college there are 60% boys. In an examination 70% students passed. Among the boys 360 passed, which is 75% of the boys.

57. Present the following information in a tabular form by computing the figures which are not directly given.

In a certain interview, there were 150 candidates of which 56% were males. 36 candidates were successful in the interview. The proportion of males to females in the successful candidates is 5 : 4.

58. Present the following information in a tabular form determining the figures which are not given.

Out of 800 employees appeared for a promotion test, 320 were married. Among 240 who were unsuccessful, 96 were married.

59. Present the following information in a table after computing figures those are not given.

A morbidity survey revealed the following information. Out of 240 persons exposed to small-pox, 112 were attacked. Out of 240 persons, 152 had been vaccinated and of those only 48 were attacked.

60. Prepare a statistical table using for the following information. Also find the figures which are not given directly.

Employed graduates	= 286
Unemployed graduates	= 48
Employed undergraduates	= 450
Unemployed undergraduates	= 216

61. Present the following data in a statistical table by computing the figures which are not directly supplied.

No. of fathers with dark eyes and sons with dark eyes = 50

No. of fathers without dark eyes and sons with dark eyes = 90

No. of fathers with dark eyes and sons without dark eyes = 80

No. of fathers without dark eyes and sons without dark eyes = 780.

62. A social worker conducted a survey which revealed the information as follows :

In 1980 the number of readers in literature, fiction and other type of books in a city library were 10000, 50000 and 10000 respectively.

In 1990 the corresponding figures were 12000, 52000 and 9000.

Present the above data in a tabular form.

63. A survey on musical entertainments gave the following results.

Total number of citizens interviewed was 6000, of which 40 % were females.

Among males 5 % liked classical music, 10 % liked light music, 8 % liked western music and the remaining preferred film songs. The corresponding figures for females were 10 %, 12 %, 6 % respectively.

Present the above information in a suitable table.

64. A locality was divided in three areas : administrative, main city and suburbs. A survey of housing conditions gave the following information.

There were 70,00,000 building of which 20,00,000 were in suburbs and 1,50,000 were in administrative area. In main city, 80 % buildings were inhabitated and remaining were under construction. The corresponding figures for suburbs were 75 % and 25% respectively. In administrative area, 4000 buildings were under construction.

Present the following information in a statistical table by computing the figures which are not directly given.

65. A census report gave the following data regarding a certain locality.

Among 35 crores of population, 24 crores persons were belonged to agricultural category. Among the agricultural category 7 crores were self supporting whereas 3 crores were earning dependents and remaining were non-earning. In non-agricultural category the number of self supporting and non-earning dependents were respectively   3.5 crores and 6 crores. The rest of the persons were earning dependents.

Present the above information in a suitable statistical table by computing the figures which are not directly supplied.

66. A manufacturing company found the scraps purchased, was of the following types.

Scrap A contains 65 % aluminium, 20 % iron, 2 % copper, 2 % manganese, 3 % magnesium and 8 % silicon.

Scrap B contains aluminium, iron, copper, manganese, and magnesium respectively 70 %, 15 %, 3 %, 2 % and 4 %.

Compute the figures which are not directly given and present the information in tabular form.

67. Complete the following table showing data related to examination result.

Class \ Year	F.Y.	S.Y.	T.Y.	Total
First class	148	82	–	–
Second class	192	95	38	–
Pass class	–	108	–	210
Fail	20	–	90	150
Total	–	325	275	1000

68. Complete the following table by finding values of a, b, c, d, e, f, g, h regarding the number of passengers travelling from city A to B.

Mode of transport	Male	Female	Total
S.T. Bus	800	a	1250
Train	b	750	2250
Aeroplane	4 c	c	d
Private vehicle	e	100	6 d
Own vehicle	350	150	f
Total	g	h	5000

69. In a sample study about tea drinking habits in towns A and B following data were obtained :

Town A	Town B
52% of the people were male	50% of the people were males
65% of the people were tea drinkers	75% of the people were tea drinkers
40% of the people were male tea drinkers	42% of the people were male tea drinkers

G. Miscellaneous Problems :

70. Among a group of students, 10% scored marks below 20, 20% scored marks between 20 and 40, 35% scored marks between 40 and 60, 20% scored marks between 60 and 80, and the remaining 30 students scored marks between 80 and 100.

(a) Using the information prepare a frequency distribution of marks of students.

(b) If minimum 40 marks are required for passing, how many students have passed the examination ?

(c) If maximum 60 marks are required for getting first class, how many students secured first class ?

71. Prepare a frequency distribution for each of the following :

   (a) Mid-value   :   47.5   52.5   57.5   62.5

       Frequency   :   4   9   17   10

   (b) Class-mark   :   4   8   12   16   20

       Frequency   :   24   45   20   10   1

72. Following is a frequency distribution of heights in cm.

Classes	150-154	55-159	160-164	165-169	170-174
Frequency	2	17	29	21	1

   (a) Obtain class boundaries of each of the classes.

   (b) Determine the class width.

73. Present the following information in a frequency distribution.

   In a branch of a certain co-operative bank, 50 % fixed deposits are less than ₹ 5000. Thirty percent fixed deposits are of the amount ₹ 5,000 to ₹ 10,000. The number of fixed deposits of amount in between ₹ 10,000 to ₹ 20,000 is 150. It is 15 % of total deposits. The remaining 5 % deposits are of amount more than ₹ 20,000.

74. Find the frequencies a, b, c, d in the following frequency distribution.

Class	0 – 10	10 – 20	20 – 30	30 – 40	Total
Frequency	a	b	c	d	100

   Given that : (i) d = 3 a (ii) b : c = 7 : 3 (iii) c : d = 3 : 5

Answers 2.1

12.

Class	157-160	160-163	163-166	166-169	169-172	172-174
Frequency	7	9	8	14	10	2

13.

Class	25-29	30-34	35-39	30-44	45-49	50-54	55-59
Frequency	1	0	3	6	6	6	7

Class	60-64	65-69	70-74	75-79	80-84
Frequency	4	4	1	1	1

14. (i)   8

   (ii)   Less than cumulative frequencies 12, 35, 82, 90, 93, 95.

   (iii) yes   (iv) 90 (v) more than cumulative frequencies 95, 83, 60, 13, 5, 2

   (vi)   13 (vii) 60 and above (viii) except the last class all have same width, which is 10

      Class marks :   15,   25,   35,   45,   55,   not defined.

15. (i)   yes (ii) class boundaries 0 – 19.5, 19.5 – 39.5, 39.5 – 59.5, 59.5 – 79.5, 79.5 – 99.5.

     Class boundaries are not same as class limits.

   (iii) Class marks 9.5, 29.5, 49.5, 69.5, 89.5.

     All classes have same width which is 20.

   (iv) Less than cumulative frequencies 8, 34, 58, 70, 75.

     No. of students having marks less than or equal to 59 is 58.

   (v)   More than cumulative frequencies 75, 67, 41, 17, 5.

     No. of students having marks more than or equal to 60 is 17.

16. (i) 142 (ii) 5 (iii) 149.5 – 154.5 (iv) 155 – 159 (v) 72

17. (i) inclusive (ii) 94.5 (iii) 99.5 – 105.5 (iv) 158 (v) 138.

18. (i) inclusive (ii) 24.5 (iii) 39.5 – 49.5 (iv) 90 (v) 64.

19. (i) inclusive (ii) Below 30, Above 71 (iii) 14 (iv) 65.5 (v) 50.5 – 60.5.

20. (i) inclusive (i) 39.5 – 59.5 (iii) 20 (iv) 29.5 (v) 75.

21. (i) exclusive (ii) 18 (iii) 450 (iv) 300 – 400 (v) 100.

22. (i) 79.5 – 89.5 (ii) 10 (iii) 80 – 89 (iv) 56.

23. (i) 1749.5 (ii) 500 (iii) 37 (iv) 53 (iv) 1500 – 1999.

24. 12, 27, 35, 38, 39.

25. Less than cumulative frequencies : 12, 27, 57, 65, 67.

   More than cumulative frequencies : 67, 55, 40, 10, 2.

26. 50, 42, 30, 15, 5.

27. No, less than cumulative frequency cannot be decreasing.

28. (a)

Class	0-10	10-20	20-30	30-40	40-50
Frequency	1	7	27	11	4

   (b)

Class	01-20	20-30	30-40	40-50	50-60	60-70
Frequency	15	20	37	36	12	4

29.

Class	Frequency
500 – 1000	4
1000 – 1500	4
1500 – 2000	33
2000 – 2500	31
2500 – 3000	26
above 3000	2

30.

Class	0-1	1-3	3-5	5-8	8-12	12-16
Frequency	12	46	148	166	128	20
More than cum. frequency	520	508	462	314	148	20

31.

Class	145-150	150-155	155-160	160-165	165-170	170-175
Frequency	7	12	22	38	30	21
More than cum. frequency	7	19	41	79	109	130

E :

40. Pie diagram

41. (a) Pie diagram, (b) private, (c) co-operative.

42. (a) Pie, (b) other industries, (c) chemical, food, drug.

43. Pie diagram.

F :

46.

	Grocery	Vegetables	Medicine	Textile	Novelty
1981	625	220	188	483	64
1982	675	242	175	536	143
1983	653	210	165	612	131

Foot note : Figures are in thousand ₹

47.

	A	B	C
U.K.	100	6.7	40
Asia	10	2.5	5.7
Africa	3	1.5	2.1
Europe	15	5	5
U.S.A	2	0	0

Foot note : Figures are in thousand ₹

48.

	Wheat	Rice	Jowar	Pulses
1972 - 73	1.020	0.81	1.667	0.1188
1973 -74	1.192	0.83	1.790	0.1220

Foot note : Figures are in million tonnes.

49.

	X		Y		Z	
	Boys	**Girls**	**Boys**	**Girls**	**Boys**	**Girls**
Arts	240	160	120	80	300	200
Science	480	320	240	160	600	400
Commerce	480	320	240	160	600	400

50.

	Wild cat			**Development**		
	Oil	**Gas**	**Dry**	**Oil**	**Gas**	**Dry**
1987	6	4	30	660	77	105
1988	6	4	36	300	77	64

51.

	1960		**1961**		**1962**	
	BG	**MG**	**BG**	**MG**	**BG**	**MG**
Compensated	286	235	258	269	215	320
Non-compensated	7	49	7	77	2	108
	249		267		220	

Foot Note : BG = Broad gauge, MG = Meter gauge

52.

	Arts		**Science**	
	Male	**Female**	**Male**	**Female**
Rural	900	100	175	25
Urban	500	100	125	75

53.

	Arts		**Science**	
	Gents	**Ladies**	**Gents**	**Ladies**
Maharashtrian	7150	2100	5850	1400
Non-Maharashtrain	1200	300	1800	200

54.

	Export	**Import**
1984	320	250
1985	340	260
1986	340	240
1987	310	204

Note : Figures are in crore ₹

55.

Demand	Prices		
	Decreased	Not changed	Increased
Decreased	3	2	8
Not changed	0	1	2
Increased	2	0	2

56.

	Passed	Failed
Boys	360	120
Girls	200	120

57.

	Successful	Unsuccessful
Male	20	64
Female	16	50

58.

	Successful	Unsuccessful
Married	224	96
Unmarried	336	144

59.

	Vaccinated	Non-vaccinated
Attacked	48	64
Not-attacked	104	24

60.

	Graduates	Undergraduates
Employed	286	450
Unemployed	48	216

61.

Son Father	Dark eyes	Without dark eyes
Dark eyes	50	90
Without dark eyes	80	780

62.

Year	Literature	Fiction	Other
1980	10	50	10
1990	12	52	9

Note : Figures are in thousands.

63.

	Classical	Light	Western	Film song
Female	240	288	144	1728
Male	180	360	288	2772

64.

	Administrative	Main city	Suburbs
Inhabited	146	3880	1500
Other	4	970	500

Note : Figures are in thousands.

65.

	Self supporting	Earning dependents	Non-earning
Agricultural	7.0	3.0	14.0
Non-agricultural	3.5	1.5	6.0

Note : Figures are in crores.

66.

Scrap	Aluminium	Iron	Copper	Man-ganese	Magne-sium	Silicon
A	65	20	2	2	3	8
B	70	15	3	2	4	6

67.

	F.Y.	S.Y.	T.Y.	Total
First class	148	82	85	315
Second class	192	95	38	325
Pass class	40	108	62	210
Fail	20	40	90	150
Total	400	325	275	1000

68.

	Male	Female	Total
S.T. Bus	800	450	1250
Train	1800	750	2250
Aeroplane	80	20	100
Private vehicle	500	100	600
Own vehicle	350	150	500
Total	3530	1470	5000

G :

70. (a)

Class	0-20	20-40	40-60	60-80	80-100
Frequency	20	40	70	40	30

(b) 140 (c) 70.

71.

(a)

Class	Frequency
45-50	4
50-55	9
55-60	17
60-65	10

(b)

Class	Frequency
2-6	24
6-10	45
10-14	20
14-18	10

72. (a) 149.5 – 154.5, 154.5 – 159.5, 159.5 – 164.5, 164.5 – 169.5, 169.5 – 174.5

(b) Classes are of same width, class width = 5.

73.

Class	Below 5000	5000-1000	10000-20000	Above 20000
Frequency	500	300	150	50

74.

Class	0-10	10-20	20-30	30-40
Frequency	10	42	18	30

⊐⊐⊐

Chapter **3**...

Measures of Central Tendency

Contents ...

Key Words :

Central Tendency, Average, Arithmetic Mean, Deviation, Combined Mean, Median, Deciles, Percentiles, Box Plot, Cumulative Frequency, Mode, Empirical Relation.

Objectives :

Averages are tools of summarizing data, finding representative. It also facilitates the comparison. The methods of determining averages are illustrated in this chapter. The third and fourth aspects of statistics are analysis and interpretation. Averages help in both analysis and interpretation.

3.1 Introduction

We have studied in the previous chapters the various methods of summarizing data and its graphical representation. However it becomes essential to condense the data into a single value. Such a single value is treated as a representative of data and it is referred to an **average** or **central value** or measure of **central tendency.** It is desired that all the important properties of the observations in the data should be represented in the average. The word average is very commonly used in day-to-day life,

For example : Average marks, average profit, average run-rate of a team in one day. A single value is suitable for comparison. Therefore, average is essential quantity. Average is a value around which most of the observations are clustered, hence this single value itself gives clear idea regarding phenomenon under study.

There are several types of averages used in practice according to the type of data and purpose. In this chapter we study three important averages viz. mean, median and mode.

3.2 Objectives or Requisites of Ideal Average

The following are the objectives of average :

1. To obtain a single representative quantity for the entire data.

2. To facilitate comparison.

There are several averages in use, hence it is necessary to discuss the requisites of good or ideal average. **The following are requisites of good average :**

1. It should be simple to understand and easy to calculate.

2. It should be rigidly defined.

3. It should be based on all observations in the data.

4. It should be capable of further mathematical treatment.

5. It should be least affected by extreme observations.

3.3 Arithmetic Mean (A.M.)

This is very commonly used and widely applicable average.

Definition : Arithmetic mean (A.M.) or mean is a sum of observations divided by number of observations i.e.

$$\text{A.M.} = \frac{\text{Sum of the observations}}{\text{Number of observations}}$$

According to the different types of data calculation of A.M. differs slightly. We consider these cases as given below :

Case (i) Individual observations or ungrouped data :

Suppose $x_1, x_2, \ldots , x_n$ is a set of n observations by definition, arithmetic mean will be

$$\text{A.M.} = \frac{x_1 + x_2 + \ldots + x_n}{n} \qquad \ldots (3.1)$$

Numerator of right side of (3.1) can be symbolically written as $\sum x$ i.e. $x_1 + x_2 + \ldots + x_n$.

Symbol $\sum$ (sigma) represents the sum. Further it is a customary to denote A.M. by $\bar{x}$. Hence

$$\text{A.M.} = \bar{x} = \frac{\sum x}{n}$$

Case (ii) Discrete frequency distribution :

Suppose $x_1, x_2, \ldots, x_n$ are values with $f_1, f_2, \ldots , f_n$ as the corresponding frequencies. Clearly to find the sum of observations we need to add observation x_1, f_1 times, observation

x_2, f_2 times and so on. Hence sum of observations will be $f_1x_1 + f_2x_2 + ... + f_nx_n$ and total number of observations will be $f_1 + f_2 + ... + f_n$. Hence,

$$\bar{x} = \frac{f_1x_1 + f_2x_2 + ... + f_nx_n}{f_1 + f_2 + ... + f_n}$$

Using $\sum$ notation we get

$$\bar{x} = \frac{\sum fx}{\sum f}$$

Case (iii) Continuous frequency distribution :

In this case, frequency is associated to the entire class and not to any specific single value. This creates difficulty in choosing x_1, x_2, ..., x_n.

For calculation purpose we make a reasonable assumption that the frequency is associated with mid-point of class or equivalently the frequency is distributed over the respective class uniformly. Thus, taking x_1, x_2, ..., x_n as the mid-values of class intervals we calculate mean by the same formula discussed in case (ii), i.e.

$$\bar{x} = \frac{\sum f \cdot x}{\sum f} = \frac{\sum f \cdot x}{N}$$

Illustration 1 : *Calculate the arithmetic mean of marks scored by a student in 7 subjects given below : 61, 68, 69, 63, 70, 60, 78.*

Solution :

$$\bar{x} = \frac{\text{Total marks scored}}{\text{Number of subjects}}$$

$$\bar{x} = \frac{61 + 68 + 69 + 63 + 70 + 60 + 78}{7} = \frac{469}{7} = 67$$

Fig. 3.1

It can be noticed in the above illustration that the observations are nearer to 60, so for convenience we assume the mean to be 60 and obtain the sum of excess of marks. It will be $1 + 8 + 9 + 3 + 10 + 10 + 18 = 49$. We find the average of excess and add in the assumed mean. Thus mean will be $60 + 49/7 = 67$.

The above discussion leads to a short-cut method of finding arithmetic mean.

Short-cut Method or Derivation Method or Assumed Mean Method :

This method reduces the calculations involved in finding mean. Following are the steps in the computational procedure of mean.

(1) Decide a suitable figure 'a' which is referred as assumed mean.

(2) Subtract 'a' from each observation, the difference so calculated is called deviation from 'a', we denote deviation by 'd'.

(3) Find sum of deviations

   $\sum d$ in case of individual observations.

   $\sum fd$ in case of frequency distribution.

(4) Use the following formula and find the mean :

$$\bar{x} = a + \frac{\sum d}{n} \quad \text{in case of individual observations}$$

and

$$\bar{x} = a + \frac{\sum fd}{N} \quad \text{in case of frequency distribution.}$$

Illustration 2 : *Calculate arithmetic mean for the following frequency distribution :*

Observation (x)	103	110	112	118	95
Frequency (f)	4	6	10	12	3

Solution : We solve the problem by both the methods.

1. **Direct method :**

x	f	f.x
103	4	$103 \times 4 = 412$
110	6	$110 \times 6 = 660$
112	10	$112 \times 10 = 1120$
118	12	$118 \times 12 = 1416$
95	3	$95 \times 3 = 285$
Total	**N = 35**	**$\sum fx = 3893$**

∴ $\bar{x} = \dfrac{\sum fx}{\sum f} = \dfrac{3893}{35} = 111.2286$

2. **Deviation method :**

Taking assumed mean a = 100, we prepare the following table and use deviation method.

x	Deviations d = x – a d = x – 100	f	f·d
103	3	4	12
110	10	6	60
112	12	10	120
118	18	12	216
95	– 5	3	– 15
	Total	**N = 35**	**$\sum fd = 393$**

Thus $\qquad \bar{x} = a + \dfrac{\Sigma fd}{N} = 100 + \dfrac{393}{35} = 100 + 11.2286 = 111.2286$

Step-deviation method : We have seen that deviation method reduces the calculations when the observations are large in magnitude. Sometimes the observations or deviations are multiples of some number. Especially when we deal with frequency distribution of continuous variables, deviations are found to be multiple of class width. In this situation step-deviation method is advisable.

Steps in the computational procedure are given below :

(1) Decide a suitable figure 'a'. (assumed mean a).

(2) Subtract 'a' from each observation and find deviation d (or class mark) i.e.

$$d = x - a.$$

(3) Divide d, obtained in (2) by convenient figure 'h' (or by class width). This figure is called as step-deviation.

i.e. $\qquad d' = \dfrac{d}{h}$

(4) Find sum of step deviations

$\Sigma d'$ $\quad$ in case of individual observations

$\Sigma fd'$ $\quad$ in case of frequency distribution.

(5) Use the following formula to find the mean

$$\bar{x} = a + \left(\dfrac{\Sigma d'}{n} \times h \right) \qquad \text{in case of individual observations}$$

and

$$\bar{x} = a + \left(\dfrac{\Sigma fd'}{N} \times h \right) \qquad \text{in case of frequency distribution.}$$

Illustration 3 : The following is a distribution of monthly salaries of the employees of a firm.

Salaries in ₹	No. of employees
0 – 500	2
500 – 1000	8
1000 – 1500	12
1500 – 2000	23
2000 – 2500	25
2500 – 3000	20
3000 – 3500	9
3500 – 4000	1

Compute arithmetic mean of salaries.

Solution : We use step-deviation method to find the mean.

Class	Mid-values	d = x – 1750	$d' = \dfrac{d}{500}$	f	fd'
0 – 500	250	– 1500	– 3	2	– 6
500 – 1000	750	– 1000	– 2	8	– 16
1000 – 1500	1250	– 500	– 1	12	– 12
1500 – 2000	1750	0	0	23	0
2000 – 2500	2250	500	1	25	25
2500 – 3000	2750	1000	2	20	40
3000 – 3500	3250	1500	3	9	27
3500 – 4000	3750	2000	4	1	4
Total	–	–	–	100	62

$$\bar{x} = a + \left(\frac{\sum fd'}{N} \times h \right)$$

Note that a = 1750, $\sum$ fd' = 62, N = 100 and h = 500.

Hence, $\bar{x} = 1750 + \dfrac{62}{100} \times 500$

∴ $\bar{x} = 1750 + 310 = 2060$

Thus average salary is ₹ 2,060.

Effect of change of origin and Scale on Arithmetic mean :

Change of origin means to add or to subtract a constant from each observation. Thus, if the original variable is denoted by x than x – a or x + a is a variable obtained by shifting the origin (where a is a constant). The new variable x – a is also referred as deviation. In this situation arithmetic mean need not be obtained again however from the earlier mean we can determine the mean after the change of origin.

(1) If y = x – a then $\bar{y} = \bar{x} - a$.

(2) If y = x + a then $\bar{y} = \bar{x} + a$.

Similarly, changing of scale means to multiply or to divide the observations by a constant. Thus, if x is the variable x/c or cx is a variable obtained by changing the scale, c being constant. In this case also we need not find the arithmetic mean once again due to change in scale. The change of scale is similar to step deviation. However the same relation is observed between old variable and the variable after changing the scale. We summarize the rules below :

(3) If $y = \dfrac{x}{c}$ then $\bar{y} = \dfrac{\bar{x}}{c}$.

(4) If $y = cx$ then $\bar{y} = c\bar{x}$.

(5) If $y = ax + b$ then $\bar{y} = a\bar{x} + b$.

(6) If $y = \dfrac{x - a}{c}$ then $\bar{y} = \dfrac{\bar{x} - a}{c}$.

Illustration 4 : Suppose the arithmetic mean of 50 observations is 120. Find the arithmetic mean if each observation is

(i)   increased by 10

(ii)   decreased by 5

(iii)   doubled

(iv)   reduced to one third

(v)   doubled and then increased by 5

(vi)   increased by 5 and then doubled.

Solution : This illustration explains the change of origin and scale (or linear transformations). Let x = original variable = y = New variable.

(i) $y = x + 10$, $\bar{y} = \bar{x} + 10 = 120 + 10 = 130$

(ii) $y = x - 5$, $\bar{y} = \bar{x} - 5 = 120 - 5 = 115$

(iii) $y = 2x$, $\bar{y} = 2\bar{x} = 2 \times 120 = 240$

(iv) $y = \dfrac{x}{3}$, $\bar{y} = \dfrac{\bar{x}}{3} = \dfrac{120}{3} = 40$

(v) $y = 2x + 5$, $\bar{y} = 2\bar{x} + 5 = 2 \times 120 + 5 = 245$

(vi) $y = 2(x + 5)$, $\bar{y} = 2(\bar{x} + 5) = 2(120 + 5) = 250$.

3.4 Merits and Demerits of Arithmetic Mean

Arithmetic mean possesses most of the requisites of good average. Hence it is widely used. We state below its merits and demerits :

Merits :

1.   It is easy to calculate and simple to follow.

2.   It is based on all observations.

3.   It is rigidly defined.

4.   It possesses sampling stability.

5.   It is capable of further mathematical treatment. Given the means and sizes of two or more groups we can find mean of combined group. We can find the total given the mean and number of observations.

Demerits :

1. It is applicable only for quantitative data.

2. It is unduly affected by extreme observations.

3. It cannot be computed for frequency distribution with open end class.

4. It cannot be determined graphically.

5. Sometimes arithmetic mean may not be an observation in a data. *For example,* arithmetic mean of number of T.V. sets sold daily is 5.25.

3.5 Mean of Combined Groups

Many times it is required to compute mean of two groups combined together. If means and sizes of groups are known we can determine the combined mean i.e. mean of combined group.

Let $\bar{x}_1$ be the arithmetic mean of first group of size n_1. Similarly $\bar{x}_2$ be mean of second group of size n_2, then the combined mean is derived as follows :

$$\bar{x}_1 = \frac{(\text{Sum of observations in first group})}{n_1}$$

hence, $\qquad n_1 \bar{x}_1 = $ Sum of observations in first group

Similarly $\qquad n_2 \bar{x}_2 = $ Sum of observations in second group.

Thus, the combined mean $\bar{x}_c$ is

$$\bar{x}_c = \frac{\left(\begin{array}{c}\text{Sum of the observations in} \\ \text{first group}\end{array}\right) + \left(\begin{array}{c}\text{Sum of the observations} \\ \text{in second group}\end{array}\right)}{(\text{Size of first group}) + (\text{Size of second group})}$$

$$\bar{x}_c = \frac{n_1 \bar{x}_1 + n_2 \bar{x}_2}{n_1 + n_2}$$

Illustration 5 : *Arithmetic mean of weight of 100 boys is 50 kg and the arithmetic mean of 50 girls is 45 kg. Calculate the arithmetic mean of combined group of boys and girls.*

Solution : Let $\bar{x}_1$ and n_1 be the mean and size of group of boys and $\bar{x}_2$ and n_2 be the mean and size of group of girls. So that $n_1 = 100$, $\bar{x}_1 = 50$, $n_2 = 50$, $\bar{x}_2 = 45$. Hence, combined mean is

$$\bar{x}_c = \frac{n_1 \bar{x}_1 + n_2 \bar{x}_2}{n_1 + n_2} = \frac{(100 \times 50) + (50 \times 45)}{100 + 50}$$

$$= \frac{7250}{150} = 48.3333$$

Illustration 6 : *The mean weekly salary paid to 300 employees of a firm is 1,470 ₹ There are 200 male employees and the remaining are females. If mean salary of males is 1,505 ₹ Obtain the mean salary of females.*

Solution : Suppose $\bar{x}_1$ and n_1 are mean and group size of males. $\bar{x}_2$ and n_2 are mean and size of group of females, $\bar{x}_c$ is mean of all the employees considered together.

Now,
$$\bar{x}_c = \frac{n_1 \bar{x}_1 + n_2 \bar{x}_2}{n_1 + n_2}$$

∴
$$1470 = \frac{(200 \times 1505) + (100 \times \bar{x}_2)}{200 + 100}$$

∴
$$1470 = \frac{301000 + 100\, x_2}{300}$$

∴
$$441000 = 301000 + 100\, \bar{x}_2$$

∴
$$4410 = 3010 + \bar{x}_2$$

∴
$$\bar{x}_2 = 1,400\ ₹$$

3.6 Median

We have seen that arithmetic mean cannot be calculated for qualitative observations like beauty, debating skill, honesty, blindness. Moreover if a frequency distribution includes open end class, mean does not exist and it is unduly affected by extreme observations. In order to overcome these drawbacks, other measures of central tendency, median or mode are used.

Illustration : The arithmetic mean of 38, 43, 41, 39, 52, 48, 60, 167 is 61. This cannot be the representative value of the data, because among 8 observations, 7 are smaller than arithmetic mean. Thus incase extreme observations are widely separated from most of the observations, arithmetic mean does not remain suitable, whereas median is suitable.

Definition : Median is the value of middle most observation in the data when the observations are arranged in increasing (or decreasing) order of their values.

Thus, median is the central observation. It divides the data into two equal parts. There are equal number of observation above as well as below the median. It is also called as **positional average**.

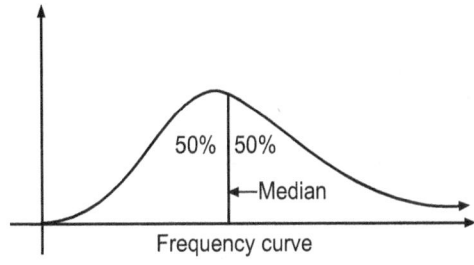

Fig. 3.2

(i) Computation of Median for Ungrouped data :

It may be noticed that in case of individual observations or ungrouped data computation of median does not require any formula. It can be determined by inspection.

Suppose n is the number of observations in the data. If n is odd then there is only one middle most observation which is $\frac{(n+1)^{th}}{2}$ observation. On the other hand if n is even then there are two middle most observations which are $(n/2)^{th}$ and $(n/2 + 1)^{th}$. In this case we take median to be mean of these two middle most observations. We follow the procedure described below for calculating median.

Step 1 : Arrange the observations in increasing (or decreasing) order.

Step 2 : Compute the median by the following criteria :

Median = The value of $(n + 1)/2$ th observation if n is odd.

$$\text{Median} = \frac{\left(\begin{array}{c}\text{The value of } (n/2)^{th}\\ \text{observation}\end{array}\right) + \left(\begin{array}{c}\text{The value of } (n/2 + 1)^{th}\\ \text{observation}\end{array}\right)}{2} \quad \text{if n is even}$$

Illustration 7 : *Following are the temperatures recorded in a certain city, observed in a certain week.*

$$35,\ 38,\ 40,\ 39,\ 35,\ 36,\ 37$$

Obtain the median temperature.

Solution : The ordered arrangement of 7 observations is

$$35,\ 35,\ 36,\ \boxed{37},\ 38,39,\ 40$$

Since, n = 7 is odd we get,

Median = The value of $(n + 1)/2^{th}$ observation

= The value of 4th observation = 37.

Illustration 8 : *The following are the sales in ₹ for 6 days in a certain week.*

$$3020, 4120, 3600,\ 3250, 3830, 4000$$

Obtain the median sale.

Solution : The ordered arrangement of 6 observations is

$$3020,\ 3250,\ \boxed{3600,\ 3830}\ ,4000,4120$$

Since n = 6 is even we get two middle observations. Hence

$$\text{Median} = \frac{\left(\begin{array}{c}\text{The value of } (n/2)^{th}\\ \text{observation}\end{array}\right) + \left(\begin{array}{c}\text{The value of } (n/2 + 1)^{th}\\ \text{observation}\end{array}\right)}{2}$$

$$\text{Median} = \frac{\left(\begin{array}{c}\text{The value of } 3^{rd}\\ \text{observation}\end{array}\right) + \left(\begin{array}{c}\text{The value of } 4^{th}\\ \text{observation}\end{array}\right)}{2} = \frac{3600 + 3830}{2} = 3715\ ₹$$

(ii) Computation of Median for Continuous frequency distribution : Suppose N is the total frequency. Since the variable under consideration is continuous we can estimate the value of $(N/2)^{th}$ observation. Hence regardless of N whether it is even or odd in continuous frequency distribution we take median to be the value of $(N/2)^{th}$ observation.

Computational procedure :

Step 1 : Obtain the class boundaries.

Step 2 : Obtain less than cumulative frequencies.

Step 3 : Locate the median class. Where median class is the class in which median i.e. $(N/2)^{th}$ observation falls. In other words, it is in a class where less than cumulative frequency is equal to or exceeds N/2 for the first time.

Step 4 : Apply the formula and find the median.

$$\text{Median} = l + \left(\frac{N/2 - c.f.}{f} \times h \right)$$

where,

l = Lower boundary (extended class limit) of the median class

N = Total frequency

c.f. = Less than cumulative frequency of the class just **preceding** to median class.

f = Frequency of median class

h = Class width

Illustration 9 : *Calculate median for the following frequency distribution :*

Marks	below 20	21-40	41-60	61-80	81-100
No. of students	1	9	32	16	7

Solution :

Class boundaries	Frequency	Less than cumulative frequency
0 – 20.5	1	1 < N/2
20.5 – 40.5	9	c.f. = 10 < N/2
40.5 – 60.5 Median class	f = 32	42 > N/2
60.5 – 80.5	16	58
80.5 – 100	7	65 = N

Median = The value of N/2 i.e. 32.5^{th} observation.

Median class : 40.5 – 60.5,

because N/2 exceeds less than cumulative frequency for the first time in this class.

Therefore, $l = 40.5$, N/2 = 32.5, c.f. = 10, f = 32, h = 20.

Hence,

$$\text{Median} = l + \left(\frac{N/2 - c.f.}{f}\right) \times h$$

$$= 40.5 + \frac{32.5 - 10}{32} \times 20$$

$$= 54.5625$$

3.7 Median – by Graphical Method

Median can be obtained graphically by means of ogive curve. Plot less than cumulative frequency curve taking upper boundaries on x-axis, and less than cumulative frequency on y-axis. Draw a line parallel to x-axis passing through point N/2 on y-axis. From the point of intersection of the line and ogive curve, draw a perpendicular to x-axis. The value at the foot of perpendicular is the median.

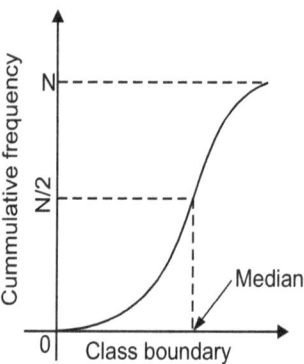

Fig. 3.3

Illustration 10 : *Obtain the median, from the following frequency distribution using formula and also graphically.*

Monthly Salary (₹)	1400-1600	1600-1800	1800-2000	2000-2200	2200-2400	2400-2600
Frequency	12	30	55	40	35	28

Solution : Here the classes are continuous, hence they can be used as they are :

Class	Frequency	Less than type cumulative frequency
1400 – 1600	12	12
1600 – 1800	30	42
1800 – 2000	55	97
2000 – 2200	40	137
2200 – 2400	35	172
2400 – 2600	28	200 = N

$$\text{Median} = \left(\frac{N}{2}\right)^{th} \text{observation}$$

$$= \left(\frac{200}{2} = 100\right)^{th} \text{observation}$$

Median lies in the (2000 – 2200) class, since 100 lies between less than cumulative frequencies 97 and 137,

$$\text{Median} = l + \left(\frac{N/2 - c.f.}{f}\right) \times h$$

$$= 2000 + \left(\frac{100 - 97}{40}\right) \times 200$$

$$= 2015$$

To obtain median graphically we use less than type cumulative frequency curve.

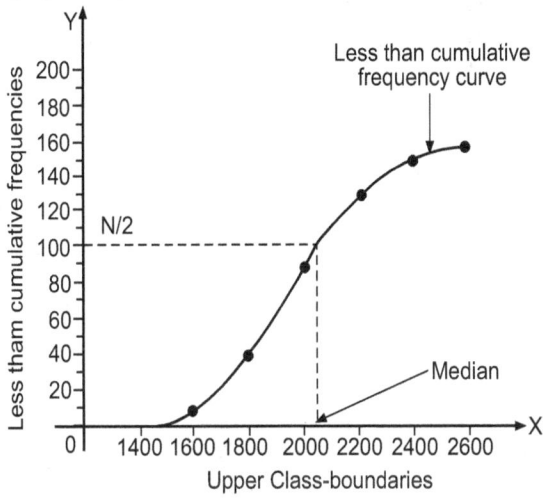

Fig. 3.4

3.8 Merits and Demerits of Median

Merits :

1. It is easy to understand and easy to calculate.
2. It is not affected due to extreme observations.
3. It can be computed for a distribution with open end classes.
4. It can be determined graphically.
5. It is applicable to qualitative data also. In this case observations are arranged in order according to the quality and the middle most observation can be obtained. The quality of this item is taken to be average quality or median quality.

Demerits :

1. It is not based on all the observations, hence it is not proper representative.
2. It is not capable of further mathematical treatment.
3. It is not as rigidly defined as the arithmetic mean.

3.9 Quartiles

Quartiles : Earlier we have seen that median divides the total number of observations into two equal parts. Similarly in order to make four equal parts we use quartiles, for making 10 equals parts we use deciles and for making 100 equal parts we use percentiles, when the observations are ordered.

Definition : The observations Q_1, Q_2, Q_3 which divide the total number of observations into 4 equal parts are called *quartiles.*

Median, quartiles are called **partition values** in common. The procedure of obtaining median is used to compute other partition values with appropriate changes. To obtain the partition values of series of individual observations, many calculations or formulae are not required. However, to compute partition values of a continuous frequency distribution, corresponding formula of median can be suitably modified. In this case, first of all less than cumulative frequency is determined. Using these cumulative frequencies a class in which partition value lies is decided and then using the formula, partition value is determined.

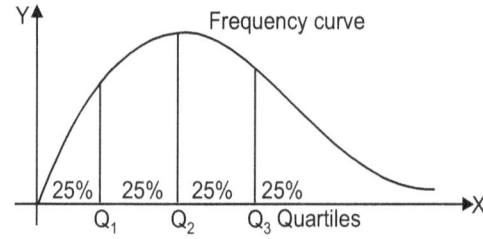

Fig. 3.5

$$\text{First quartile } (Q_1) \;=\; l + \left(\frac{\dfrac{N}{4} - \text{c.f.}}{f} \right) \times h$$

$$\text{Second quartile } (Q_2) \;=\; l + \left(\frac{\dfrac{N}{2} - \text{c.f.}}{f} \right) \times h$$

$$\text{Third quartile } (Q_3) \;=\; l + \left(\frac{\dfrac{3N}{4} - \text{c.f.}}{f} \right) \times h$$

Note :

1. Quartiles are not equispaced. However, area under the curve between any two successive quartiles is same. Therefore area between any two successive quartiles is 25% of the total area under the frequency curve.

2. Quartiles can be obtained graphically using less than cumulative frequency curve. The procedure is similar to that of median.

3. Minimum $< Q_1 < Q_2 < Q_3 <$ Maximum.

Illustration 11 : Compute the quartiles for the following series of observations.

26, 30, 35, 5, 6, 7, 9, 20, 40, 45, 11, 18, 15, 49, 60.

Solution : To find the quartiles first we arrange the observations in increasing (or decreasing) order of their magnitudes. Ordered arrangement will be

5, 6, 7, $\boxed{9}$, 11, 15, 18, $\boxed{20}$, 26, 30, 35, $\boxed{40}$, 45, 49, 60.

First quartile or lower quartile Q_1

$$= \left(\frac{(n+1)}{4}\right)^{th} \text{ observation}$$

$$= \left(\frac{15+1}{4} = 4\right)^{th} \text{ observation} = 9$$

Second quartile or median Q_2

$$= \left(\frac{n+1}{2}\right)^{th} \text{ observation}$$

$$= \left(\frac{15+1}{2} = 8\right)^{th} \text{ observation} = 20$$

Third quartile or upper quartile Q_3

$$= \left(\frac{3(n+1)}{4}\right)^{th} \text{ observation}$$

$$= \left(\frac{3(15+1)}{4} = 12\right)^{th} \text{ observation} = 40.$$

Illustration 12 : Obtain the quartiles from the following frequency distribution using formula and also graphically.

Monthly Salary (₹)	1400-1600	1600-1800	1800-2000	2000-2200	2200-2400	2400-2600
Frequency	12	30	55	40	35	28

Solution : Here the classes are continuous, hence they can be used as they are :

Class	Frequency	Less than type cumulative frequency
1400 – 1600	12	12
1600 – 1800	30	42
1800 – 2000	55	97
2000 – 2200	40	137
2200 – 2400	35	172
2400 – 2600	28	200 = N

$$Q_1 = \left(\frac{N}{4}\right)^{th} \text{ observation} = \left(\frac{200}{4} = 50\right)^{th} \text{ observation.}$$

$$\text{First quartile } (Q_1) = l + \left(\frac{\frac{N}{4} - c.f.}{f}\right) \times h$$

Since we have to consider 50th observation, and $42 < 50 < 97$, we have to consider the class of less than cumulative frequency in which partition value lies. Therefore, $1800 - 2000$ is the first quartile class.

∴ Q_1 lies in $(1800 - 2000)$ class

∴

$$Q_1 = 1800 + \frac{50 - 42}{55} \times 200 = 1800 + 29.0909 = 1829.0909$$

$$Q_2 = \text{Median} = \left(\frac{N}{2}\right)^{th} \text{ observation}$$

$$Q_2 \text{ class} : (2000 - 2200) = l + \left(\frac{N/2 - c.f.}{f}\right) \times h$$

$$= 2000 + \frac{100 - 97}{40} \times 200 = 2000 + 15 = 2015$$

$$Q_3 = \left(\frac{3N}{4}\right)^{th} \text{ observation} = 150^{th} \text{ observation}$$

Q_3 class : $2200 - 2400$

$$Q_3 = l + \frac{(3N/4) - c.f.}{f} \times h$$

$$= 2200 + \frac{150 - 137}{28} \times 200 = 2292.86$$

To obtain Q_1, Q_2, Q_3 graphically we use less than type cumulative frequency curve.

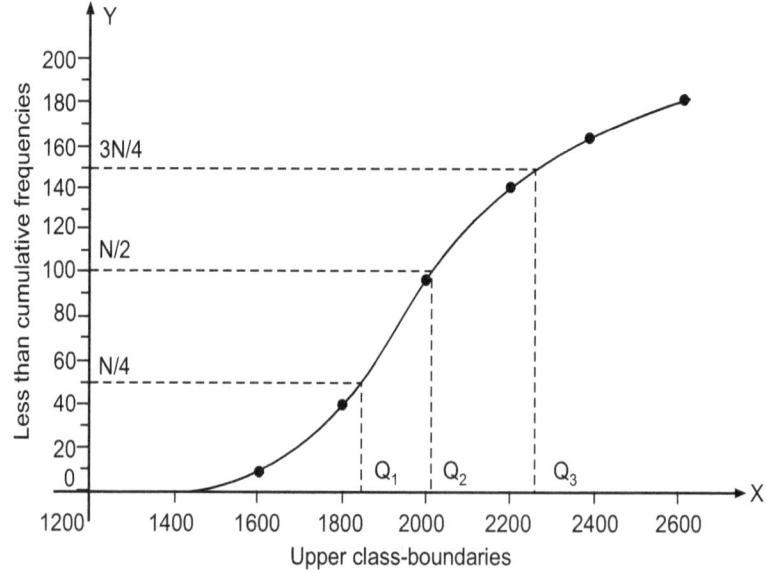

Fig. 3.6

3.10 Box and Whisker Plot

There is one more way of graphical representation of data known as box and whisker plot.

To draw box plot we find the three quartiles and the extreme observations. We illustrate the procedure by the following example.

Illustration 13 : Construct box plot to represent the data given below

26, 30, 35, 5, 6, 7, 9, 20, 40, 45, 11, 18, 15, 49, 60.

Solution : Clearly the ordered arrangement is

5, 6, 7, $\boxed{9}$, 11, 15, 18, $\boxed{20}$, 26, 30, 35, $\boxed{40}$, 45, 49, 60.

Note that the minimum is 5, maximum is 60 and the three quartiles are respectively 9, 20, 40. We take observations from minimum to maximum on line and put the rectangular box to include the first quartile and the third quartile. Thus the length of box is $Q_3 - Q_1$. In this case it is $40 - 9 = 31$. We divide the box in two boxes by putting horizontal line at median.

The box pot is drawn below.

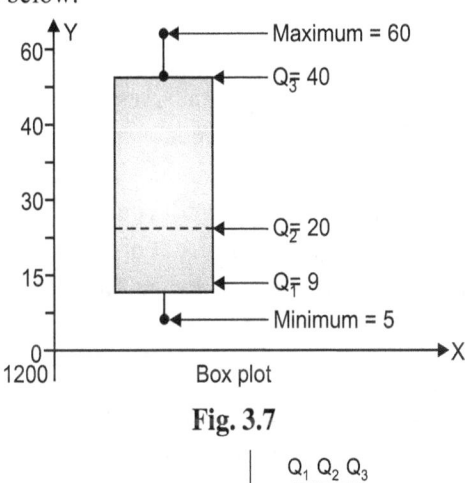

Fig. 3.7

Note : The box plot may be horizonal also.

Uses of box plot :

1. It gives the idea about the spread of data.

2. The box represents the interquartile range $Q_3 - Q_1$ of the data. In other words it gives the range in which middle 50% observations lie.

3. It gives the idea about the symmetry of the data around the median.

4. Median divides the data in two equal parts, box plot gives idea about how the observations are clustered or spread in each part of data.

5. The box plot facilitates the comparison of the aspects (i) central tendency, (ii) spread, (iii) symmetry.

3.11 Mode

It is yet another measure of central tendency developed to overcome the drawbacks of arithmetic mean. Apart from this, in some situations mode is the proper average.

Definition : The observation with maximum frequency or the most repeated observation is called as mode.

It is clear from earlier discussion that the general nature of frequency curve is bell shaped in majority of situations. Thus initially frequency is small, it increases and reaches the maximum and then it declines. The value on x-axis at which the maxima or the peak of the frequency curve appears is a mode.

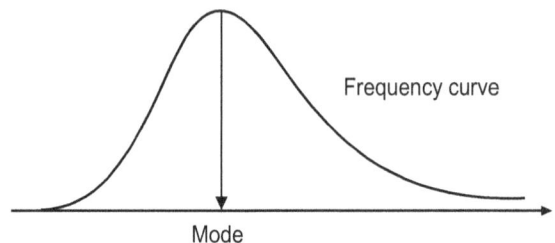

Fig. 3.8

In case of election results, a political party with largest votes (i.e. maximum frequency) is considered as representative. Thus, it is mode or modal opinion. In this situation, mode is the appropriate average. Similarly, to estimate the crop yield, too good quality or too poor quality crop is not considered. A quality of crop most commonly found is taken into account, which is nothing but mode. In titration experiment, out of three readings a repeated reading is taken to be final reading. It is mode and not the arithmetic mean. Thus in number of situations mode is appropriate.

(i) Computation of mode for Individual observations and Discrete frequency distribution : In this case we can find the observation with the largest frequency just by inspection. If the largest frequency occurs twice (or more), then we say there are two (or many) modes.

Illustration 14 : *Find the mode of the following frequency distribution :*

x	10	11	12	13	14	15
f	2	5	10	21	12	13

Solution : Since maximum frequency is associated with observation 13, the mode is 13.

(ii) Computation of mode for Continuous frequency distribution :

Step 1 : Obtain the class – boundaries.

Step 2 : Locate the modal class. Modal class is class in which mode lies or a class with the largest frequency.

Step 3 : Apply the formula and find the mode.

$$\text{Mode} = l + \left(\frac{f_m - f_1}{2f_m - f_1 - f_2}\right) \times h$$

where, l = Lower boundary (or extended class limit) of modal class

f_m = Frequency of (or extended class limit) modal class

f_1 = Frequency of pre-modal class

f_2 = Frequency of post-modal class

h = Width of modal class

Illustration 15 : *Calculate modal income from the following income distribution :*

Daily income (₹)	30 and below	31-60	61-90	91-120	121-150	above 150
No. of Persons	22	198	110	95	42	33

Solution :

Class boundaries	Frequency
below 30.5	f_1 = 22
30.5 – 60.5	f_m = 198 Modal class
60.5 – 90.5	f_2 = 110
90.5 – 120.5	95
120.5 – 150.5	42
above 150.5	33

Modal class is 31–60. Since the corresponding frequency is the highest.

Here we get l = 30.5, f_m = 198, f_1 = 22, f_2 = 110, h = 30

$$\text{Mode} = l + \left(\frac{f_m - f_1}{2f_m - f_1 - f_2}\right) \times h$$

$$= 30.5 + \frac{198 - 22}{2 \times 198 - 22 - 110} \times 30 = 50.5$$

Note :

1. If the maximum frequency is repeated, to find the mode uniquely, a method of grouping is adopted and a modal class is determined. The method of grouping is beyond the scope of book.

2. Mode cannot be determined if modal class is at the extreme. (i.e. the maximum frequency occurs at the beginning or at the end of the frequency distribution.)

3. Modal, pre-modal and post-modal classes should be of the same width.

4. If $f_1 = f_2$ then mode is the class-mark of modal class.

(iii) Computation of mode – by Empirical relation : Arithmetic mean, mode and median are averages, hence we expect that those should be identical in value. However, this is true only in ideal situation. It is true whenever the frequency curve is perfectly symmetric and bell-shaped. For a moderately asymmetric unimodal frequency distribution the following empirical relationship holds approximately.

Mean – Mode ≈ 3 (Mean – Median)   ... (3.2)

In some situations mode is ill-defined (see notes 1, 2 stated above). To overcome this difficulty in computing mode, the empirical relation (1) is used. If any two averages included in (3.2) are known, the remaining third can be computed. Therefore, if mean and median are known, then mode can be determined.

The empirical relation cannot be theoretically proved. Karl Pearson has stated it on the basis of vast experience. This relationship is observed to be valid for number of data sets after actual computations.

(iv) Computation of mode – by graphical method : Mode can be obtained graphically with the help of histogram. Mode is the x-co-ordinate of point P or the value at foot of perpendicular from P to x-axis, shown in Fig. 3.9.

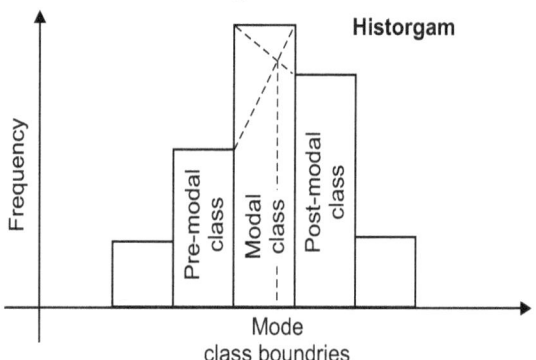

Fig. 3.9 : Histogram

Merits and Demerits of mode :

Merits :

1. It is simple to understand and easy to compute.
2. It is applicable for qualitative and quantitative data.
3. It is not affected by extreme observations.
4. It can be computed for distribution with open end classes.
5. It can be determined graphically.

Demerits :

1. It is not based on all the observations.
2. It is not capable of further mathematical treatment.
3. It is not rigidly defined like arithmetic mean.
4. It is indeterminate if the modal class is at the extreme of the distribution.

Note : It is possible to have two modes, such frequency distribution is called as bimodal frequency distribution. Sometimes bimodal frequency distribution is an indication of mixture of two frequency distributions.

For example, operator or machine is changed in manufacturing process. In medical sciences, two types of anaemia viz. microcytic and macrocytic are found in same population which give bimodal frequency curve.

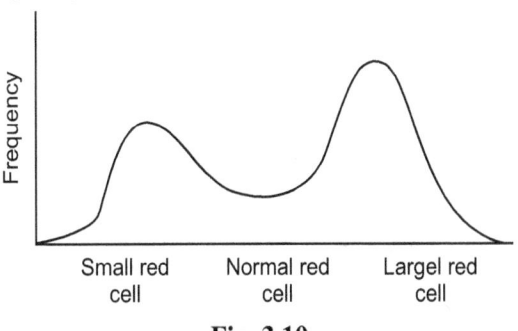

Fig. 3.10

Illustration 16 : *Calculate arithmetic mean and mode for the following data :*

Monthly salary (₹)	Number of workers
Below 400	0
Below 600	4
Below 800	14
Below 1000	33
Below 1200	45
Below 1400	49
Below 1600	50

Solution : We need to prepare frequency distribution from the given cumulative frequency distribution.

Class	Frequency	Mid-values x	$u = \dfrac{x - 900}{200}$	fu
400 - 600	4 – 0 = 4	500	– 2	– 8
600 - 800	14 – 4 = 10	700	– 1	– 10
800 - 1000	33 – 14 = 19	900	0	0
1000 - 1200	45 – 33 = 12	1100	1	12
1200 - 1400	49 – 45 = 4	1300	2	8
1400 - 1600	50 – 49 = 1	1500	3	3
Total	50	–	–	5

$$\text{Mean} = a + \frac{\sum fu}{N} \times h, \text{ where } a = 900, \sum fu = 5, N = 50, h = 200$$

$$= 900 + \frac{5}{50} \times 200 = 920 \text{ ₹}$$

Modal class : 800 – 1000

$$\text{Mode} = l + \left(\frac{f_m - f_1}{2 f_m - f_1 - f_2}\right) \times h$$

Here $l = 800$, $f_m = 19$, $f_1 = 10$, $f_2 = 12$, $h = 200$

$$\therefore \text{ Mode} = 900 + \left(\frac{19 - 10}{38 - 10 - 12}\right) \times 200 = 912.5$$

Illustrative Examples

Example 3.1 : *From the following data find the missing frequencies, it is given that mean is 15.3818 and total frequency is 55.*

Class	9-11	11-13	13-15	15-17	17-19	19-21
Frequency	3	7	–	20	–	5

Solution : Let the missing frequencies be a and b

Class	Mid-value x	Frequency f	f · x
9 - 11	10	3	30
11 - 13	12	7	84
13 - 15	14	a	14a
15 - 17	16	20	320
17 - 19	18	b	18b
19 - 21	20	5	100
Total	–	$35 + a + b = N = 55$	$534 + 14a + 18b = \sum fx$

We get two equations from the given information

i.e. $35 + a + b = 55$ ($\because$ Total frequency N = 55)

$\therefore$ $a + b = 20$ ... (1)

$$\bar{X} = \frac{\sum fx}{N} \text{ gives}$$

$$15.3818 = \frac{534 + 14a + 18b}{55}$$

$\therefore$ $845.999 = 534 + 14a + 18b$

$\therefore$ $14a + 18b = 311.999$ ... (2)

Solving (1) and (2) we get, a = 12.0002, b = 7.9998.

After rounding-off the values, a = 12 and b = 8.

Thus, frequency of the class 11 - 13 is 12 and that of 17 - 19 is 8.

Example 3.2 : *Find the arithmetic mean given that* $\sum (x - 10) = 230$ *and n = 50.*

Solution : Let $d = x - 10$, $a = 10$, hence $\sum d = 230$

$$\therefore \quad \text{Mean} = a + \frac{\sum d}{n} = 10 + \frac{230}{50} = 14.6$$

Example 3.3 : *Arithmetic mean of 50 items is 104. While checking, it was noticed that observation 98 was misread as 89. Find the correct value of mean.*

Solution :

$$\text{Incorrect mean} = 104 = \frac{\text{Incorrect sum}}{n}$$

$\therefore$ Incorrect sum $= 104 \times 50 = 5200$

Correct sum = Incorrect sum + Correct observation − Incorrect observation

$$= 5200 + 98 - 89 = 5209$$

$\therefore$ Correct mean $= \dfrac{\text{Correct sum}}{n}$

$$= \frac{5209}{50} = 104.18.$$

Example 3.4 : *The number of washing machines sold in a shop per day are distributed as follows. Find median*

No. of machines sold	0	1	2	3	4	5
No. of days	6	10	4	3	3	1

Solution : Let X = No. of machines sold, f = No. of days.

X	f	Less than type cumulative frequency
0	6	6
1	10	16
2	4	20
3	3	23
4	3	26
5	1	27 = n

$$\text{Median} = \text{The value of } \left(\frac{n+1}{2} = \frac{27+1}{2} = 14\right)^{th} \text{ observation in the}$$

ordered arrangement

$$= 1$$

Example 3.5 : *A salesman has given a target to complete average daily sales of ₹ 1000. In a particular week, average sales of first 6 days is ₹ 980. What should be his sales on seventh day in order to make-up the target ?*

Solution : Here we use average as arithmetic mean

$$\bar{X} = \frac{\sum x}{n} = \frac{\sum x}{7} = 1000$$

∴   Total sales for 7 days $= \sum x = n\bar{X} = 7 \times 1000 = 7000 ₹$

The average of first 6 days $= \frac{\sum x}{6} = 980.$

Total sales for 6 days $= 6 \times 980 = 5880 ₹$

Sales required on 7th day $= 7000 - 5880 = 1120 ₹$

Example 3.6 : *The median of a group of 100 observations is computed to be 70. While verifying, it was found that the observation 13 was misread as 31. Find the correct median.*

Solution : Note that the median is 70. The observation 31 is to be replaced by correct observation as 13. This change does not affect the middle most observation in the ordered arrangement, hence median will remain same. Thus the median after correction is 70.

Note : *However, arithmetic mean will change.*

Example 3.7 : *Calculate mode of the following frequency distribution*   **(P.U. 1999)**

Class	50–100	100–150	150–200	200–250	250–300	300–350	350–400
Frequency	5	15	25	18	12	3	2

Solution : Modal class $= (150 - 200)$

$$\text{Mode} = l + \left(\frac{f_m - f_1}{2f_m - f_1 - f_0}\right) \times h = 150 + \left(\frac{25 - 18}{50 - 18 - 15}\right) \times 50$$

$$= 150 + \left(\frac{7}{17}\right) \times 50 = 170.5882$$

Example 3.8 : *Following is a frequency distribution regarding the number of family members, number of earning members in a certain locality.*

Income per month	No. of families	No. of family members	
		Earners	Non-earners
0 – 2000	22	25	40
2000 – 3000	59	75	143
3000 – 4000	70	91	179
4000 – 6000	25	57	136
6000 – 10000	15	42	85
10000 – 14000	9	30	17
Total	200	320	600

Calculate :

1. Average monthly income per family
2. Average monthly income per earning member
3. Per capita income
4. Average family size
5. The median family income.

Solution :

Income	Mid-point (x)	No. of families (f)	f.x	Less than cumulative frequency
0 – 2000	1000	22	22000	22
2000 – 3000	2500	59	147500	81
3000 – 4000	3500	70	245000	151
4000 – 6000	5000	25	125000	176
6000 – 10000	8000	15	120000	191
10000 – 14000	12000	9	108000	200
Total		200	767500	–

1. Average monthly income per family $= \dfrac{\sum fx}{\sum f} = \dfrac{767500}{200} = 3837.5\ ₹$

2. Average monthly income per earning member $= \dfrac{\text{Total income}}{\text{No. of earning members}}$

$$= \dfrac{767500}{320} = 2398.44\ ₹$$

3. Per capita income $= \dfrac{\text{Total income}}{\text{Total population}} = \dfrac{7675000}{320 + 600} = 834.24\ ₹$

   (Total population = No. of earners + No. of non-earners.)

4. Average family size $= \dfrac{\text{Total number of earners and non-earners}}{\text{Total number of families}}$

$$= \dfrac{320 + 600}{200} = \dfrac{920}{200} = 4.6$$

5. The median of family income.

   Median = The value of $\left(\dfrac{N}{2} = \dfrac{200}{2} = 100\right)^{\text{th}}$ observation

$$= l + \left(\dfrac{\dfrac{N}{4} - \text{C.F.}}{f}\right) h = 3000 + \left(\dfrac{100 - 81}{70}\right) \times 1000 = 3271.43\ ₹$$

Example 3.9 : *The monthly income (₹) of 10 families in a village is as follows :*

1200, 1000, 1100, 1250, 950, 1300, 1350, 1150, 1200, 1050.

Find Mean, Median and Mode of this Income Distribution.   **(April 2010)**

Solution :   Mean $= \dfrac{\sum x}{n} = \dfrac{11550}{10} = 1155$

The ordered arrangement to find the median is as follows :

950, 1000, 1050, 1100, $\boxed{1150, \ 1200}$, 1200, 1250, 1300, 1350.

$$\text{Median} = \text{The value of} \left(\dfrac{n+1}{2} = \dfrac{11}{2} = 5.5\right)^{th} \text{observation}$$

$$= \dfrac{5^{th} \text{ observation} + 6^{th} \text{ observation}}{2}$$

$$= \dfrac{1150 + 1200}{2}$$

$$= 1175 \ ₹$$

$$\text{Mode} = \text{Observation with maximum frequency}$$

$$= 1200 \ ₹$$

Thus, Mean $= ₹ \ 1155$, Median $= ₹ \ 1175$, mode $= 1200 \ ₹$

Example 3.10 : *The following data relates to age distribution of 50 persons :*

Age (years)	Frequency
20-30	3
30-40	7
40-50	14
50-60	16
60-70	8
70-80	2

Find mode of above distribution   **(April 2010)**

Solution :   Modal class : 50 – 60

$$\text{Mode} = l + \dfrac{f_m - f_0}{2f_m - f_0 - f_1} \times h$$

$l = 50$, $f_m = 16$, $f_0 = 14$, $f_1 = 8$, $h = 10$.

∴ $\text{Mode} = 50 + \left(\dfrac{16 - 14}{32 - 14 - 8}\right) \times 10$

$$= 52 \text{ years}$$

3.12 Choice of an Average

Proper choice of an average is essential, otherwise results based on it will not be reliable. The choice depends upon the type of data and purpose of collection of data or survey. We have already discussed the various situations suitable for each average. Once again we summarize the same in short.

In majority of situations A.M. is preferred, G.M. is used to compute average of changes, growth rates, interest rates etc., whereas H.M. is used to compute average speeds, rates specified in terms of units per Re. etc.

In case of quantitative data and frequency distributions having open end class, means cannot be computed, median or mode are suitable.

Sometimes single average is not sufficient as descriptive measure of data, we use two or more averages.

Limitations of Averages :
1. Mean, mode, median are proper representatives for bell-shaped frequency distributions.
2. Averages cannot give the idea about the internal variation among the items.
3. Averages cannot give the idea about the nature of data.

Illustration 17 : The following data gives dividend paid by two companies.

Year	1985	1986	1987	1988	1989
Company A	40%	30%	20%	15%	15%
Company B	10%	20%	20%	35%	35%

A.M. of dividends paid by companies A and B are same and the common value is 24%. However, company B is prospering and A is declining. This nature of data cannot be focused by averages.

Case study : Shriram Oxygen Ltd. is a company in manufacturing of industrial oxygen based in an industrial area of Washi, Navi Mumbai. There are in all about 1000 employees in this company. They are of various grades. For example, there is a managing director, about 10 directors, 30 senior general managers, about 200 managers, 150 officers and rest are workers of different grades. Company's monthly salary budget is about ₹ 30 lac.

Management of this company is of the opinion to increase the productivity by not increasing the man power but through increasing the salary of existing employees.

Existing salary of managing director is approximately ₹ 1 lacs per month, directors get around ₹ 75,000/- per month, general manager gets around ₹ 50,000 whereas workers salary varies from ₹ 20,000 to ₹ 50,000 as per their grades.

Company has a revised budget of ₹ 40 lac per month. Company would like to know about what is the average salary per month. Whether to find mean would be appropriate or should median be used. What would be average revised salary per month ?

Points to Remember

1. Arithmetic mean $(\bar{x}) = \dfrac{\Sigma x}{n}$ for ungrouped data

    $= \dfrac{\Sigma fx}{\Sigma f}$ for frequency distribution.

2. Median $= l + \left(\dfrac{\dfrac{N}{2} - c.f.}{f} \right) \times h$.

3. Mode $= l + \left(\dfrac{f_m - f_1}{2f_m - f_1 - f_2} \right) \times h$

4. If $y = ax + b$, then $\bar{y} = a\bar{x} + b$, $y = \dfrac{x - c}{d}$ then $\bar{y} = \dfrac{\bar{x} - c}{d}$

5. Combined arithmetic mean $= \dfrac{n_1 \bar{x} + n_2 \bar{y}}{n_1 + n_2}$

6. Median can be obtained graphically using ogive curves.

7. Mode can be obtained graphically using histogram.

8. Arithmetic mean is the best average.

9. Arithmetic mean cannot be determined by graph.

Exercise 3.1

A. Theory Questions :

1. What do you mean by central tendency ? Explain the purpose of measures of central tendency.

2. State the requisites of an ideal average.

3. Define mean, median, mode, quartiles and state the formula for each, in case of (i) individual observations (ii) frequency distributions.

4. Discuss merits and demerits of (i) mean, (ii) median, (iii) mode.

5. Explain graphical method of determination of (i) median (ii) mode (ii) quartiles.

Exercise 3.2

B. Discrete Series :

6. Monthly consumption of electricity in units of a certain family in a year is given below :

    210, 207, 315, 250, 240, 232, 216, 208, 209, 215, 300, 290.

    Compute the mean, median and mode consumption of electricity.

7. The marks obtained by 12 students are given below :

    30, 55, 50, 40, 50, 60, 55, 62, 55, 45, 61, 65

    Calculate mean, median and mode for the above data.

8. Compute the mean, mode and median for the following data :

$$68, 49, 38, 41, 49, 54, 89, 99, 67$$

9. Find the mean, median and mode of the following observations :

$$61, 62, 63, 62, 63, 62, 64, 64, 60, 65.$$

10. In a set of 50 items, arranged in ascending order of magnitude the values of 24th, 25th and 26th items are 40, 42 and 45 respectively. Find the median. Also find the median if the number of observations was 51.

11. Calculate mean and median weight of the group of students with weights (in kg) given below :

$$51, 52, 53, 51, 53, 54, 54, 50, 55, 53.$$

If a new group of students with weights in kg as 50, 56, 58, 57, 60 is added to the original group, find mean and median of combined group.

12. Compute median of the following series

$$5, 20, 18, 12, 0, 21, 18, 26, 5, 15, 20.$$

13. The following figures represent the number of books issued at the counter of commer college library on 8 different days.

$$96, 98, 75, 80, 102, 100, 94, 75.$$

Calculate the median and mode of the data.

14. Compare the average runs scored by cricters A and B using arithmetic mean.

Cricketer	Runs scored				
A	5	20	90	75	100
B	40	35	60	65	50

15. The weekly income of 10 families in a village is as follows :

$$1200, 1000, 1100, 1250, 950, 1300, 1350, 1150, 1200, 1050.$$

Find the mean, mode, median of the income distribution.

C. Frequency Distribution :

16. Find the mean, mode and median of the following data.

X	5	6	7	8	9	10	11	12
Frequency	8	10	9	6	5	4	4	1

17. Find the mean, median and mode of the following frequency distribution.

Marks	0 - 20	20 - 40	40 - 60	60 - 80	80 - 100
No. of frequency	5	12	32	40	11

18. Find arithmetic mean, mode and median of following frequency distribution.

Marks	0 - 20	20 - 40	40 - 60	60 - 80	80 - 100
No. of students	4	8	9	20	9

19. Compute arithmetic mean, mode and median of the following frequency distribution.

Weight in kg.	30 - 40	40 - 50	50 - 60	60 - 70	70 - 80
No. of students	3	5	12	20	10

20. Determine arithmetic mean, mode and median of marks from the data given below :

Marks	0 - 10	10 - 20	20 - 30	30 - 40	40 - 50
No. of students	1	3	10	4	2

21. The monthly profit in rupees of 100 shops are distributed as follows :

Profit (in ₹) per shop	0 - 100	100 - 200	200 - 300	300 - 400	400 - 500	500 - 600
No. of shops	12	18	27	20	17	6

(i) Calculate the mode for above data. (ii) Find mode graphically.

22. A study of a certain operation shows the following distribution for 180 workers. Calculate the median. Also find it graphically.

Class interval (in seconds)	10 - 30	30 - 50	50 - 70	70 - 90	90 - 110
Frequency	10	40	80	35	15

23. Find the mean, mode and median and quartiles for the following data :

Class	100 - 200	200 - 300	300 - 400	400 - 500
Frequency	15	20	10	5

24. Compute the median and quartiles for the following frequency distribution. Also find it graphically.

Dividend (%)	0 - 20	20 - 40	40 - 60	60 - 80	80 - 100
No. of companies	20	35	15	8	2

25. Find the mean, mode, median and quartiles of the following frequency distribution.

Weight (kg)	30 - 40	40 - 50	50 - 60	60 - 70	70 - 80
No. of students	4	5	7	3	1

26. Find mode for the following frequency distribution of income of 70 workers :

Income (₹)	Less than 1000	1000-2000	2000-3000	3000-4000	4000-5000	Above 5000
No. of Workers	08	14	13	25	07	03

27. The following data relates to age distribution of 50 persons :

Age (Years)	Frequency
20-30	3
30-40	7
40-50	14
50-60	16
60-70	8
70-80	2

Find mode of above distribution.

28. Following is the frequency distribution of sales of companies :

Sale (00,000 ₹)	0-20	20-40	40-60	60-80	80-100
No. of companies	05	18	20	12	05

Find the mode.

29. Following is the frequency distribution of percentage of dividend declared by companies :

Dividend %	10-15	15-20	20-25	25-30	30-35
No. of companies	15	20	35	10	5

Find the mode.

30. Calculate median and quartiles graphically for the following distribution :

Class	5-15	15-25	25-35	35-45	45-55
Frequency	5	15	20	15	5

31. Draw the histogram for the following frequency distribution :

Sales (in thousand ₹)	0-20	20-40	40-60	60-80	80-100
No. of companies	5	18	20	12	5

Hence locate the mode.

D. Missing Values :

32. If mean of the following frequency distribution is 15.82 find the missing value of ∗.

X	10	12	13	17	∗	25	18	30
Frequency	25	17	13	15	14	8	6	2

33. Find the missing frequency of the following frequency distribution if the arithmetic mean is 26.90.

Class	10 - 15	15 - 20	20 - 25	25 - 30	30 - 35	35 - 40	40 - 45
Frequency	5	6	8	∗	7	5	4

34. You are given the following complete frequency distribution. It is known that the total frequency is 100 and the median is 44. Find the missing frequencies. Also compute the mean after finding missing frequencies.

Class	Frequency	Class	Frequency
10-20	5	50-60	–
20-30	12	60-70	10
30-40	–	70-80	4
40-50	20		

35. Mean daily salary of 50 employees in a firm is ₹ 188.40. Frequency distribution of salaries of these employees in which some frequencies are missing is given below :

Salary	140-160	160-180	180-200	200-220	220-240
Frequency	6	–	17	–	5

Find the missing frequencies.

36. The daily expenditure of 100 families is given below :

Expenditure	20-29	30-39	40-49	50-59	60-69
No. of families	14	–	27	–	15

If the mode of the distribution is 43.5, find the missing frequencies.

E. Combined Mean :

37. Find the combined mean of the following data :

Group I $\bar{x}_1$ = 2100 n_1 = 100

Group II $\bar{x}_2$ = 1500 n_2 = 200

38. Average monthly sale of certain departmental store for first 11 months was ₹ 56000. Due to repairs and renewal of shop in the last month the sales dropped down to ₹ 8000. Find the average monthly sales in the year.

39. Obtain the combined mean profit per salesman from the following data

	Mean profit per salesman	No. of salesman
Shop 1	2000	5
Shop 2	3000	12
Shop 3	5000	3

40. Find the combined arithmetic mean and salary given that :

Group	Male	Female
No. of employees	100	50
Arithmetic mean of salary	6000 ₹	5100 ₹

41. Given

Group 1	Group 2
$n_1 = 100$	$n_2 = 100$
$\Sigma x = 600$	$\Sigma y = 800$

Find $\bar{x}$, $\bar{y}$ and combined mean of the two groups.

F. Miscellaneous Problems :

42. A set of 10 values has arithmetic mean 20. Find the arithmetic mean if, (i) each value is doubled and then increased by 2 (ii) each value is increased by 5 and then doubled. (iii) each value is decreased by 5 (iv) each value is increased by 3.

43. The arithmetic mean of 10 items is 30. What will be mean, if each item is doubled ?

44. If n = 10 and $\Sigma (x - 5) = 90$ find the mean.

45. Obtain the average bonus per employee for the following frequency distribution.

Salary Group (₹)	1000-2000	2000-4000	4000-6000	above 6000
Bonus (₹)	300	400	450	500
Frequency	5	12	5	3

46. Calculate median and mode wage from the following data : (i) by using the formula (ii) by graphical method :

Wages in ₹	No. of workers
above 130	520
above 140	470
above 150	399
above 160	210
above 170	105
above 180	45
above 190	7

47. Find the median and mode of the following data by computational method and graphical method :

No. of days absent	No. of students
less than 5	29
less than 10	224
less than 15	465
less than 20	582
less than 25	634
less than 30	644
less than 35	650
less than 40	653
less than 45	655

48. Obtain the mean, median and mode from following data :

Monthly Rent (in ₹)	No. of families
221 - 240	6
241 - 260	9
261 - 280	11
281 - 300	14
301 - 320	20
321 - 340	15
341 - 360	10
361 - 380	8
381 - 400	7

49. Average of marks of 30 candidates was 40. Later on it was found that a score of 47 was misread as 74. Find the correct average.

50. The mean weight of 98 students as calculated from a frequency distribution is 50 kg. It was later found that the frequency of the class 30-40 was wrongly taken as 8 instead of 10. Calculate the correct arithmetic mean.

51. A salesman has given a target to complete average daily sales of ₹ 5000. In a particular week average of first 6 days is ₹ 4990. What should be his sales on seventh day in order to make up the target ?

Answers 3.2

6. Mean = 241, Median = 224, No mode.

7. Mean = 52.33, Mode = Median = 55.

8. Mean = 61.56, Mode = 49, Median = 54.

9. Mean = 62.6, Median = 62.5, Mode = 62

10. 43.5, 45

11. Original data : Mean 52.6, Median 53, Combined data : Mean = 53.8, Median 53

12. 18

13. Mode = 75, Median = 95

14. $\bar{X}_A = 58 > \bar{X}_B = 50$.

15. Mean = 1155, mode = 1200, Median = 1175.

16. Mean = 7.4894, Mode = 6, median = 7.

17. Mean = 58, Median = 60.2857, Mode = 64.32

18. Mean = 58.8, Median = 64, Mode = 65,

19. Mean = 60.8, Mode = 64.44, Median = 62.5,

20. Mean = 26.8, Mode = 25.3846, Median = 26,

21. 256.25

22. 60

23. Mean = 260, Mode = 233.33, Median = 250, Q_1 = 162.5, Q_3 = 325.

24. Median = 25.7142, Q_1 = 20, Q_3 = 31.43.

25. Mean = 51, Mode = 53.3333, Median = 53.333, Q_1 = 42, Q_3 = 58.57.

26. 3400

27. 52

28. 42.

29. 21.875.

30. Q_1 = 21.67, Q_2 = 30, Q_3 = 38.3333.

31. By histogram 42

32. 24

33. 15

34. Missing frequencies 25, 24, Mean = 44.2

35. 12, 20

36. 23, 21

37. 1700

38. 52,000

39. 3050

40. ₹ 5700

41. $\bar{X}$ = 6, $\bar{Y}$ = 8, Combined mean = 7.

42. (i) 45 (ii) 50 (iii) 15 (iv) 23

43. 60

44. 14

45. 402

46. Median = 157.3545, Mode = 155.8416

47. Median = 12.1473, Mode = 11.35

48. Mean = Median = 310.5, Mode = 311.409

49. 39.5

50. 49.7

51. ₹ 5600

Objective Questions

1. Arithmetic mean of a group is 20. If each observation is increased by 5, find the mean of new observations.

2. State the imperical relation between mean, mode and median.

3. If n = 10, $\sum (x - 6) = 30$, find $\bar{x}$.

4. State the mode of following frequency distribution :

Class	0-10	10-20	20-30	30-40	40-50
Frequency	7	10	22	10	8

5. If each frequency is doubled, then what will happen to the arithmetic mean.

6. If frequency distribution has open end class, which average will be possible to compute.

7. Individual observations are not known but the total of 10 observations is known. Suggest the average which can be computed.

8. Suggest the average which you can compute if all the observations except the largest and smallest are known.

Answers

1. 25

3. 9

4. 25

5. Will not change

6. Mode, Median

7. Mean

8. Median

❏❏❏

Chapter 4

Measures of Dispersion

Contents ...

Key Words :

Dispersion, Deviation, Relative Dispersion Absolute Dispersion, Maximum, Minimum, Range, Coefficient Of Range, Standard Deviation (S.D.), Coefficient of Variation (C.V.), Variance.

Objectives :

The reliability of average is more if dispersion is less. Measures of dispersion is a tool which summerizes the internal variation or variation within the observations. The techniques of measurement of dispersion are discussed in this chapter. Statistics is in existence because of variation. Statistician has to talk in terms of S.D. and C.V. There are some situations such as genetics, biodiversity etc. where larger S.D. or C.V. has its importance.

4.1 Introduction

We have seen that, average condenses information into a single value. However, average alone is not sufficient to describe the frequency distribution completely. There may be two frequency distributions or data sets with same means but those may not be identical.

Illustration : Marks of students A, B, C in 5 subjects are as follows :

Student	Marks					A.M.
A	51	52	50	48	49	50
B	30	35	50	65	70	50
C	0	15	45	95	95	50

Notice that the average marks of all students are the same but they differ in variation. Clearly we can say that A is more consistent than B and B is more consistent than C.

For further study and analysis it becomes essential to measure the extent of variation. Observations are scattered or dispersed from central value. This variation is called as *dispersion*. Thus, next important aspect of comparison or study of frequency distribution or data sets is dispersion. Moreover it plays very important role in further analysis.

Average remains good representative, if dispersion is less (i.e. if the observations are close to it). Thus, dispersion decides the reliability of average.

4.2 Measures of Dispersion

In this chapter we study the following measures of dispersion : (i) range and (ii) standard deviation. These measures have the same units as that of the observation, for example, ₹, cm., hours., etc., and the measures are called as **absolute measures of dispersion.**

Absolute and Relative Measures of Dispersion

It can be very well seen that absolute measures possess units and hence create difficulty in comparison of dispersion for two or more frequency distributions or data sets. *For example :* For a group of persons, variation in height and variation in weight is to be compared. Height may be in cm and weight may be in kg. Therefore, comparison is not possible until a unitless quantity is available. Therefore, with respect to every absolute measure of dispersion, relative measure of dispersion is defined. Relative measure can be obtained by dividing the absolute measure by corresponding average. Such a relative measure is called as coefficient of the respective absolute measure.

4.3 Range and Coefficient of Range

Range is a crude measure of dispersion. However, it is the simplest measure and suitable if the extent of variation is small.

Definition : If L is the largest observation and S is the smallest observation then range is the difference between L and S. Thus,

$$\text{Range} = L - S$$

and the corresponding relative measure is

$$\text{Coefficient of range} = \frac{L - S}{L + S}$$

In case of frequency distribution lower limit of first and upper limit of last class intervals are taken to be the smallest and the largest observations respectively.

Note : Requisites of good measures of dispersion are same as those of average.

Merits of Range : (1) It is simple to understand and easy to calculate.

(2) It is rigidly defined.

Demerits of Range : (1) It is not based on all observations. It does not give proper idea regarding variation between the extreme observations.

For example : Range of 0, 3, 5, 200 is same as that of 0, 50, 100, 150, 200, however, variation patterns are different.

(2) It cannot be determined for frequency distribution with open end class.

Applications of Range :

Range is suitable measure of dispersion in case of small group with less variation. (i) It is widely used in the branch of statistics known as Statistical Quality Control. (ii) The changes in prices of shares lowest and highest observations are used. (iii) Temperature at a certain place is recorded using maximum and minimum value. (iv) Range used in medical sciences to check whether blood pressure, hemoglobin count etc. is normal.

Illustration 1 : *Compute range and coefficient of range for the following data :*
100, 24, 14, 105, 21, 35, 106.

Solution : Here,

$$\text{Smallest observation (S)} = 14$$
$$\text{Largest observation (L)} = 106$$
$$\text{Range} = L - S = 106 - 14 = 92$$
$$\text{Coefficient of range} = \frac{L-S}{L+S} = \frac{92}{106+14}$$
$$= \frac{92}{120} = 0.7667$$

Illustration 2 : *Determine the range and the coefficient of range for the following data :*

Electricity consumption per month	:	100–150	150–300	300–450	450–600
No. of families	:	28	56	43	23

Solution :

$$\text{Range} = \text{Largest observation (L)} - \text{Smallest observation (S)}$$
$$= 600 - 100 = 500$$
$$\text{Coefficient of range} = \frac{L-S}{L+S} = \frac{500}{700} = \frac{5}{7}.$$

4.4 Quartile Deviation or Semi-interquartile Range

The range uses only two extreme items. Hence, any change in the inbetween observations is not going to affect the range. This is a main drawback of range. Moreover in many situations extreme items are widely separated from remaining items.

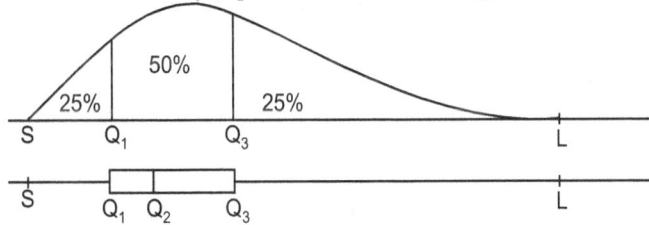

Fig. 4.1

In this situation range will overestimate the dispersion. Thus, range fails to give true picture of dispersion. In order to overcome these drawbacks range of middle 50% items is computed.

Clearly the middle 50% items lie inbetween the two quartiles Q_1 and Q_3. The measure of dispersion based on these quartiles is given below :

Quartile Deviation (Q.D.) or Semi-Interquartile Range $= \dfrac{Q_3 - Q_1}{2}.$

And the corresponding relative measure is

Coefficient of Quartile Deviation $= \dfrac{Q_3 - Q_1}{Q_3 + Q_1}$

Illustrative Examples

Example 4.1 : Compute (i) range and coefficient of range, (ii) quartile deviation and coefficient of quartile deviation for the following data :

100, 24, 14, 105, 21, 35, 106, 16, 100, 72, 68, 103, 61, 90, 20.

Solution : (i) Here, Smallest observation (S) = 14

Largest observation (L) = 106

$$\text{Range} = L - S = 106 - 14 = 92$$

$$\text{Coefficient of range} = \frac{L-S}{L+S} = \frac{92}{106+14} = \frac{92}{120}$$

$$= 0.7667$$

(ii) To find quartile deviation, we arrange the observations in ascending order as follows :

14, 16, 20, $\boxed{21}$, 24, 35, 61, 68, 72, 90, 100, $\boxed{100}$, 103, 105, 106

$$Q_1 = \text{The value of } \left(\frac{n+1}{4} = \frac{15+1}{4} = 4\right)^{th} \text{ item in the ordered arrangement}$$

$$= 21$$

$$Q_3 = \text{The value of } \left(\frac{3(n+1)}{4} = \frac{3 \times 16}{4} = 12\right)^{th} \text{ item in the ordered arrangement}$$

$$= 100$$

$$\therefore \quad Q.D. = \frac{Q_3 - Q_1}{2} = \frac{100 - 21}{2} = 39.5$$

$$\text{Coefficient of Q.D.} = \frac{Q_3 - Q_1}{Q_3 + Q_1} = 0.6529$$

Example 4.2 : Compute Q.D. and Coefficient of Q.D. for the following frequency distribution.

Daily Wages (in ₹)	below 35	35–40	40–45	45–50	50–55	55–60	60–65	above 65
No. of workers	12	18	22	26	36	23	19	8

Solution :

Class	Frequency	Less than type cumulative frequency	
below 35	12	12	
35–40	18	30	
40–45	22	52..............	... → Q_1 class
45–50	26	78	
50–55	36	114	
55–60	23	137..............	... → Q_3 class
60–65	19	156	
above 65	8	164 = N	

$$Q_1 = \text{The value of } \left(\frac{N}{4} = \frac{164}{4} = 41\right)^{st} \text{observation}$$

Therefore, (40 – 45) is Q_1 class

∴ $$Q_1 = l + \frac{N/4 - c.f.}{f} \times h = 40 + \frac{41 - 30}{22} \times 5 = 42.5$$

$$Q_3 = \text{The value of } \left(\frac{3N}{4} = \frac{3 \times 164}{4} = 123\right)^{rd} \text{observation}$$

Therefore, Q_3 lies in (55 – 60)

∴ $$Q_3 = l + \frac{3N/4 - c.f.}{f} \times h = 55 + \frac{123 - 114}{23} \times 5 = 56.9565$$

∴ $$Q.D. = \frac{Q_3 - Q_1}{2} = \frac{56.9565 - 42.5}{2} = 7.2283$$

$$\text{Coefficient of Q.D.} = \frac{Q_3 - Q_1}{Q_3 + Q_1} = \frac{55.9565 - 42.5}{55.9565 + 42.5} = 0.1454$$

Remark : One of the requisites of a good measure is that, it should be based on all the observations. However, Q.D. depends upon only two partition values. Therefore, it is not affected by any changes except the upper and lower quartile.

4.5 Mean Deviation and Coefficient of Mean Deviation

A prime requirement of a good statistical measure is that it should be based on all the observations. It is not satisfied by both the range and quartile deviation. Here we discuss the measure of dispersion which take into account all the observations. Naturally, the use of deviations taken from a certain point of reference is appropriate. Preferably we take deviations from arithmetic mean (A.M.). We require to combine all these deviations into a single value. One of the appropriate techniques is to take arithmetic mean. However, the sum of deviations taken from A.M. is zero. Therefore, A.M. of deviations fails to serve the purpose. A.M. behaves like a centre of gravity, it balances both positive and negative deviations giving total zero. Hence, it is required to get rid of the algebraic signs of deviations. This can be done in two ways : (a) taking absolute deviations (b) taking squares of the deviations.

Definition : The arithmetic mean of absolute deviations from any average (mean or median or mode) is called as mean deviation about the respective average.

(i) Mean deviation (M.D.) about mean :

$$= \frac{\sum |d|}{n} \text{ for individual observations, where } |d| = |x - \bar{x}|$$

$$= \frac{\sum f|d|}{N} \text{ for frequency distribution where } N = \sum f$$

Relative measure of dispersion is

Coefficient of M.D. about mean $= \dfrac{\text{M.D. about mean}}{\text{Mean}}$

(ii) M.D. about mean :

$$= \frac{\sum |d|}{n} \text{ for individual observations where } |d| = |x - \text{median}|$$

$$= \frac{\sum f \cdot |d|}{N} \text{ for frequency distribution}$$

Relative measure of dispersion is

Coefficient of M.D. about median $= \dfrac{\text{M.D. about median}}{\text{Median}}$

(iii) M.D. about mode :

$$= \frac{\sum |d|}{n} \text{ for individual observations where } |d| = |x - \text{mode}|$$

$$= \frac{\sum f |d|}{N} \text{ for frequency distribution}$$

Relative measure of dispersion is

Coefficient of M.D. about mode $= \dfrac{\text{M.D. about mode}}{\text{Mode}}$

Computational Procedure :

Step 1　　: Obtain the required average (mean or mode or median).

Step 2　　: Obtain the absolute deviation $|d| = |x - \text{average}|$ for each observation.

Step 3　　: Find the sum of $|d|$ as $\sum |d|$ for individual observation and $\sum f |d|$ for frequency distribution.

Step 4　　: Compute M.D. as

$$\frac{\sum |d|}{n} \quad \text{for individual observations and}$$

$$\frac{\sum f |d|}{N} \quad \text{for frequency distribution.}$$

Step 5　　: Obtain coefficient of M.D. (if required) by formula $\dfrac{\text{M.D.}}{\text{Average}}$.

Example 4.3 : Compute (i) M.D. about mean and coefficient of M.D. about mean (ii) M.D. about median and coefficient of M.D. about median for the prices per 10 kg of sugar for 7 days in a certain week. 80, 82, 79, 78, 85, 80, 83.

Solution :

(i) Arithmetic mean $= \dfrac{\Sigma x}{n} = \dfrac{567}{7} = 81$

x	80	82	79	78	85	80	83	Total
$|d| = |x - 81|$	1	1	2	3	4	1	2	14

M.D. about mean $= \dfrac{\Sigma |d|}{n} = \dfrac{14}{7} = 2 ₹$

Coefficient of M.D. about mean $= \dfrac{\text{M.D. about mean}}{\text{Mean}} = \dfrac{2}{81} = 0.0247.$

(ii) To find the median we use the ordered arrangement :

78, 79, 80, $\boxed{80}$, 82, 83, 85

Median $= \left(\dfrac{n+1}{2}\right)^{th}$ i.e. 4th observation $= 80.$

x_i	80	82	79	78	85	80	83	Total
$|d| = |x - 80|$	0	2	1	2	5	0	3	13

M.D. about median $= \dfrac{\Sigma |d|}{n} = \dfrac{13}{7} = 1.8571 ₹$

Coefficient of M.D. about median $= \dfrac{\text{M.D. about median}}{\text{Median}} = \dfrac{1.8571}{80} = 0.0232$

Example 4.4 : Obtain M.D. about (i) mean (ii) median and the absolute measure of dispersion in each case for the following frequency distribution.

Class	2–4	4–6	6–8	8–10
Frequency	3	4	2	1

Solution : First we find mean and median which we need for further calculations.

Class	Mid-values X	f	fx	Cumulative frequency
2–4	3	3	9	3
4–6	5	4	20	7
6–8	7	2	14	9
8–10	9	1	9	10
Total	–	10	52	–

$\text{Mean} = \dfrac{\Sigma fx}{N} = 5.2$

Median = The size of $(N/2)^{th}$ i.e. 5th observation.

Median class : 4 – 6

$\text{Median} = l + \dfrac{N/2 - c.f.}{f} \times h$ ($l = 4$, N/2 = 5, c.f. = 3, h = 2)

$\therefore$ Median = 5

x	f	$\lvert x - \bar{x} \rvert$	$f \lvert x - \bar{x} \rvert$	$\lvert x - Me \rvert = \lvert x - 5 \rvert$	$f \lvert x - Me \rvert$
3	3	2.2	6.6	2	6
5	4	0.2	0.4	0	0
7	2	1.8	3.6	2	4
9	1	3.8	3.8	4	4
Total	10	–	14.8	–	14

$\text{M.D. about mean} = \dfrac{\Sigma f \lvert x - \bar{x} \rvert}{N} = \dfrac{14.8}{10} = 1.48$

$\text{Coefficient of M.D. about mean} = \dfrac{\text{M.D.}}{\text{Mean}} = \dfrac{1.48}{5.2} = 0.2846$

$\text{M.D. about median} = \dfrac{\Sigma f_i \lvert x_i - Me \rvert}{N} = \dfrac{14}{10} = 1.4$

$\text{Coefficient of M.D. about median} = \dfrac{1.4}{5} = 0.28$

Minimality property of M.D. : Among all mean deviations, mean deviation about median is minimum.

Therefore, in order to avoid the effect of choice of average, mean deviation about median is preferred.

Merits of M.D. :

1. It is simple to understand and easy to calculate.
2. It is rigidly defined.
3. It is based on all observations.

Demerits of M.D. :

1. It is not applicable for qualitative data.
2. Since algebraic signs of deviations are ignored, it is not applicable for further mathematical treatment.
3. It cannot be computed for the frequency distribution with open end class.

A serious drawback mentioned in demerits of M.D. (2) can be overcome by taking squares of the deviations. Based on the squares of deviations a measure of dispersion is defined and it is discussed below :

4.6 Standard Deviation and Coefficient of Variation

Here we discuss a measure of dispersion which satisfies most of the requisites of good measure and free from the drawbacks present in the other measures of dispersion.

Definition : The positive square root of mean of squares of the deviations taken from arithmetic mean is called as **standard deviation** (S.D.)

It is denoted by σ (read as sigma, a lower case Greek letter).

Therefore, $\sigma = \sqrt{\dfrac{\sum (x - \bar{x})^2}{n}}$ for individual observations

$\qquad = \sqrt{\dfrac{\sum f (x - \bar{x})^2}{N}}$ for frequency distributions

After simplification we can have computational formula for σ in more suitable form as follows :

$$\sigma = \sqrt{\dfrac{\sum x^2}{n} - \bar{x}^2}\qquad \text{for individual observations}$$

$$= \sqrt{\dfrac{\sum fx^2}{N} - \bar{x}^2}\qquad \text{for frequency distribution.}$$

where, $\bar{x}$ is a arithmetic mean.

Note : The quantity σ^2 is called as **variance.** Prof. R. A. Fisher has suggested the term variance.

Relative measure of S.D. is called coefficient of variation.

Coefficient of Variation : Prof. Karl Pearson suggested the relative measure of standard deviation. It is called as coefficient of variation (C.V.)

It is given by C.V. $= \dfrac{\text{S.D}}{|\text{A.M.}|} \times 100 = \dfrac{\sigma}{|\bar{x}|} \times 100\%$ ... (4.1)

Coefficient of variation is always expressed in percentage.

Remarks : (1) R.H.S. of (4.1) includes the multiplier 100, because $\dfrac{\sigma}{|\bar{x}|}$ is too small in many cases. Thus, for convenience it is multiplied by 100.

2. Frequently we need to compare dispersions of two or more groups. If the values in data set are large in magnitude, naturally variation among them will be proportionately larger.

For example, S.D. of weights of a group of elephants will be larger than that of a group of human beings. Suppose S.D. of weights of a group of elephants is 15 kg and that of human beings is also 15 kg. In this case we cannot say, both the groups have identical variation. This is because average weight of a group of elephants is larger than that of the average weight of a group of persons. Therefore for comparing variations between two different data sets, a measure based on the ratio of σ and $\bar{x}$ would be appropriate. This is achieved in coefficient of variation. It measures variation in all data sets using a common yard stick; moreover it is free from units.

3.   According to Prof. Karl Pearson, C.V. is the percentage variation in mean whereas S.D. gives the total variation in the mean.

Uses of Coefficient of Variation :

It is already discussed that for comparison of variability, homogeneity, stability, uniformity, consistency, a unitless measure of dispersion is coefficient of variation (C.V.).

In manufacturing process C.V. is very important quantity. Larger the C.V., larger is the variation and poorer is the quality. In quality control section every effort is made to improve upon the quality, which means the items to be manufactured as per specifications. The extent of deviation from specifications can be measured by C.V. Thus, C.V. is unit of measurement of variation.

Almost all industries reduced the C.V. of their goods to considerable extent in last 50 years. This was due to competition. In pharmaceutical industries C.V. is as low as 1 or less than 1. The variation in weight of tablets is almost negligible.

Earlier the Japanese industrial product and American industrial product have same average quality, however, there was considerable difference in C.V. C.V. of Japanese goods was less than 5 times than that of American goods.

As a result of low C.V. the Japanese goods were more popular.

If C.V. is increased how it affects is explained below with the following example. Suppose we purchase a bag or pauch of edible oil packed by a automatic filling machine. Suppose the volume of oil is expected to be 1 litre. If the machine is set for C.V. = 1, (since C.V. = 0 is impossible). Using statistical laws we can conclude that approximately 99.73% of the bags filled by machine will contain oil in the range 970 ml to 1030 ml. This range is reasonable for user. Instead if the machine is set to C.V. = 5, then 14% bags will found to contain 900 ml to 950 ml oil, another 2.1% will found to contain oil between 850 ml to 900 ml. Approximately 16% bags will contain 900 ml or less oil. Thus alongwith average one have take extreme care to reduce C.V.

Let us discuss an example from automobile industry. Suppose company A and B manufacture scooters which give 50 km per litre. Suppose C.V. of company A is 1 and that of company B is 5.

Among the scooters manufactured by company A, 99.73% will run 48.5 to 51.5 per litre. On the other hand among the scooters manufactured by company B, 14% will run 45 to 47.5 km per litre and 2.1% will run 42.5 to 45 km per litre. Thus, in case of C.V. = 5 about 16.1% customers will be unhappy. Although averages are same, they differ in C.V. which has considerable effect.

C.V. of industrial product depends upon raw material. Hence, a good quality of raw material ultimately give homogeneous end product.

In chemical and pharmaceutical industries C.V. is reduced by thorough mixing, pounding to convert raw material into homogeneous end product.

C.V. and Least Count :

Use of proper measuring instrument is also a way to check whether C.V. is maintained properly. If appropriate instrument is not used, C.V. will be inflated. As a thumb rule in industry.

Least count $\approx \dfrac{1}{10}$ specified range.

For example, if the inner diameter of cylinder is required to be between 0.95 cm and least count of the instrument should be $\left(\dfrac{1}{10}\right)^{th}$ of the specified range which $\dfrac{1}{10}(1.05 - 0.95)$

$= 0.01$ cm $= 0.1$ mm.

Illustration 3 : *Compute S.D. and C.V. for the following data :*

$$36, 15, 25, 10, 14.$$

Solution :

						Total
x	36	15	25	10	14	100
x^2	1296	225	625	100	196	2442

$$\bar{x} = \frac{\Sigma x}{n}$$

$$= \frac{100}{5} = 20$$

$$\sigma = \sqrt{\frac{\Sigma x^2}{n} - \bar{x}^2}$$

$$= \sqrt{\frac{2442}{5} - 20^2}$$

$$= \sqrt{88.4} = 9.4021$$

$$\text{C.V.} = \frac{\sigma}{|\bar{x}|} \times 100$$

$$= 45.2105 \%$$

In order to reduce the bulk of calculation similar to mean we can use 'deviation method' and 'step deviation method' to calculate S.D.

S.D. by Deviation Method :

Step 1 : Decide assumed mean 'a'

Step 2 : Let d = x – a. Compute deviation 'd'.

Step 3 : Find sum of deviations and sum of squares of deviations

$\Sigma d, \Sigma d^2,$ for individual observations.

$\Sigma fd, \Sigma fd^2,$ for frequency distribution.

Step 4 : Apply formula and find S.D. as follows :

$$\sigma = \sqrt{\frac{\Sigma d^2}{n} - \left(\frac{\Sigma d}{n}\right)^2} \qquad \text{for individual observations}$$

$$\sigma = \sqrt{\frac{\Sigma fd^2}{N} - \left(\frac{\Sigma fd}{N}\right)^2} \qquad \text{for frequency distribution}$$

Illustration 4 : *Compute S.D. and C.V. of marks scored by 10 candidates given below :*

54, 61, 64, 69, 58, 56, 49, 57, 55, 50.

Solution : Let a = 57, d = x − 57

x	54	61	64	69	58	56	49	57	55	50	Total
d	− 3	4	7	12	1	− 1	− 8	0	− 2	− 7	3
d²	9	16	49	144	1	1	64	0	4	49	337

$$\sigma = \sqrt{\frac{\Sigma d^2}{n} - \left(\frac{\Sigma d}{n}\right)^2} = \sqrt{\frac{337}{10} - \left(\frac{3}{10}\right)^2}$$

$$= \sqrt{33.61} = 5.7974$$

C.V. requires $\bar{x}$, hence $\bar{x} = a + \dfrac{\Sigma d}{n} = 57.3$

$$\text{C.V.} = \frac{\sigma}{|\bar{x}|} \times 100 = \frac{5.7974}{57.3} \times 100 = 10.1176\,\%$$

S.D. by Step Deviation Method :

Step 1 : Decide assumed mean 'a'.

Step 2 : Find the deviations, d = x − a.

Step 3 : Find the step deviations, $d' = \dfrac{d}{h}$.

Step 4 : Find the sum of d' and d'².

$\Sigma d', \Sigma d'^2$ for individual observations

$\Sigma fd', \Sigma fd'^2$ for frequency distribution

Step 5 : Apply the formula.

$$\sigma = \sqrt{\frac{\Sigma d'^2}{n} - \left(\frac{\Sigma d'}{n}\right)^2} \times h \qquad \text{for individual observations.}$$

$$\sigma = \sqrt{\frac{\Sigma fd'^2}{N} - \left(\frac{\Sigma fd'}{N}\right)^2} \times h \qquad \text{for frequency distribution.}$$

Illustration 5 : *Calculate the standard deviation and coefficient of variation for the frequency distribution of marks of 100 candidates given below :*

Marks	0–20	20–40	40–60	60–80	80–100
Frequency	5	12	32	40	11

Solution : We use step-deviation method to find σ.

Class	Mid-values x	Freq. f	$d' = \dfrac{x-50}{20}$	$f \times d'$	$f \times d'^2$
00 - 20	10	5	– 2	– 10	$-10 \times -2 = 20$
20 - 40	30	12	– 1	– 12	$-12 \times -1 = 12$
40 - 60	50	32	0	0	0
60 - 80	70	40	1	40	$40 \times 1 = 40$
80 - 100	90	11	2	22	$22 \times 2 = 44$
Total	–	100	–	40	$\sum fd'^2 = 116$

Here, a = 50, h = 20, N = 100

$$\text{Mean} = a + \frac{\sum fd'}{N} \times h$$

$$= 50 + \frac{40}{100} \times 20 = 58$$

$$\text{S.D.} = \sqrt{\frac{\sum fd'^2}{N} - \left(\frac{\sum fd'}{N}\right)^2} \times h$$

$$\sigma = \sqrt{\frac{116}{100} - \left(\frac{40}{100}\right)^2} \times 20 = 20$$

$$\text{C.V.} = \frac{\sigma}{|\bar{x}|} \times 100$$

$$= \frac{20}{58} \times 100 = 34.4828 \%$$

Merits of S.D. :

1. It is based on all observations.
2. It is rigidly defined.
3. It is capable of further mathematical treatment.
4. It does not ignore algebraic signs of deviations.
5. It is not much affected by sampling fluctuations.

Demerits of S.D. :

1. It is difficult to understand and to calculate.
2. It cannot be computed for a distribution with open end class.
3. It is unduly affected due to extreme deviations.
4. It cannot be calculated for qualitative data.

Important Notes :

1. If all the observations are increased (or decreased) by a constant, S.D. remains the same.

2. If each of the observation is multiplied by constant K, then S.D. is K times the original S.D.

3. If all the observations are equal, S.D. is zero (why ?).

4. If data contains only one observation, S.D. is zero (why ?)

As far as variance is concerned smaller variance is better in many situations. However there are some situations in genetical sciences where larger variance is better.

Variance and standard deviation are used in number of situations. Some of them are discussed below :

(a) Precision of an instrument is inversely proportional to variance. Therefore precision = k/variance.

(b) In portfolio analysis, risk is described in terms of variance of prices of shares.

(c) For the comparison of performance of two or more instruments, machines, coefficient of variation is used.

(d) The spread of variable is approximately taken as $\left(\bar{x} - 3\sigma, \bar{x} + 3\sigma\right)$.

Thus standard deviation helps in estimating lower limit and upper limit of the items.

4.7 Standard Deviation of Combined Group

Suppose there are two groups with sizes n_1, n_2 having arithmetic means $\bar{x}_1$, $\bar{x}_2$; standard deviations σ_1, σ_2 respectively. Then the mean of combined group is

$$\bar{x}_c = \frac{n_1 \bar{x}_1 + n_2 \bar{x}_2}{n_1 + n_2}$$

Let $d_1 = \bar{x}_1 - \bar{x}_c$ and $d_2 = \bar{x}_2 - \bar{x}_c$. Then S.D. of combined group is given by.

$$\sigma_c = \sqrt{\frac{n_1 (\sigma_1^2 + d_1^2) + n_2 (\sigma_2^2 + d_2^2)}{n_1 + n_2}}$$

Illustration 6 : *A group of 50 items have mean and standard deviation 61 and 8 respectively. Another group of 100 observations has mean and standard deviation 70 and 9 respectively. Find mean and standard deviation of combined group.*

Solution : We are given that : $n_1 = 50$, $\bar{x}_1 = 61$, $\sigma_1 = 8$, $n_2 = 100$, $\bar{x}_2 = 70$ and $\sigma_2 = 9$. Therefore combined mean

$$\bar{x}_c = \frac{n_1 \bar{x}_1 + n_2 \bar{x}_2}{n_1 + n_2}$$

$$= \frac{(50 \times 61) + (100 \times 70)}{50 + 100} = 67$$

$$\therefore \quad d_1 = \bar{x}_1 - \bar{x}_c = 61 - 67 = -6 \quad \text{and} \quad d_2 = \bar{x}_2 - \bar{x}_c = 70 - 67 = 3.$$

∴   Combined S.D. is

$$\sigma_c = \sqrt{\frac{n_1\left(\sigma_1^2 + d_1^2\right) + n_2\left(\sigma_2^2 + d_2^2\right)}{n_1 + n_2}}$$

$$\sigma_c = \sqrt{\frac{50\,(64 + 36) + 100\,(81 + 9)}{150}}$$

$$= 9.6609$$

Illustration 7 : *The mean weight of 150 students is 60 kg. The mean weight of boys is 70 kg, with standard deviation of 10 kg. For girls the mean weight is 55 kg with standard deviation of 15 kg. Find the number of boys and combined standard deviation.*

Solution : Let there be n_1 boys with mean $\bar{x}_1$ and S.D. σ_1. Similarly, there be n_2 girls with mean $\bar{x}_2$ and standard deviation σ_2. Hence, we get : $n_1 + n_2 = 150$, $\bar{x}_c = 60$, $\bar{x}_1 = 70$, $\bar{x}_2 = 55$, $\sigma_1 = 10$, $\sigma_2 = 15$.

$$\bar{x}_c = \frac{n_1\bar{x}_1 + n_2\bar{x}_2}{n_1 + n_2}$$

∴ $$60 = \frac{70n_1 + 55n_2}{n_1 + n_2}$$

$$60n_1 + 60n_2 = 70n_1 + 55n_2$$

$$n_2 = 2n_1 \qquad\qquad \text{... (1)}$$

Note that

$$n_1 + n_2 = 150$$

∴ $$n_1 + 2n_1 = 150 \qquad\qquad \text{... from (1)}$$

$$n_1 = 50$$

∴   Number of boys = 50.

We get $d_1 = \bar{x}_1 - \bar{x}_c = 70 - 60 = 10$ and

$$d_2 = \bar{x}_2 - \bar{x}_c = 55 - 60 = -5$$

∴   Combined standard deviation

$$\sigma = \sqrt{\frac{n_1\left(\sigma_1^2 + d_1^2\right) + n_2\left(\sigma_2^2 + d_2^2\right)}{n_1 + n_2}}$$

∴ $$\sigma = \sqrt{\frac{50\,(100 + 100) + 100\,(225 + 25)}{150}}$$

$$= 15.2753 \text{ kg.}$$

Illustration 8 : *The mean and standard deviation of 10 observations were 9.5 and 2.5 respectively. If one more observation with value 15 is included in the group, obtain the mean and standard deviation of these 11 observations.*

Solution : Let there be two groups, first group of original 10 observations and second group of new single observation. Hence,

$$n_1 = 10, \qquad n_2 = 1$$

$$\bar{x}_1 = 9.5, \qquad \bar{x}_2 = 15 \text{ (why ?)}$$

$$\sigma_1 = 2.5, \qquad \sigma_2 = 0 \text{ (why ?)}$$

Combined mean

$$\bar{x}_c = \frac{n_1\bar{x}_1 + n_2\bar{x}_2}{n_1 + n_2}$$

$$= \frac{10 \times 9.5 + 15}{11} = 10$$

$\therefore \ d_1 = \bar{x}_1 - \bar{x}_c = -0.5$ and $d_2 = \bar{x}_2 - \bar{x}_c = 5$

$\therefore$

$$\sigma_c = \sqrt{\frac{10\,(6.25 + 0.25) + (25 + 0)}{11}}$$

$$= 2.8604$$

Illustrative Examples

Example 4.5 : *The number of runs scored by cricketers A and B in 5 test matches are shown below :*

A	5	20	90	76	102	90	6	108	20	16
B	40	35	60	62	58	76	42	30	30	20

Find (i) which cricketer is better in average ? (ii) which cricketer is more consistent ?

Solution :

$$\text{Mean of A} = \frac{\sum x}{n} = \frac{533}{10} = 53.3$$

$$\text{S.D. of A} = \sqrt{\frac{\sum x^2}{n} - \left(\frac{\sum x}{n}\right)^2}$$

$$= \sqrt{\frac{45161}{10} - (53.3)^2}$$

$$= 40.9293$$

$\therefore \qquad$ C.V. of A $= 76.79\%$

$$\text{Mean of B} = \frac{\sum y}{n} = \frac{453}{10} = 45.3$$

$$\text{S.D. of B} = \sqrt{\frac{\sum y^2}{n} - \left(\frac{\sum y}{n}\right)^2} = \sqrt{\frac{23373}{10} - (45.3)^2}$$

$$= 16.8882$$

$\therefore$ C.V. of B $= 37.28\%$

(i) A gives better average runs (mean A > mean B)

(ii) B is more consistent (C.V. of B < C.V. of A)

Example 4.6 : *Arithmetic mean and standard deviation of 12 items are 22 and 3 respectively. Later on it was observed that the item 32 was wrongly taken as 23. Compute correct mean, standard deviation and coefficient of variation.*

Solution :

Incorrect sum $(\sum x) = n \times$ Incorrect mean $= 12 \times 22 = 264$

$$\text{Correct } \sum x = \text{Incorrect } \sum x + \text{Correct item} - \text{Incorrect item}$$

$$\sum x = 264 - 23 + 32 = 273$$

$$\text{Correct mean} = \frac{273}{12} = 22.75$$

$$\sigma^2 = \frac{\sum x^2}{n} - (\bar{x})^2$$

$\therefore$ $n\left[\sigma^2 + (\bar{x})^2\right] = \sum x^2$

$\therefore$ Incorrect $\sum x^2 = n\left[\sigma^2 + (\bar{x})^2\right]$ with σ and $\bar{x}$ incorrect.

$$= 12\,(9 + 484) = 5916$$

$$\text{Correct } \sum x^2 = \text{Incorrect } \sum x^2 + (\text{Correct item})^2 - (\text{Incorrect item})^2$$

$$= 5916 + 32^2 - 23^2 = 6411$$

$$\text{Correct } \sigma = \sqrt{\frac{\sum x^2}{n} - \left(\frac{\sum x}{n}\right)^2}\qquad \text{with correct } \sum x^2 \text{ and } \sum x$$

$$= \sqrt{\frac{6411}{12} - (22.75)^2}$$

$$= \sqrt{16.6875} = 4.0850$$

$$\text{Correct C.V.} = \frac{\sigma}{|\bar{x}|} \times 100 = 17.9562\%$$

Example 4.7 : *For a set of 90 items the mean and standard deviation are 59 and 9 respectively. For 40 items selected from those 90 items the mean and standard deviation are 54 and 6 respectively. Find the mean and standard deviation of the remaining items.*

Solution : We have

Group 1	**Group 2**	**Combined Group**
$n_1 = 40$	$n_2 = 50$	$n = 90$
$\bar{x}_1 = 54$	$\bar{x}_2 = ?$	$\bar{x}_c = 59$
$\sigma_1 = 6$	$\sigma_2 = ?$	$\sigma_c = 9$

To find $\bar{x}_2$ we use $\bar{x}_c$.

$$\bar{x}_c = \frac{n_1\bar{x}_1 + n_2\bar{x}_2}{n_1 + n_2} \text{ gives}$$

$$59 = \frac{40 \times 54 + 50\,\bar{x}_2}{90}$$

∴ $$\bar{x}_2 = 63.$$

∴ $$d_1 = \bar{x}_1 - \bar{x}_c = -5, \ d_2 = \bar{x}_2 - \bar{x}_c = 4$$

$$\sigma_c^2 = \frac{n_1(\sigma_1^2 + d_1^2) + n_2(\sigma_2^2 + d_2^2)}{n_1 + n_2}$$

$$81 = \frac{40(36 + 25) + 50(\sigma_2^2 + 16)}{90}$$

∴ $$\sigma_2 = 9.$$

Example 4.8 : *Given that : $n = 10$, $\sum(x - 20) = 8$, $\sum(x - 20)^2 = 762$. Find mean and S.D.*

Solution : Let $d = x - 20$, Hence $\bar{x} = 20 + \dfrac{\sum d}{n} = 20.8$

$$\text{S.D.} = \sqrt{\frac{\sum d^2}{n} - \left(\frac{\sum d}{n}\right)^2} = \sqrt{\frac{762}{10} - \left(\frac{8}{10}\right)^2} = 8.6925$$

Example 4.9 : *Compute standard deviation of the following frequency distribution :*

Weight (in Kg)	30–40	40–50	50–60	60–70	70–80
No. of standards	3	5	12	20	10

Solution :

Class	mid point (x)	frequency (f)	$d' = \dfrac{x - 55}{10}$	fd'	fd'^{2}
30–40	35	3	– 2	– 6	12
40–50	45	5	– 1	– 5	5
50–60	55	12	0	0	0
60–70	65	20	1	20	20
70–80	75	10	2	20	40
Total		50	–	29	77

$$\sigma = h \cdot \sqrt{\frac{\sum fd'^2}{\sum f} - \left(\frac{\sum fd'}{\sum f}\right)^2} = 10\sqrt{\frac{77}{50} - \left(\frac{29}{50}\right)^2} = 10.9709$$

Example 4.10 : *The following data represents the goals scored by two teams in foot ball matches.*

Number of goals scored	0	1	2	3	4
No. of matches by Team A	20	12	8	3	2
No. of matches by Team B	18	10	7	6	4

Which team scores more goal in a average ? Which team is more consistent ?

Solution : In order to test the consistency, we have to determine coefficient of variation.

   Let   X = Number of goals scored.

          f = Number of matches played.

	Team A					Team B		
X	**f**	**fx**	**fx²**		**X**	**f**	**fx**	**fx²**
0	20	0	0		0	18	0	0
1	12	12	12		1	10	10	10
2	8	16	32		2	7	14	28
3	3	9	27		3	6	18	54
4	2	8	32		4	4	16	64
Total	**45**	**45**	**103**		**Total**	**45**	**58**	**156**

$$\bar{X} = \frac{\Sigma fx}{\Sigma f} = \frac{45}{45} = 1 \qquad\qquad \bar{X} = \frac{\Sigma fx}{\Sigma f} = \frac{58}{45} = 1.2889$$

$$\sigma = \sqrt{\frac{\Sigma fx^2}{\Sigma f} - \bar{X}^2} \qquad\qquad \sigma = \sqrt{\frac{\Sigma fx^2}{\Sigma f} - \bar{X}^2}$$

$$= \sqrt{\frac{103}{45} - \left(\frac{45}{45}\right)^2} \qquad\qquad = \sqrt{\frac{156}{45} - 1.2889^2}$$

$$= 1.13529 \qquad\qquad\qquad = 1.3437$$

$$\text{C.V. (A)} = \frac{\sigma}{\bar{X}} \times 100 \qquad\qquad \text{C.V. (B)} = \frac{\sigma}{\bar{X}} \times 100$$

$$= 113.529 \% \qquad\qquad\qquad = 104.25 \%$$

Conclusion : 1. Since $\bar{X}_B > \bar{X}_A$, team B is better in average performance.

2. Since C.V. (B) < C.V. (A), team B is more consistent than A.

Example 4.11 : The following is information regarding portfolios A and B.

Portfolio	Average return	Risk (variance)
A	10 % ($\bar{X}$)	15 (σ_1^2)
B	20 % ($\bar{Y}$)	30 (σ_2^2)

We assume that the portfolios are independent, find the average return and combined risk if (i) equal investment in both portfolios is considered (ii) 25% of the shares are from portfolio A and the remaining from portfolio B.

Case (i) : If we invest 50 % amount of total in each portfolio then

$$\text{Average return (R)} = 0.5\,\overline{X} + 0.5\,\overline{Y} \qquad (\textbf{Result} : \text{If } Z = ax + by, \text{ then } \overline{Z} = a\,\overline{x} + b\,\overline{y})$$
$$= 0.5 \times 10 + 0.5 \times 20 \qquad\qquad\qquad \text{Here } a = b = 0.5$$
$$= 15$$

$$\text{Combined risk} = 0.5^2\,\sigma_1^2 + 0.5^2\,\sigma_2^2 \qquad (\textbf{Result} : \sigma_{ax+by}^2 = a^2\,\sigma_x^2 + b^2\,\sigma_y^2)$$
$$= 11.25$$

Thus the combined risk reduces.

Case (ii) : If we invest 25 % in portfolio A and 75 % in portfolio B then

$$\text{Average return} = 0.25\,\overline{X} + 0.75\,\overline{Y} \qquad (a = 0.25,\ b = 0.75,\ \overline{z} = a\,\overline{x} + b\,\overline{y})$$
$$= 17.5\ \%$$

$$\text{Combined risk} = 0.25^2\,\sigma_1^2 + 0.75^2\,\sigma_2^2 \qquad (a^2\sigma_1^2 + b^2\,\sigma_2^2)$$
$$= 17.81$$

Note : One can determine the percentage of investment in each portfolio so that the total risk is minimum, similarly one can find investment pattern that will maximise the total return. The details are beyond the scope of book.

Example 4.12 : *Compute Range and Coefficient of Range for the daily wages (₹) of 8 workers in a factory : 90, 120, 150, 80, 120, 125, 105, 75.*

Solution : Largest observation (L) $= 150$
Smallest observation (S) $= 75$
Range $= L - S = 150 - 75 = 75$
$$\text{Coefficient of range} = \frac{L-S}{L+S} = \frac{75}{150+75} = \frac{75}{225} = \frac{1}{3}$$

Example 4.13 : *Compute Standard Deviation for the following data :*
15, 18, 22, 25, 10.

Solution :

						Total
x	15	18	22	25	10	90
x^2	225	324	484	625	100	1758

$$\text{Standard deviation } (\sigma) = \sqrt{\frac{\sum x^2}{n} - \overline{X}^2}$$

$$n = 5,\ \overline{X} = \frac{\sum x}{n} = \frac{90}{5} = 18$$

$$\therefore \qquad\qquad \sigma = \sqrt{\frac{1758}{5} - 18^2}$$
$$= \sqrt{351.6 - 324} = \sqrt{27.6}$$
$$= 5.2536$$

Example 4.14 : *Two workers on the same job show the following results over long period of time :*

	Worker 'A'	Worker 'B'
Mean time of completing the job (in minutes)	30	25
Standard deviation	6	4

(i) *Which worker appears to be more consistent in the time he requires to complte the job ? Why ?*

(ii) Which worker is faster in completing the job ? Why ?

Solution : (i) Consistency is compared by coefficient of variation (C.V.).

$$\text{C.V. (A)} \ = \ \frac{\sigma_A}{\bar{X}_A} \times 100 \ = \ \frac{6}{30} \times 100 \ = 20\%$$

$$\text{C.V. (B)} \ = \ \frac{\sigma_B}{\bar{X}_B} \times 100 \ = \ \frac{4}{25} \times 100 = 16\%$$

Since C.V. (B) $<$ C.V. (A), where B is more consistent.

(ii) Worker is faster if the mean time required is smaller, since $\bar{X}_B = 25 < \bar{X}_A = 30$, Worker B is more faster.

Case Study :

Parag Infotech Pvt. Ltd. is a company to provide a software solutions. Directors of the company have taken a decision to double the capital and expand it in a big way. In view of this company decides to recruit at least 50 computer engineers. Company invited applications from fresh computer engineering graduates having at least 70% marks at their final examination. Company also expected furnish details of marks obtained from their SSC examination onwards.

Company received 200 applications. Most of the applications have secured marks between 70% to 73% in their final examination. Due to short of time to recruit, company is not interested to conduct personal interview of all the applicants but to select 70 of the best applicants for personal interview of the final selection. Company feels that 2% to 3% variation in final examination marks may be due to chance and has no effect in the performance.

Statisticians have advised to company to use the concept of measures of dispersion. Discuss the use of range and standard deviation in this regard to take the proper decision.

Points to Remember

1. Range = Largest observations – Smallest observation.

   $$\text{Coefficient of range} = \frac{\text{Largest observation} - \text{Smallest observation}}{\text{Largest observation} + \text{Smallest observation}}$$

2. Standard deviation (S.D.) $= \sigma = \sqrt{\dfrac{\sum x^2}{n} - \bar{X}^2}$ for discrete series

   $$= \sqrt{\frac{\sum fx^2}{\sum f} - \bar{X}^2} \text{ for frequency distribution}$$

3. Coefficient of variation (C.V.) $= \dfrac{\sigma}{\bar{X}} \times 100\%$.

4. C.V. is used for the comparison of variation.

Exercise 4.1

A. Theory Questions :

1. What is dispersion ? What purpose does it serve in the study of distribution ?
2. What type of measures will you use for comparison of dispersion in different distributions ? Mention any two of such measures.
3. Explain relative measure of dispersion and state its utility.
4. Define : Range, and standard deviation. State the formula for each incase of ungrouped data and frequency distribution.
5. Compare critically the two measures of dispersion : range and standard deviation.
6. State the merits and demerits of each of the following measures of dispersion : range and S.D.
7. Explain why S.D. is the best measure of dispersion.
8. What is utility of C.V. ?

Exercise 4.2

B. Discrete Series :

1. Find the standard deviation of the following data : 2, 3, 5, 2, 7, 5, 7, 6, 11, 12.
2. Find the arithmetic mean and standard deviation of the following series
   14, 8, 11, 10, 13, 16, 5, 9, 12, 2.
3. Monthly consumption of electricity in units of a certain family in a year is given below :

   210, 207, 315, 250, 240, 232, 216, 208, 209, 315, 300, 200.

   Compute   (i)   range and coefficient of range

   (ii)   standard deviation and coefficient variation.

4. Calculate the range and coefficient of range for the following data :

    88, 52, 67, 38, 59, 46. Also compute standard deviation.

5. Monthly consumption of electricity in units of six families in a city is given below. Compute coefficient of variation.

    210, 207, 315, 320, 250, 240.

6. Compute the (i) range and the coefficient of range (ii) quartile deviation and coefficient of quartile deviation for the following data :

    8, 12, 10, 18, 28, 17, 20, 22, 12, 10, 16.

    Also find the new range, coefficient of range quartile deviation and coefficient of quartile deviation in which each observation is doubled.

7. Calculate the range and the coefficient of range for the following data :

    125, 140, 110, 105, 130, 95, 115, 125, 80.

8. Compute the (i) range and coefficient of range (ii) quartile deviation and coefficient of quartile deviation for the data given below :

    52, 45, 60, 53, 48, 65, 42, 45, 60, 55, 58.

9. The prices of shares of a company from Monday to Friday are as follows :

Days	Mon.	Tues.	Wed.	Thur.	Fri.
Price (₹)	524	502	544	519	558

    Calculate the range and the coefficient of range.

10. Compute the (i) standard deviation (ii) mean deviation about mean (iii) coefficient of mean deviation about the mean for the following data :

    15, 18, 22, 25, 10.

11. Calculate the (i) coefficient of variation (ii) mean deviation about the median for the following series :

    12, 18, 15, 20, 16.

12. Find the (i) standard deviation and coefficient of variation (ii) mean deviation about median (iii) coefficient of mean deviation about median for the following data :

    6, 4, 5, 3, 12, 10.

13. Which of the following two series A and B is more stable ? Why ?

A	4	4	2	3	6	8	2	0	1	− 1
B	8	7	5	5	6	7	4	3	4	1

14. Using coefficient of variation find which of the following batsman is more consistent in scoring :

Score of A	42	115	6	73	7	19	119	36	84	29
Score of B	47	12	76	42	4	51	37	48	13	0

15. Compare the variation between the weight and the height of a group of 10 persons using coefficient of variation.

Sr. No.	1	2	3	4	5	6	7	8	9	10
Weight (kg)	70	65	65	64	69	63	65	70	71	62
Height (cm)	170	140	151	145	165	167	156	160	153	168

C. Frequency Distribution :

16. A survey conducted to determine distance travelled (in kms) per litre of petrol by newly introduced motorcycle gives the following distribution :

Distance (km)	40-45	45-50	50-55	55-60	60-65
No. of Motorcycles	10	17	23	40	10

Find the (i) standard deviation (ii) quartile deviation and coefficient of quartile deviation (iii) mean deviation about median and coefficient of mean deviation about median.

17. Find the variance for the following frequency distribution :

Class	5-15	15-25	25-35	35-45	45-55
Frequency	05	15	12	18	08

18. Compute the standard deviation for the following data :

Marks	0.-10	10-20	20-30	30-40	40-50
No. of Students	3	7	25	20	5

19. Calculate the coefficient of variation (C.V.) for the following data :

Class	0-10	10-20	20-30	30-40	40-50	50-60
Frequency	5	9	15	21	6	4

20. Calculate the standard deviation and coefficient of variation for the following frequency distribution :

X	2	4	6	8	10
Frequency	2	4	14	8	2

21. Find the standard deviation from the following data :

Marks	0 - 10	10 - 20	20 - 30	30 - 40	40 - 50
Frequency	10	16	30	32	12

22. Find the (i) standard deviation and coefficient of variation (ii) quartile deviation and coefficient of quartile deviation of distribution of daily wages.

Daily wages	1 - 20	21 - 40	41 - 60	61 - 80	81 - 100
Frequency	5	32	45	17	1

23. Compute the coefficient of variation for the following data :

Class	0 - 20	20 - 40	40 - 60	60 - 80	80 - 100
Frequency	6	32	45	17	0

24. Obtain the standard deviation for the following data :

Class	20 - 40	40 - 60	60 - 80	80 - 100
Frequency	6	8	4	2

25. Compute the standard deviation of the following frequency distributions :

Marks	0 - 10	10 - 20	20 - 30	30 - 40	40 - 50
No. of students	1	3	10	4	2

26. Find the coefficient of variation for the following data :

Size of item	2	4	6	8	10	12
No. of items	6	10	20	24	12	8

27. A share broker studied 100 companies and obtained the following data for the year 2012-13.

Divident declared (%)	0 - 8	8 - 16	16 - 24	24 - 32	32 - 40
No. of companies	15	30	40	10	5

Calculate the mean and the standard deviation of the above data and obtain the coefficient of variation.

28. Two automatic tea filling machines A and B tested for the performance. Machines are supposed to fill 500 gm. tea in each packet. A random sample of 100 filled packets on each machine showed the following distribution.

Weight in gm.	Frequency A	Frequency B
485–490	12	10
490–495	18	15
495–500	20	24
500–505	22	20
505–510	24	18
510–515	4	13

Which machine is more consistent ? Why ?

D. Combined Standard Deviation :

29. Find combined deviation from the following data :

Workers	Number	Average Salary	Standard Deviation
Male	80	1520	06
Female	20	1420	05

30. Two workers on the same job show the following results over long period of time :

	Worker 'A'	Worker 'B'
Mean time of completing the job (in minutes)	30	24
Standard Deviation	6	4
Number of jobs	10	10

(i) Which worker appears to be more consistent in the time he requires to complete the job ? Why ?

(ii) Which worker is faster in completing the job ? Why ?

(iii) Find the combined mean and standard deviation of the two workers together.

31. For a set of 50 items, the mean and standard deviation are 60 and 3 respectively. For another set of 100 items, the mean and standard deviation are 63 and 4 respectively. Find the mean and the standard deviation of combined group.

32. Information about the daily salaries of employees in firms A and B is stated below :

Firm	No. of employees	Mean Salary	S.D. of Salary
A	60	₹ 400	₹ 10
B	40	₹ 500	₹ 11

(i) Which firm gives more amount as salary ?

(ii) Which firm has smaller variation in salary ?

(iii) Find the combined mean and S.D. of two firms.

33. Information regarding daily salaries of two companies A and B is given below :

	Company A	Company B
No. of workers	600	400
Mean salary	₹ 180	₹ 200
S.D. of salary	₹ 9	₹ 10

(i) Which company pays larger salary ?
(ii) Which company has less variation in salaries ?
(iii) Find combined mean and S.D. of two firms A and B.

34. Find the combined standard deviation of groups A and B taken together given that :

Group	Size	Arithmetic mean	Standard deviation
A	100	60	6
B	200	63	4

35. Find the combined mean and standard deviation from the following data.

Group	Arithmetic mean	S.D.	Size
A	50	10	100
B	55	11	150

36. Find the arithmetic means of each group from the following data :

Group	S.D.	C. V.
1	16	40%
2	20	50%

37. The arithmetic mean and standard deviation of a group of 50 items are 61 and 8 respectively. In a second group of 100 items they are 70 and 9 respectively. Find the combined mean and S.D. of the two groups.

38. The means of two samples of sizes 50 and 100 are 40 and 25 respectively. The standard deviations of those samples are 10 and 8 respectively. Obtain the combined standard deviation.

39. The arithmetic mean and the standard deviation of the values of 100 items in a group are 80 and 5 respectively. In a second group of 25 items, each item has a value equal to 60. Find the combined standard deviation of two groups taken together.

40. Calculate the combined variance of the two groups of items.

	Group I	Group II
No. of observations	40	60
Arithmetic mean	25	30
Standard deviation	6	4

E. Miscellaneous Problems :

41. The arithmetic mean and standard deviation of 20 observations are 10 and 2 respectively. Later on it was noticed that item 8 taken was incorrect. Calculate arithmetic mean and standard deviation if

(i) the wrong item is omitted.

(ii) the wrong item is replaced by 12.

42. The mean and standard deviation of 100 observations are 40 and 5.1 respectively. It was later discovered that an observation 40 was misread as 50. Calculate correct mean and standard deviation.

43. If $n = 10$, $\Sigma (x - 120) = 20$, $\Sigma (x - 120)^2 = 200$. Find the mean and the standard deviation.

44. If $n = 100$, $\Sigma x = -20$, $\Sigma x^2 = 220$, find standard deviation and coefficient of variation.

45. Find the standard deviation of set A, Set B, Set C and Set D and comment on findings.

Set A :	1	2	3	4	5
Set B :	11	12	13	14	15
Set C :	10	20	30	40	50
Set D :	4	4	4	4	4

46. The range, arithmetic mean and standard deviation of 10 items are 20, 62, 10 respectively. If each observation is increased by 5, what will be the range, arithmetic mean and standard deviation.

Answers 4.2

1. 3.2558.

2. $\bar{X} = 10, \sigma = 4$

3. (i) 115, 0.2233   (ii) 41.95, 17.35%

4. Range = 50, Coefficient of range = 0.3968, $\sigma = 16.1314$

5. 45.4239%

6. Range = 20, Coefficient of range = 0.5555, Q.D. = 5, Coefficient of Q.D. = 1/3.
    New range = 40, New coefficient of range = 0.5555, New Q.D. = 5,
    New coefficient of Q.D. = 1/3.

7. Range = 60, Coefficient of range = 0.2727

8. Range = 23, Coefficient of range = 0.215, Q.D. = 7.5, Coefficient of Q.D. = 0.1429.

9. Range = 56, Coefficient of range = 0.0528

10. 5.2536, M.D. = 4.4, Coefficient of M.D. = 0.2444.

11. 16.75%, M.D. = 2.2.

12. $\sigma = 3.2489$, C.V. = 48.73%, M.D. = 2.5, Coefficient of M.D. = 0.4167.

13. Series B more stable, C.V. (A) = 89.1898% C.V. (B) = 40%

14. B is more consistent C.V. (A) = 75.54 %, C.V. (B) = 70.82 %

15. C.V. (weight) = 4.67 % < C.V. (height) = 6.18 %

16. 5.7383, Q.D. = 4.3566, Coefficient of Q.D. = 0.08103, M.D. = 4.85,
    Coefficient of M.D. = 0.0882.

17. 144.14

18. 9.5029

19. $\sigma = 12.8279$, C.V. 43.73%

20. $\sigma = 1.9137$, C.V. = 30.5378

21. S.D. = 11.4891

22. S.D. = 16.4572, C.V. = 35.85 %, Q.D. = 12.1944, Coefficient of Q.D. = 0.1349.

23. 36.3505

24. S.D. = 18.8680

25. 9.6307

26. 37.3625 %

27. $\bar{x}$ = 16.8, σ = 8.1584, C.V. = 48.56 %

28. C.V. (A) = 1.4294 %   C.V. (B) = 1.5084 %, Machine A is more consistent.

29. 40.42029

30. (i)   C.V. (A) = 20% > C.V. (B) = 16.6667%, B is more consistent

    (ii) B (iii) Combined mean = 27, Combined S.D. = 5.9161

31. Combined mean = 62, Combined S.D. = 3.9581

32. (i)   B (ii) C.V. (A) = 2.5% > C.V. (B) = 2.2%, B has smaller variation

    (iii) Combined mean = 440, Combined S.D. = 50.0839

33. (i)   B (ii) Both name same C.V. = 5%, both are equal in variation

    (iii) Combined mean = 188, Combined S.D. = 14.2969%

34. 4.97

35. $\bar{x}_c$ = 53, σ_c = 10.8904

36. 40, 40

37. $\bar{x}_c$ = 67, σ_c = 9.6605

38. 11.225

39. σ_c = 9.1651

40. σ_c = 5.477

41. (i)   Mean = 10.1053, S.D. = 1.9922   (ii) Mean = 10.2, S.D. = 1.99

42. Mean = 39.9, S.D. = 5

43. Mean = 116, S.D. = 22.9783

44. S.D. = 1.4697, C.V. = 734.8469%

45. σ_A = σ_B = $\sqrt{2}$, σ_C = $10\sqrt{2}$, σ_D = 0.

46. Range = 20, $\bar{x}$ = 67, σ = 10.

Objective Questions

1. Find the standard deviation of 2, 2, 2, 2, 2.
2. If the standard deviation of 1, 2, 3, 4, 5 is $\sqrt{2}$ then state the standard deviation of
   (a) 11, 12, 13, 14, 15 (b) 10, 20, 30, 40, 50 (c) – 1, – 2, – 3, – 4, – 5.
3. If each observation is doubled what will be the standard deviation ?
4. If each observation is increased by 5, what will be the standard deviation ?
5. Suppose there are two groups with following details :

Group	A	B
Size	10	10
Arithmetic mean	50	50
Standard deviation	4	6

Find the standard deviation of the combined groups.

Answers

1. 0   2. (a) $\sqrt{2}$ (b) $10\sqrt{2}$ (c) $\sqrt{2}$
2. S.D. will be doubled.
3. S.D. will be change.
5. $\sigma_c = \sqrt{26}$.

❒❒❒

Chapter **5**...

Correlation and Regression

Contents ...

Key Words :

Bivariate Data, Correlation, Scatter Diagram, Covariance, Karl Pearson's Coefficient of Correlation, Ranks, Rank Correlation, Regression Lines, Regression Coefficients, Coefficient of Determination, Standard Error of Regression Estimate.

Objectives :

In this chapter we study the technique to bivariate data to know whether there is any interrelationship between them. A particular type of relationship viz. the extent of linear relationship is being measured using correlation. Such measure is developed for quantitative and qualitative data.

(5.1)

The relation between correlated variables can be established using regression analysis. It is useful in forecasting or prediction of one variable when the value of other variable is known. The estimates are more reliable if the r^2 is larger.

5.1 Introduction

Many a times we come across situations where two variables are interrelated. For example : (i) Marks and intelligence quotient of students. (ii) Rainfall and agricultural production. (iii) Demand and price of a certain commodity. (iv) Income and expenditure of a family. (v) Height of son and that of father. In these situations we may be interested in examining the relation between the two variables. Such interrelated variables are called as *correlated variables.* The extent of linear relation between the two variables is called as *correlation.*

Bivariate Data :

In order to determine correlation, we require data regarding two concerned variables. These data are called as *bivariate data.* Suppose X and Y are the variables under consideration.

Whenever the variables X and Y are the variables measured on the same item, they are likely to be correlated. For example, the income of family (X) and the expenditure of family (Y). We record the values of X and Y for each of the families under study. Suppose it gives a set of n pairs (x_1, y_1); (x_2, y_2); ... ; (x_n, y_n) where x is income and y is the expenditure of the family. This set of n pairs is a **bivariate data.** When n is large, for convenience the data are expressed in bivariate frequency distribution or two-way frequency distribution. In this case we make m classes of X and n classes of Y. Like univariate classification, pairs (x, y) are classified by using tally marks (i, j)th class. Number of tally marks is denoted by f_{ij}.

Remark : Note that (x_i, y_i) is an ordered pair. First component in every pair is observation on variable X and second component is on variable Y. In the further analysis the components X_i and Y_i are inseparable, i.e. we cannot rearrange the pairs as (x_1, y_{10}) or (x_3, y_4) etc.

5.2 Types of Correlation

Positive Correlation, Negative Correlation, No Correlation

It may be noticed that in some cases, increase in value of one variable is associated with increase in value of other variable or decrease in value of one variable is associated with decrease in value of other variable. Correlation between these variables is said to be **positive**.

For example : Marks and intelligence quotient. In this case, there is a positive correlation between these variables.

On the other hand in some other situations increase in value of one variable is accompanied by decrease in value of other variable and vice-versa. Here the changes in values of two variables are in opposite direction. Correlation between these variables is said to be **negative**.   **(April 2010)**

For example : Consider supply and price of commodity. Clearly if supply of commodity is more, price falls down and if there is a scarcity of a commodity, then price goes up. Hence, there is a negative correlation between supply and price of a commodity.

Soimetimes, change in one variable is not related to change in other variable then we say that there is **no correlation**.

For example : Height of student and his examination score.

There are several measures of correlation of which three are in general used :
(i) Scatter diagram, (ii) Product moment correlation coefficient and (iii) Rank correlation.

5.3 Scatter Diagram

In order to visualise the correlation between two variables, the first step is scatter diagram.

Suppose $\{(x_i, y_i); i = 1, 2, \ldots, n\}$ are bivariate data on two variables x and y.

If these n pairs are plotted on a graph paper, taking one of the variable on X axis and other on Y axis, we get a diagram called as *Scatter diagram.* With the help of scatter diagram we get a general idea about the existence of correlation and the type of correlation. However, it fails to give correct numerical value of correlation. It is easy but crude and approximate method of measuring correlation. In this method we need to find out correlation by visual judgement only. We classify scatter diagrams broadly into
5 categories which are depicted below in Fig. 5.1 to Fig. 5.8.

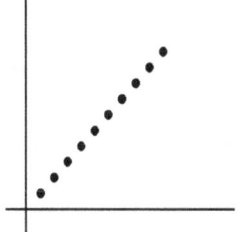

Fig. 5.1 : Positive perfect correlation

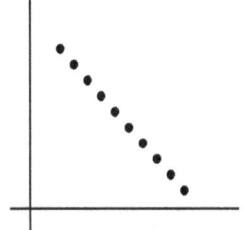

Fig. 5.2 : Negative perfect correlation

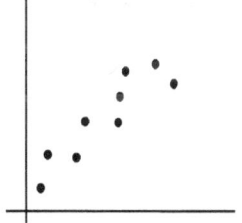

Fig. 5.3 : Positive correlation

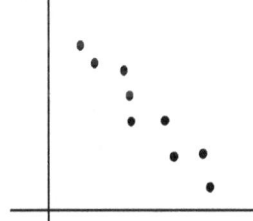

Fig. 5.4 : Negative correlation

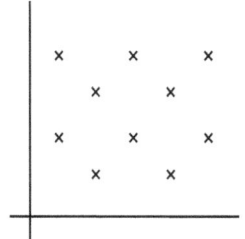

Fig. 5.5 : No correlation

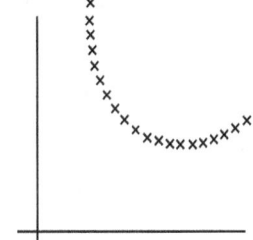

Fig. 5.6 : Non-linear correlation

Fig. 5.7 : No Correlation   **Fig. 5.8 : No Correlation**

In Fig. 5.1 and Fig. 5.3 we see that the changes in value of one variable and changes in value of other variable are in the same direction. Hence, the correlation is positive or direct. Moreover in Fig. 5.1 all the points lie on the same line, hence correlation is perfect positive.

In Fig. 5.2 and Fig. 5.4 we see that changes in values of one variable and those of other variable are in opposite direction. Hence, the correlation is negative or inverse. Specifically in Fig. 5.2 we observe that points fall on the same line. This is an indication of negative perfect correlation. In Fig. 5.5 we see that the points are scattered in a haphazard manner without showing any particular pattern. This is an indication of almost no correlation. In Fig. 5.6 points show non-linear pattern.

In Fig. 5.7 and 5.8 one of the variables is not really a variable. It is a constant. It does not increase or decrease for any type of change in the other variable. Thus, change in one variable is not at all associated with that of in the other variable. Hence, in this situation, there is no correlation between the two variables. This type of scatter diagram will be observed in the following situations. For example : Suppose X is Interest on debenture, Y is Dividend paid on shares. X is fixed, whereas Y depends upon company's profit. Clearly there is no correlation between X and Y.

Thus, we can draw conclusions regarding correlation between two variables by means of scatter diagram.

5.4 Merits and Demerits of Scatter Diagram

Merits :

1. Scatter diagram is the simplest method of studying correlation.

2. It is easy to understand.

3. It is not influenced by extreme values.

Demerits :

1. It does not give a numerical measure of correlation.

2. It is a subjective method.

3. It cannot be applied to qualitative data.

Illustration 1 : *Following table gives aptitude score (X) and creativity (Y).*

X	63	61	62	52	69	72	55	67	80	73
Y	69	65	67	60	72	86	62	75	82	83

Draw scatter diagram and comment on the type of correlation between X and Y.

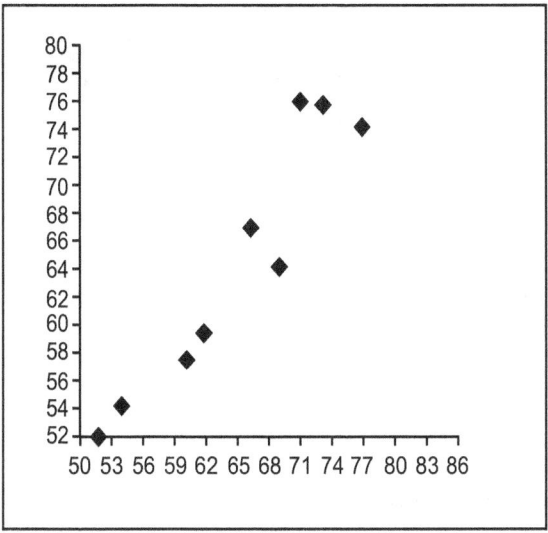

Fig. 5.9

Interpretation : There exist positive correlation of high degree between X and Y.

5.5 Covariance

We introduce the concept of covariance. It will be required to study correlation and regression critically. The drawbacks of scatter diagram as a measure of correlation can be overcome by covariance. The covariance is the joint mutual variation between two variables.

Covariance : The covariance between X and Y is denoted by Cov (X, Y) and is defined as

$$\text{Cov (X, Y)} = \frac{\sum (x - \bar{x})(y - \bar{y})}{n}$$

The computational formula after simplification will be

$$\text{Cov (X, Y)} = \frac{\sum xy}{n} - \bar{x}\,\bar{y}$$

Remark : (1) Cov (X, Y) is similar to variance.

Note that $\text{Var (X)} = \dfrac{\sum x^2}{n} - \bar{x}^2$ can be expressed as $\text{Var (X)} = \dfrac{\sum x \cdot x}{n} - \bar{x} \cdot \bar{x}$. Here

replacing the second x by y and second $\bar{x}$ by $\bar{y}$ we get, $\dfrac{\sum xy}{n} - \bar{x}\,\bar{y}$.

(2) Cov (X, Y) = Cov (Y, X).

(3) Cov (X, X) = Var (X).

(4) Cov (X, constant) = 0.

(5) Covariance may be negative, positive, zero whereas variance is non-negative.

(6) If a, b, h, k are constants then

$$\text{Cov (X} - a, \text{Y} - b) = \text{Cov (X, Y)}$$

$$\text{Cov}\left(\frac{X-a}{h}, \frac{Y-b}{k}\right) = \frac{1}{hk}\,\text{Cov (X, Y)}, \quad h \neq 0,\ k \neq 0$$

5.6 Karl Pearson's Coefficient of Correlation (Or Product Moment Correlation Coefficient)

If X and Y are correlated, then we get scatter diagrams of the following types. Here we plot the deviations $(x - \bar{x}, y - \bar{y})$.

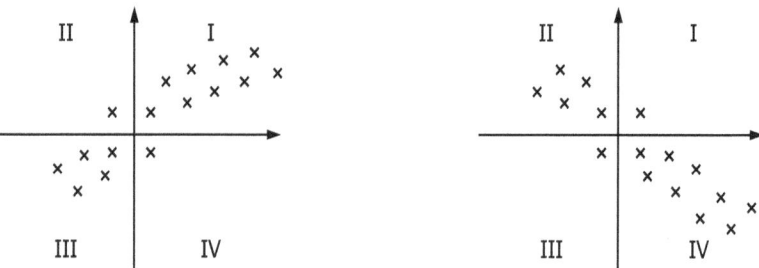

Fig. 5.10 : Positive Correlation   **Fig. 5.11 : Negative Correlation**

Let us examine the two situations independently. In Fig. 5.10 of positive correlation, observe that both the co-ordinates have same sign, either positive or negative. Thus, $\sum (x - \bar{x}) (y - \bar{y}) > 0$. In other words Cov $(x, y) > 0$ for positively correlated variables. On the other hand in Fig. 5.11, one of the co-ordinates is always negative. Hence, $\sum(x - \bar{x}) (y - \bar{y}) < 0$. That is Cov $(x, y) < 0$ for negatively correlated variables. Also, covariance measures the extent of joint variation between x and y. Due to these properties of covariance, a relative measure of correlation is defined using covariance. It is discussed below :

Karl Pearson's coefficient of correlation : Karl Pearson's coefficient of correlation is denoted by r and it is defined as follows :

$$r = \frac{\sum (x - \bar{x}) (y - \bar{y})}{\sqrt{\sum (x - \bar{x})^2 \times \sum (y - \bar{y})^2}} \qquad \ldots (5.1)$$

where $\bar{x}$ and $\bar{y}$ are arithmetic means of x and y respectively. Formula given by (5.1) can be put in simplified way for calculation purpose.

$$r = \frac{\sum xy - n \bar{x} \bar{y}}{\sqrt{(\sum x^2 - n\bar{x}^2)(\sum y^2 - n\bar{y}^2)}} \qquad \ldots (5.2)$$

or $$r = \frac{\frac{1}{n}\sum xy - \bar{x} \bar{y}}{\sigma_x \sigma_y} \qquad \ldots (5.3)$$

where, σ_x = standard deviation of x, σ_y = standard deviation of y.

Using covariance, correlation will be

$$r = \frac{Cov (X, Y)}{\sigma_x \sigma_y} \qquad \ldots (5.4)$$

The above (5.1), (5.2), (5.3), (5.4) formulae give one and the same numerical value; however according to convenience and type of data available we choose formula.

In most of the cases where raw or unsummerised data are given we use formula (b).

To study the algebraic properties the formulae (d) or (a) are most suitable.

Properties of correlation coefficient 'r' :

1.   Correlation coefficient 'r' lies between –1 and 1 (i.e. $-1 < r < 1$).

Interpretation : If $r > 0$ the correlation is positive and if $r < 0$. The correlation is negative. If $r = 0$ we say the variables are uncorrelated. Larger the numerical value of r more close is the extent of relationship between the variables. In general for $|r| > 0.8$, we consider high correlation. If $|r|$ is between 0.3 to 0.8 we say that correlation is considerable. If $|r| < 0.3$ we say that correlation is negligible. If $r = 1$ we say there is perfect positive correlation whereas if $r = -1$ we say that there is perfect negative correlation. The above interpretation is general. For more valid interpretation one has to take into account value of n also. Details are beyond the scope of book.

2.   Correlation coefficient does not change due to change of origin. In other words if a constant is added or subtracted from each observation, correlation coefficient remains same. Corr $(x \pm a, y \pm b) = $ Corr (x, y).

3.   Correlation remains numerically same under the change of scale. In other words if we divide or multiply each observation by constant correlation remains same numerically.

$$\text{Corr (ax, by)} = \text{Corr (x, y)} \quad \text{if a and b have same algebraic signs.}$$
$$= -\text{Corr (x, y)} \quad \text{if a and b have opposite algebraic signs.}$$

4.   Correlation coefficient between X and Y is same as that of between Y and X.

i.e.   Corr $(x, y) = $ Corr (y, x).

5.   Corr $(x, x) = 1$,   Corr $(x, - x) = - 1$.

5.7 Computational Procedure of Correlation Coefficient

We propose two methods for computing correlation coefficient.
(i)   Direct method.
(ii)   Deviation method.

(i)   Direct method : Following are the steps involved in the calculations of Karl Pearson's correlation coefficients.

Step 1 : Obtain sum of x values i.e. $\sum x$ and hence ($\bar{x}$).

Step 2 : Obtain sum of y values, i.e. $\sum y$ and hence $(\bar{y})$.

Step 3 : Obtain sum of squares of x, i.e. $\sum x^2$.

Step 4 : Obtain sum of squares of y, i.e. $\sum y^2$

Step 5 : Obtain sum of products of x and y, i.e. $\sum xy$.

Step 6 : Find r by applying formula

$$r = \frac{\sum xy - n\bar{x}\,\bar{y}}{\sqrt{\sum (x^2 - n\bar{x}^2) \times \sum (y^2 - n\bar{y}^2)}}$$

Illustration 2 : *Following are the values of import of raw material and export of finished products in suitable units.*

Export	10	11	14	14	20	22	16	12	15	13
Import	12	14	15	16	21	26	21	15	16	14

Calculate the coefficient of correlation between the import values and export values.

(April 2011, 2013)

Solution : Let X : Quantity exported, Y : Quantity imported.

Preparing table as follows calculations can be made simple. Here we use direct method

x	y	x^2	y^2	xy
10	12	100	144	120
11	14	121	196	154
14	15	196	225	210
14	16	196	256	224
20	21	400	441	420
22	26	484	676	572
16	21	256	441	336
12	15	144	225	180
15	16	225	256	240
13	14	169	196	182
Total = 147	**170**	**2291**	**3056**	**2638**

Here n = 10, hence $\bar{x} = \dfrac{\sum x}{n} = \dfrac{147}{10} = 14.7$ and $\bar{y} = \dfrac{\sum y}{n} = \dfrac{170}{10} = 17.$

$$r = \frac{\sum xy - n\,\bar{x} \cdot \bar{y}}{\sqrt{(\sum x^2 - n\bar{x}^2) \times \sum (y^2 - n\,\bar{y}^2)}}$$

$$= \frac{2638 - 10 \times 14.7 \times 17}{\sqrt{(2291 - 10 \times 14.7^2)(3056 - 10 \times 17^2)}}$$

$$= \frac{139}{\sqrt{130.1 \times 166}}$$

$$= 0.9458$$

Interpretation : There is a high positive correlation between import of raw material and export of finished product.

(ii) Deviation method : Sometimes original values are large. In order to reduce the bulk of calculation we use deviation method. Here we subtract a convenient number from x observations, similarly we subtract some other number from y observations. Due to the property of correlation coefficient it does not affect the correlation coefficient. Procedural steps involved in this method are as follows :

Step 1 : Obtain deviations u = x – a   (a being constant)

Step 2 : Obtain deviations v = y – b   (b being constant)

Step 3 : Obtain sum of u and v. i.e. $\sum u$ and $\sum v$.

Step 4 : Obtain sum of squares of u and v. i.e. $\sum u^2$ and $\sum v^2$.

Step 5 : Obtain sum of products of u and v' i.e. $\sum uv$.

Step 6 : Find r by applying the formula.

$$r = \frac{\sum uv - n\,\bar{u}\,\bar{v}}{\sqrt{\sum (u^2 - n\,\bar{u}^2) \times \sum (v^2 - n\,\bar{v}^2)}}$$

where $\quad \bar{u} = \dfrac{\sum u}{n}$ and $\bar{v} = \dfrac{\sum v}{n}$.

Illustration 3 : Compare correlation between the heights of father and son from the following data.

Height of father (in inches) :   65   63   67   64   68   70   68   71

Height of son (in inches) :   68   65   68   65   69   68   71   70

Solution : Let x = height of father, y = height of son.

We use deviation method by taking U = X – 60 and Y = Y – 65.

x	y	u	v	u²	v²	uv
65	68	5	3	25	9	18
63	65	3	0	9	0	0
67	68	7	3	49	9	21
64	65	4	0	16	0	0
68	69	8	4	64	16	32
70	68	10	3	100	9	30
68	71	8	6	64	36	48
71	70	11	5	121	25	55
Total	–	56	24	448	104	183

$$\bar{u} = \frac{\sum u}{n} = \frac{56}{8} = 7, \ \bar{v} = \frac{\sum v}{n} = \frac{24}{8} = 3$$

$$r = \frac{\sum uv - n\bar{u}\,\bar{v}}{\sqrt{\sum (u^2 - n\bar{u}^2) \times (\sum v^2 - n\,\bar{v}^2)}}$$

$$= \frac{183 - 8 \times 7 \times 3}{\sqrt{(448 - 8 \times 7^2)(104 - 8 \times 3^2)}}$$

$$= \frac{15}{\sqrt{56 \times 32}} = 0.3543$$

Illustration 4 : *Compute correlation coefficient between supply and price of commodity using following data.*

Supply	152	158	169	182	160	166	182
Price	198	178	167	152	180	170	162

Solution : Here we use deviation method to find r.

Let x = supply, u = x – 150, y = price, v = y – 160.

x	y	u	v	u^2	v^2	uv
152	198	2	38	4	1444	76
158	178	8	18	64	324	144
169	167	19	7	361	49	133
182	152	32	– 8	1024	64	– 256
160	180	10	20	100	400	200
166	170	16	10	256	100	160
182	162	32	2	1024	4	64
Total	**–**	**87**	**87**	**2833**	**2385**	**521**

Here n = 7, $\sum u = 119$, $\sum v = 87$, $\sum u^2 = 2833$ $\sum v^2 = 2385$, $\sum uv = 521$

∴ $\bar{u} = 17$, $\bar{v} = 12.4286$

$$r = \frac{\sum uv - n\bar{u}\,\bar{v}}{\sqrt{(\sum u^2 - n\bar{u}^2) \times (\sum v^2 - n\bar{v}^2)}}$$

$$r = \frac{521 - 7 \times 17 \times 12.4286}{\sqrt{(2833 - 7 \times 17^2)(2.385 - 7 \times 12.4286^2)}}$$

$$r = \frac{-958}{\sqrt{810 \times 1303.7142}} = \frac{-958}{1027.6227}$$

$$= -0.9322$$

Interpretation : There is high negative correlation between supply and price.

Illustration 5 : *Find correlation coefficient between X and Y, given that,*

  n = 25, $\sum x = 75$, $\sum y = 100$, $\sum x^2 = 250$, $\sum y^2 = 500$, $\sum xy = 325$.

Solution : Here $\bar{x} = \frac{75}{25} = 3$, $\bar{y} = \frac{100}{25} = 4$

∴ $$r = \frac{\sum xy - n\bar{x}\,\bar{y}}{\sqrt{(\sum x^2 - n\bar{x}^2) \times \sum(y^2 - n\bar{y}^2)}}$$

$$r = \frac{325 - 25 \times 3 \times 4}{\sqrt{(250 - 25 \times 9)(500 - 25 \times 16)}}$$

$$= \frac{25}{\sqrt{25 \times 100}} = \frac{25}{50} = 0.5$$

Illustration 6 : *Compute the product moment coefficient of correlation for the following* data : *n = 100,* $\bar{x}$ *= 62,* $\bar{y}$ *= 53,* σ_x *= 10,* σ_y *= 12,* $\sum (x - \bar{x}) (y - \bar{y})$ *= 8000.*

Solution :
$$r = \frac{\sum (x - \bar{x}) (y - \bar{y})}{\sqrt{\sum (x - \bar{x})^2 \sum (y - \bar{y})^2}}$$

Dividing numerator and denominator by n we get,

$$r = \frac{\sum (x - \bar{x}) (y - \bar{y})/n}{\sqrt{\dfrac{\sum (x - \bar{x})^2}{n} \dfrac{\sum (y - \bar{y})^2}{n}}} = \frac{\sum (x - \bar{x}) (y - \bar{y})/n}{\sigma_x \, \sigma_y}$$

$$= \frac{8000/100}{10 \times 12}$$

$$= 0.6667$$

Illustration 7 : *Compute correlation coefficient between X and Y given that :*
n = 100, $\sum (x - 35) = 25$, $\sum (y - 19) = 68$, $\sum (x - 35)^2 = 167$,
$\sum (y - 19)^2 = 162$, $\sum (x - 35) (y - 19) = 130$

Solution : Let,   u = x – 35 and   v = y – 19

∴ $\bar{u}$ = 0.25 $\bar{v}$ = 0.68

$$r = \frac{\sum uv - n \bar{u} \bar{v}}{(\sum u^2 - n \bar{u}^2) \times (\sum v^2 - n \bar{v}^2)} = \frac{113}{\sqrt{160.75 \times 115.76}}$$

$$= 0.8283$$

5.8 Merits and Demerits of Karl Pearson's Coefficient of Correlation

Merits : 1. Karl Pearson's coefficient of correlation determines a single value which summarises the extent of linear relationship. It also indicates type of correlation.

2.   It depends upon all observations.

Demerits : 1. It cannot be computed for qualitative data such as honesty and intelligence, beauty and intelligence.

2.   It is unduly affected by extreme values.

3.   It measures only linear relationship.

For example : Suppose

X :	– 2	– 1	0	1	2
Y :	4	1	0	1	4

Here $\sum x = 0$, $\sum y = 10$, $\sum xy = 0$. Hence, Cov (X, Y) = $\dfrac{\sum xy}{n} - \bar{x} \bar{y} = 0$.

Therefore, Corr (X, Y) = 0. However Y = X^2, which is non-linear. Hence, correlation fails to measure non-linear relationship. Details are beyond the scope of book.

Note : To overcome the demerit (1) Spearman's rank correlation is used which is discussed below.

5.9 Rank Correlation

Karl Pearson's coefficient of correlation is the best measure of correlation, however, it poses difficulty in measuring the correlation between qualitative characteristics. If the qualitative characteristics under study are recorded using ordinal scale, we can arrange the items in ascending or in descending order according to the merit that they possess.

Ranking : Ordered arrangement of items according to merit that they possess is called as **ranking.**

Rank : The number indicating the position in ranking is called as **rank.**

Tie : Tie is said to occur in ranking if two or more items have same merit. In this case we allot common rank to these items. This rank is the average of ranks which would have been alloted if the respective items would differ in merit slightly.

In this manner bivariate qualitative data can be expressed in bivariate quantitative form. This enables to compute correlation coefficient. Spearman in 1904 suggested a measure of correlation using the ranks. Suppose we have recorded n pairs of observations on qualitative characteristics A and B. Let $x_1, x_2, \ldots x_n$ be the ranks given to the items of characteristic A. Similarly, $y_1, y_2, \ldots, y_n$ be the ranks given to the items of characteristic B. Therefore (x_i, y_i) will be the pair of ranks associated with i^{th} pair of A and B. The following are noteworthy points regarding ranks.

(i)   The ranks $x_1, x_2, \ldots, x_n$ forms a permutation of $1, 2, \ldots, n$; so also $y_1, y_2, \ldots y_n$.

(ii)   The ranks are given by arranging the items either in ascending order or in descending order of the quality. In order to compute rank correlation the items of type A and those of type B are ordered in the same way either in ascending order or in descending order.

The product moment correlation coefficient between these ranks is called as **Spearman's rank** correlation coefficient. It is denoted by R and given by the formula.

$$R = 1 - \frac{6 \sum d^2}{n(n-1)}$$

where,   d = difference between corresponding ranks of X and Y for an individual observation

d = rank of X – rank of Y

n = Number of pairs of observations.

Note : (i) Spearman's rank correlation is simple to compute as compared to Karl Pearson's coefficient of correlation. However, there is a loss of accuracy, whenever we compute it for quantitative data.

(ii)   Rank correlation can also be computed for quantitative data. In psychology, Spearman's rank correlation is most commonly used to measure the correlation between the different traits such as intelligence and mathematical aptitude, intelligence and anger, anger and aggressiveness.

(iii) Smaller the d_i's larger is the correlation. On the other hand, larger the d_i's correlation will tend to be large but it will be negative.

(iv) Since R is a Karl Pearson's coefficient of correlation between the ranks, it lies between – 1 and 1. We can prove this result independently.

Result : Spearman's rank correlation coefficient lies between – 1 and 1.

Proof : Case (i) : If there is a perfect positive correlation between two characteristics A and B, then the ranks x_i and y_i in each pair are equal. Therefore, $d_i = 0$ for each pair of observation, which gives $\sum d_i^2 = 0$.

Substituting $\sum d_i^2 = 0$ in R we get R = 1. This is one extreme situation, the other extreme situation is discussed below.

Case (ii) : Suppose the ranks are exactly opposite. This happens when there is a perfect negative correlation. The ranks will be

$$x : \quad 1 \quad\quad 2 \quad\quad\quad 3 \quad\quad \cdots\cdots$$
$$y : \quad n \quad\quad n-1 \quad\quad n-2 \quad \cdots\cdots$$

It gives R = – 1.

Illustration 8 : *Calculate Spearman's rank correlation coefficient between the following marks given by two judges in series of eight one-act plays in a drama competition.*

One-act play No.	1	2	3	4	5	6	7	8
Marks by Judge A	*81*	*72*	*60*	*33*	*29*	*11*	*56*	*42*
Marks by Judge B	*75*	*56*	*42*	*15*	*30*	*20*	*60*	*80*

Solution : Let us give ranks to marks by judge A, arranging the items in the increasing order. Similarly, we give ranks on the basis of marks given by judge B.

One-act play	Marks by A	Marks by B	Rank of A x_i	Rank of B y_i	$d_i = x_i - y_i$	d_i^2
1	81	75	8	7	1	1
2	72	56	7	5	2	4
3	60	42	6	4	2	4
4	33	15	3	1	2	4
5	29	30	2	3	– 1	1
6	11	20	1	2	– 1	1
7	56	60	5	6	– 1	1
8	42	80	4	8	– 4	16
Total	–	–	–	–	–	32

$$\text{Spearman's rank correlation} = 1 - \frac{6 \sum d_i^2}{n(n^2-1)} = 1 - \frac{6 \times 32}{8(8^2-1)}$$

$$= 1 - \frac{192}{504} = 0.6190$$

Interpretation : There is a considerable agreement between the two judges.

5.10 Rank Correlation with Ties

If two or more items have same merit or quality, then common rank is allotted to each of such items. This rank is arithmetic mean of ranks which would have been given. In case the corresponding items would differ slightly in quality or merit. The number of items getting same rank is called as length of the tie. We denote it by m. For example, suppose scores of the students are to be ranked. Let the scores be arranged in increasing order. Suppose 3rd and 4th students have same scores then we give common rank to both. It will be an arithmetic mean of 3 and 4 viz. 3.5. Hence, we give rank 3.5 to both the students. In this case length of the tie is m = 2. Suppose 6th, 7th and 8th students have same scores, then the common rank will be $\dfrac{6+7+8}{3}$ = 7. Here the length of tie will be m = 3.

In case tie occurs, $\sum d_i^2$ need to be corrected. For every tie of length m, $\sum d_i^2$ is corrected by adding $m (m^2 - 1)/12$ in it. The corrections for ties are computed separately for each of two series viz. x and y. Let us denote T_x as the total correction due to ties in x. Similarly, T_y is the total correction due to ties in y. Spearman's rank correlation formula is modified as follows :

$$R = 1 - \frac{6 \left(\sum d_i^2 + T_x + T_y \right)}{n (n^2 - 1)}$$

Actual comparisons are explained with the help of numerical example given below :

Illustration 9 : *The runs scored by eleven cricketers in two test matches M_1 and M_2 are as follows :*

Cricketer	A	B	C	D	E	F	G	H	I	J	K
Runs (M_1)	82	82	85	35	55	33	52	73	55	50	50
Runs (M_2)	50	50	93	31	66	37	87	50	62	64	65

Compute correlation between the runs scored by cricketers in the matches using (i) Spearman's rank correlation coefficient. (ii) Karl Pearson's coefficient of correlation.

Solution :

Cricketer	Runs M_1 u_i	Runs M_2 v_i	Ranks of M_1 x_i	Ranks of M_2 y_i	$d_i^2 =$ $(x_i - y_i)^2$	u_i^2	v_i^2	$u_i v_i$
A	82	50	1.5	8	42.25	6724	2500	4100
B	82	50	1.5	8	42.25	6724	2500	4100
C	85	93	1	1	0.00	7225	8649	7905
D	35	31	10	11	1.00	1225	961	1085
E	55	66	5.5	3	6.25	3025	4356	3630
F	33	37	11	10	1.00	1089	1369	1221
G	52	87	7	2	25.00	2704	7569	4524
H	73	50	4	8	16.00	5329	2500	3650
I	55	62	5.5	6	0.25	3025	3844	3410
J	50	64	8.5	5	12.25	2500	4096	3200
K	50	65	8.5	4	20.25	2500	4225	3250
Total	652	655	–	–	166.50	42569	42070	40075

(i)   To compute rank correlation coefficient, we give ranks to cricketers. We arrange the runs in decreasing order, hence in series M_1, the cricketer C scored the highest runs 85, get rank 1. Next two cricketers A and B in the ordered arrangement have same score, hence they receive common rank 1.5. So also the cricketers E and I receive common rank 5.5. Similarly J and K receive common rank 8.5. In the series M_2 cricketer A, B and H have same score hence each gets same rank 8 as the average of 7, 8 and 9. We omit 9 for allotting next rank. Therefore cricketer F who is next in the ordered arrangement gets rank 10.

Let us determine correction due to ties. Series X has three ties each of length m = 2, hence

$$T_X = \sum \frac{m\,(m^2-1)}{12} = \frac{2\,(2^2-1)}{12} + \frac{2\,(2^2-1)}{12} + \frac{2\,(2^2-1)}{12} = 1.5$$

Series Y has only one tie of length m = 3.

Hence, $$T_y = \frac{m\,(m^2-1)}{12} = \frac{3\,(3^2-1)}{12} = 2$$

$\therefore$ $$R = 1 - \frac{6\,(\sum d_i^2 + T_X + T_y)}{n\,(n^2-1)} = 1 - \frac{6\,(166.5 + 1.5 + 2)}{11\,(11^2-1)} = 0.2272$$

Interpretation : There is a poor correlation between the scores in test M_1 and those of M_2.

(ii)   To compute Karl Pearson's coefficient of correlation, we determine covariance. We denote runs in M_1 by U and runs in M_2 by V.

$\therefore$ $$\text{Cov}\,(U,\,V) = \frac{\sum u_i v_i}{n} - \left(\frac{\sum u_i}{n}\right)\left(\frac{\sum v_i}{n}\right)$$

$$= \frac{40075}{11} - \frac{652}{11} \times \frac{655}{11} = 113.7603$$

$$\sigma_u^2 = \frac{\sum u_i^2}{n} - \left(\frac{\sum u_i}{n}\right)^2 = \frac{42070}{11} - \left(\frac{652}{11}\right)^2 = 311.2896$$

$$\sigma_v^2 = \frac{\sum v_i^2}{n} - \left(\frac{\sum v_i}{n}\right)^2 = \frac{42569}{11} - \left(\frac{655}{11}\right)^2 = 324.2484$$

$\therefore$ $$r = \frac{\text{Cov}\,(U,\,V)}{\sigma_u\,\sigma_v} = \frac{113.7603}{\sqrt{311.2896 \times 324.2484}} = 0.3581$$

Interpretation : Correlation between the runs scored in the matches M_1 and M_2 is poor.

5.11 Regression As Prediction Model

In earlier discussions we have studied correlation. It gives extent of linear relationship between two variables. If two variables are correlated, we can use this correlation for prediction of variable given the other variable.

Regression : Technique of prediction on the basis of correlation is called as *regression*.

Since correlation measures the linear relation between two variables, we find a linear equation in these variables. In otherwords, we state the relation in terms of equation of straight line. Using scatter diagram we get an idea of correlation. One can obtain a line passing through these points. However, if correlation is not perfect (i.e. $r \neq \pm 1$) then several lines can be drawn through these pints. Out of those lines, how to choose the best line is a problem. So a line which minimizes the total of sum of squares of differences between true value and the value given by straight line is chosen. The principle is called as *least square principle*. The equation so obtained is called as *least square regression line*.

Using regression equation one can find relation between advertising expenses and increase in sales, similarly the relation between sales and profit.

Suppose (x_1, y_1), (x_2, y_2), ..., (x_n, y_n) are n pairs of observations on variable X and Y. Since there are two variables, there will be two regression lines.

1. Regression line of Y on X : In this case we assume y as dependent variable or *response variable* and x as independent variable or *explanatory variable*. Therefore this line can be used to predict values of y for known values of x. Suppose the equation of such a line is $y = a + bx$. Mainly we need to fix the constants a and b. This can be done by least square of differences between actual value of y and its estimate $(\hat{y})$ ($\hat{y}$ is read as y hat) obtained from equation.

$$\text{Error in estimation} = \text{True value} - \text{estimate using the line } y = a + bx$$

$$= y - \hat{y}$$

$$= y - (a + bx)$$

$$= y - a - bx$$

Sum of squares of errors is denoted by,

$$S = \sum (y - a - bx)^2$$

Using mathematical methods we choose the constants a and b so that S is minimum. These methods gives rise the following two equations in a and b

$$\sum y = na + b \sum x$$

$$\sum xy = a \sum x + b \sum x^2$$

The above equations are called as *normal equations*. Solving the normal equations simultaneously we get, a and b

$$b = \frac{n \sum xy - \sum x \cdot \sum y}{n \sum x^2 - (\sum x)^2} \quad \text{and} \quad a = b \frac{\sum x}{n} - \frac{\sum y}{n}$$

Hence, $$b = \frac{\frac{\sum xy}{n} - \bar{x}\,\bar{y}}{\sigma_x^2} \quad \text{and} \quad a = b\bar{x} - \bar{y}$$

$$\therefore \quad b = \frac{\text{Cov}(x, y)}{\sigma_x^2} \quad \text{and} \quad a = b\bar{x} - \bar{y}$$

The constant b involved in the equation is called as *regression coefficient of y on x*. Hence instead of writing it as b, henceforth we write it as b_{yx}.

$$\therefore \quad b_{yx} = \frac{\text{Cov }(x, y)}{\sigma_x^2}$$

Substituting these values of a and b in $y = a + bx$ and simplifying the same we get,

$$y - \bar{y} = b_{yx}(x - \bar{x})$$

as least square regression equation of y on x.

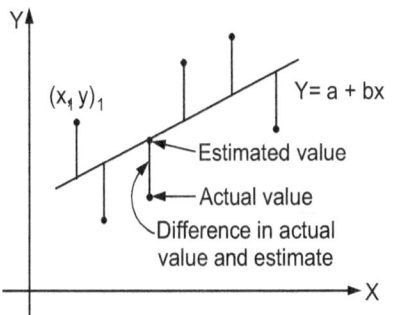

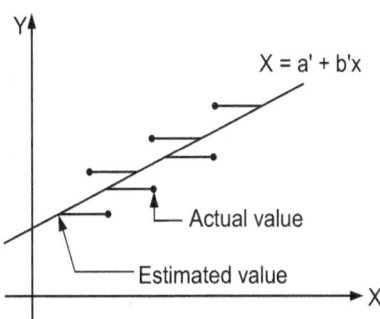

Fig. 5.12   **Fig. 5.13**

2. **Regression line of X on Y :** In this case we assume x as dependent variable and y as independent variable. This line is used to predict values of x for known values of y. Its least square equation is obtained using same technique which is used for obtaining regression equation of y on x.

Thus the equation of line will be

$$x - \bar{x} = b_{xy}(y - \bar{y})$$

Coefficient involved in the above equation is known as *regression coefficient of X on Y.*

$$\therefore \quad b_{xy} = \frac{\sum (x - \bar{x})(y - \bar{y})/n}{\sigma_y^2} = \frac{\frac{\sum xy}{n} - \bar{x}\,\bar{y}}{\sigma_y^2}$$

$$= \frac{\text{Cov }(x, y)}{\sigma^2 x}$$

Illustration 10 : *Following data gives expenditure incurred on advertisement and the sales for 10 years.*

Advertisement expenses in thousand ₹(X)	10	12	15	14	16	20	19	24	26	30
Sales in lakh ₹(Y)	5.0	5.1	5.4	5.5	5.7	5.9	6.0	7.3	7.5	7.8

(i)   Find the appropriate line of regression to estimate sales for given advertisement. Also estimate sales if advertisement expenses is ₹ 35,000.

(ii) To achieve sales target of ₹ 10 lakhs how much you need to invest in advertisement.

(iii) If company does not invest any amount in advertisement what will be the sales ?

(iv) Find the increase in sales per thousand ₹ advertisement expenses.

Solution : Let   X = Advertisement expenses

                            Y = Sales.

Here to estimate sales we need to find the regression line of Y on X, similarly to estimate expenditure required to achieve the target sales we need the regression line of X on Y.

Procedure :

(1) Prepare the table to find $\sum x, \sum y, \sum x^2, \sum y^2, \sum xy$.

(2) Find $\bar{X}, \bar{Y}, \sigma_x^2, \sigma_y^2$, Cov (X, Y), b_{xy}, b_{yx}.

(3) Determine the regression lines.

X	Y	X²	Y²	XY
10	5.0	100	25.00	50.0
12	5.1	144	26.01	61.2
15	5.4	225	29.16	81.0
14	5.5	196	30.25	77.0
16	5.7	256	32.49	91.2
20	5.9	400	34.81	118.0
19	6.0	361	36.00	114.0
24	7.3	576	53.29	175.2
26	7.5	676	56.25	195.0
30	7.8	900	60.84	234.0
Total = 186	61.2	3834	384.10	1196.6

$$n = 10, \ \bar{X} = \frac{\sum x}{n} = \frac{186}{10} = 18.6, \ \bar{Y} = \frac{\sum y}{n} = \frac{61.2}{10} = 6.12$$

$$\sigma_x^2 = \frac{\sum x^2}{n} - \bar{X}^2 = \frac{3834}{10} - 18.6^2 = 383.40 - 345.96 = 37.44$$

$$\sigma_y^2 = \frac{\sum y^2}{n} - \bar{y}^2 = \frac{384.10}{10} - 6.12^2 = 38.4100 - 37.4544 = 0.9556$$

$$\text{Cov (x, y)} = \frac{\sum xy}{n} - \bar{X}\,\bar{Y} = \frac{1196.6}{10} - 18.5 \times 6.12 = 119.660 - 113.832$$

$$= 5.828$$

$$b_{yx} = \frac{\text{Cov (x, y)}}{\sigma_x^2} = \frac{5.828}{37.44} = 0.1557$$

$$b_{xy} = \frac{\text{Cov (x, y)}}{\sigma_y^2} = \frac{5.828}{0.9556} = 6.0988$$

(i) To estimate sales (y) for given advertisement express (x), we use regression line of y on x

$$y - \bar{y} \;=\; b_{yx}\,(x - \bar{x})$$

$$y - 6.12 \;=\; 0.1557\,(x - 18.6)$$

$$y - 6.12 \;=\; 0.1557\,x - 2.89602$$

$$y \;=\; 0.1557\,x + 3.2240$$

Estimate of y for x = 35 we substitute x = 35 in the above equation

$$y \;=\; 0.1557 \times 35 + 3.2240 \;=\; 8.6735$$

Interpretation : If we spend ₹ 35,000 on advertisement then sales will be approximately ₹ 8.6735 lakhs.

(ii)   To estimate advertisement expenses (X) for achieving sales target (Y) we use regression line of X on Y.

$$x - \bar{x} \;=\; b_{xy}\,(y - \bar{y})$$

$$x - 18.6 \;=\; 6.0988\,(y - 6.12)$$

$$x - 18.6 \;=\; 6.0988\,y - 37.3247$$

$$x \;=\; 6.0988\,y - 18.7247$$

To estimate x for y = 10, substitute y = 10 in the above equation

$$\therefore \qquad x \;=\; 6.0988 \times 10 - 18.7247$$

$$=\; 42.2633 \text{ thousand } ₹$$

To achieve sales target of ₹ 10 lakhs. We have to spend ₹ 42,263.30.

(iii) To find sales when advertisement expenses is zero, we put x = 0 in the regression line of y on x.

$$y \;=\; 0.1557\,(0) + 3.224 \;=\; 3.224$$

$$y \;=\; 3.224 \text{ lakhs } ₹$$

Interpretation : If y = a + bx is equation of regression line then the intercept a is the value of y for x = 0.

(iv)   y = 0.1557 x + 3.224 is equation in which slope is 0.1557. Thus for unit increase in x, y increases by 0.1557 lakhs of ₹ Hence if we increase advertisement expenses by ₹ one thousand, sales will approximately increase by 0.1557 lakhs of ₹ or ₹ 15,570.

Geometric Interpretation of Regression line :

We can visualise the line, slope intercept geometrically in the following figure.

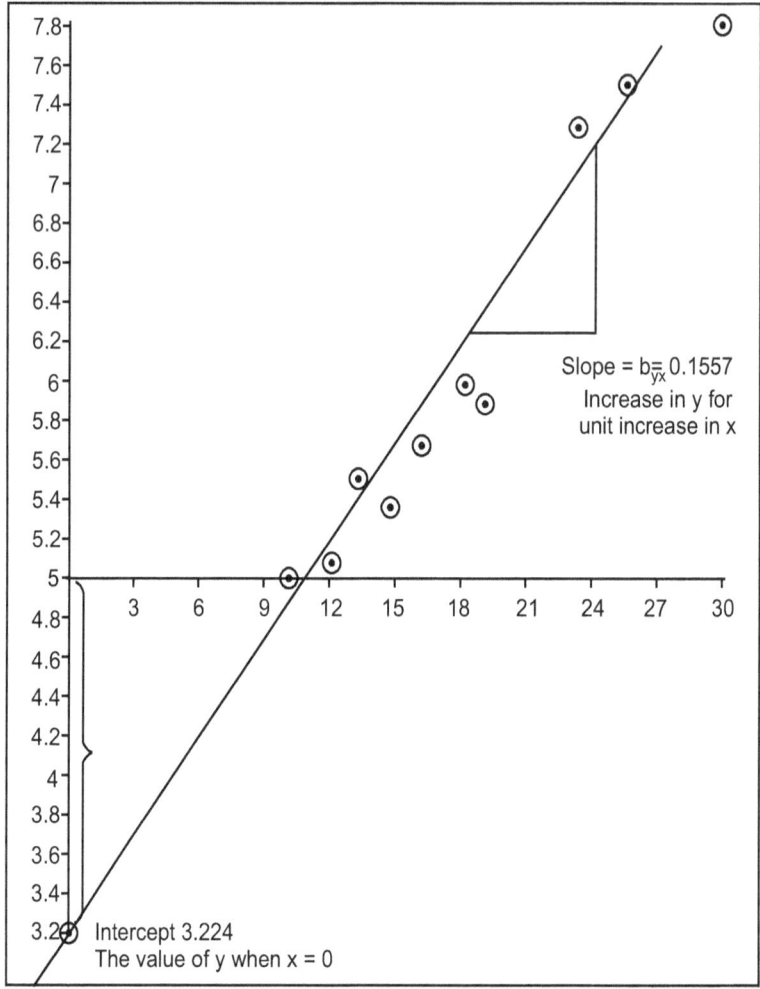

Fig. 5.14

5.12 Interpretation of Regression Coefficient

The regression line of Y on X is $y - \bar{y} = b_{yx}(x - \bar{x})$, we can write it as $Y = b_{yx} X + C$. Clearly, unit change in X will make change of b_{yx} units in Y. If b_{yx} is positive, then increase (or decrease) in X by one unit will be associated with increase (or decrease) in Y by b_{yx} units. On the other hand, if b_{yx} is negative, then increase (or decrease) in X by one unit is going to cause decrease (or increase) in Y by b_{yx} units.

For example, suppose X = supply and Y = price (₹) and the regression line is $Y = -1.2 X + 10$. Here we interpret the regression coefficient as follows. If supply (X) increases by one unit, the price is going to decrease by ₹ 1.20, or unit decrease in supply is going to cause increase in price by ₹ 1.20. Thus b_{yx} is the amount of change in Y per unit change in X.

Let X = expenditure on advertisement in ₹ and Y = annual profit in ₹ Suppose Y = 12 X + 19 is the regression line, then we interpret it as follows. For every rupee spent on advertisement, profit is estimated to rise by ₹ 12.

Coefficient of determination :

Definition : If r is the correlation coefficient then r^2 is called as coefficient of determination.

The coefficient of determination measures the **strength** of regression of Y on X. Larger the value of r^2, more powerful is the regression model. In other words, reliability in determining the Y values on the basis of X is more. Hence, it is called as the **coefficient of determination**. Also note that $|r| > r^2$; since $0 < |r| < 1$. Thus correlation coefficient overestimates the actual extent of linear relationship. Hence, in advanced studies, use of r^2 is recommended than that of r. However, a drawback of coefficient of determination is that it is always positive, hence fails to give the idea about the type of relationship between X and Y.

5.13 Applications of Correlation and Regression

There are number of fields where correlation and regression are used as tools in the analysis.

(a) In agricultural experiments, one can use regression line to estimate change in agricultural production due to various factors viz. fertilizers, irrigation facility, fertility of soil etc.

Similarly, one can study the relation between two variables such as germination time (Y) and temperature of soil (X).

Relation between alkalinity of water in a river (or pond) and growth of fungi can be studied using regression and correlation.

(b) In business and trade, correlation and regression helps in planning and forecasting to a great extent.

In portfolio analysis, β (beta) index is used quite often. Suppose Y is return on a security (a share of particular company) and X is the return on all other remaining securities measured in terms of index, then regression coefficient b_{yx} is called as beta index of a security. If β > 1, the share is treated as aggressive otherwise defensive.

(c) In medical sciences, we can find the regression line between age of a person (X) and blood pressure (Y). This helps in preparing the scale for blood pressure agewise. Further it may be used in finding abnormalities. Similarly using regression analysis one can find growth chart for a normal baby. It may be about age in months and weight or age and height.

(d) An economist may be interested to know the relationship between age and productivity index. Effect of training or education on change in total turnover can be measured using similar techniques.

(e) In portfolio analysis, risk is measured in terms of variances and covariances. If Y = return of a security, X = market return then,

Systematic risk of $Y = b_{yx}^2 \ \sigma_x^2$

Unsystematic risk of $Y = \sigma_y^2 - b_{yx}^2 \ \sigma_x^2$.

Thus the total risk σ_y^2 is partitioned into systematic and unsystematic risks.

An optimal way of investing in two or more portfolios can be obtained using linear combination, which has the least variance.

(f) We see a wonderful application of correlation in the field of physical education and sports.

Several aptitude tests are given for players. There are certain events or activities in the sport with performances correlated to each other.

For example, the performance in athletics events discuss (disc-throw), shot-put (iron ball throw) and javelin (spear throw) are correlated. Among three events correlation between any two is high positive. This indicates that the aptitude required for any of these there is same. Thus one can reduce the number of tests. Performance in one event can be used to estimate the performance in other.

5.14 Linear Regression : Cause and Effect

By means of correlation analysis we get an idea about the type of correlation and the extent of correlation between two variables. However, this does not tell us anything about cause and effect relationship. If X and Y are correlated, then we cannot say X is the cause and Y is the effect or vice versa. Even in case of perfect correlation also, we cannot conclude that one of the variable is the cause and the other is effect. If X is the cause and Y is effect, then X and Y are correlated (or dependent) but not vice-versa. It is possible that some common factors influence both X and Y, due to which they turn out to be correlated. For example, price of a commodity and demand.

Sometimes correlation between two variables is found just due to pure chance. It is called as *'spurious or non-sense correlation'*.

For example, suppose X = Number of literates in a country and Y = Number of criminals in a country. Clearly as X increases, in majority cases Y also increases; thus there is a high positive correlation between X and Y. However, we cannot say that X is cause and Y is effect. In other words, we cannot conclude that literacy is the cause of crime. Both X and Y show similar trend because of third common variable that the population. Increase (or decrease) in population will have effect on X and Y of similar kind. Hence there will be positive correlation between X and Y.

We have seen in the above discussion that the correlated variables cannot be sorted out as cause and effect. However, regression does this job. This demands two separate prediction equations for the two variables. For example, suppose X is the intelligence quotient (I.Q.) and Y is the marks in an examination. Then we can have regression line of Y on X to estimate marks in examination, given the I.Q. Here we assume that I.Q. is the cause and marks is the effect. Similarly using regression line of X on Y, we can estimate I.Q. whenever marks are available, reversing the role of cause and effect.

Suppose X is the total rainfall in a certain period and Y is the agricultural yield. In this case, there is no point in finding regression line of X on Y, as yield cannot be cause to rainfall. Regression line of Y on X makes sense and hence is of much use.

Thus we note the importance of two regression lines for prediction purposes.

Illustration 11 : *Obtain regression lines for following data* :

X	2	3	5	7	8	10	12	15
Y	2	5	8	10	12	14	15	16

Find estimate of :

(i)   *Y when X = 6.*

(ii) *X when Y = 20.*

Solution : To find regression lines we require to calculate regression coefficients b_{xy} and b_{yx}. These coefficients depend upon $\sum x$, $\sum y$, $\sum x^2$, $\sum y^2$, $\sum xy$. So we prepare the following table and simplify the calculations :

	x	y	x²	y²	xy
	2	2	4	4	4
	3	5	9	25	15
	5	8	25	64	40
	7	10	49	100	70
	9	12	81	144	108
	10	14	100	196	140
	12	15	144	225	180
	15	16	225	256	240
Total	63	82	637	1014	797

$$n = \text{number of pairs of observations} = 8$$

$$\bar{x} = \frac{\sum x}{n} = \frac{63}{8} = 7.875$$

$$\sigma^2 x = \frac{\sum x^2}{n} - \bar{x}^2 = \frac{637}{8} - (7.875)^2 = 17.6094$$

$$\bar{y} = \frac{82}{8} = 10.25$$

$$\sigma^2 y = \frac{\sum y^2}{n} - \bar{y}^2 = \frac{1014}{8} - (10.25)^2 = 21.6875$$

$$\text{Cov} (x, y) = \frac{\sum xy}{n} - \bar{x}\,\bar{y} = \frac{797}{8} - 7.875 \times 10.25 = 18.9063$$

$$b_{yx} = \frac{\text{Cov} (x, y)}{\sigma_y^2} = \frac{18.9063}{17.6094} = 1.0736$$

$$b_{xy} = \frac{\text{Cov} (x, y)}{\sigma_y^2} = \frac{18.9063}{21.6875} = 0.8718$$

Regression line of Y on X :

$$y - \bar{y} = b_{yx}(x - \bar{x})$$
$$y - 10.25 = 1.0736(x - 7.875)$$
$$y = 1.0736x + 1.7954$$

(i) Estimate of y for x = 6, can be obtained by substituting x = 6 in the above regression equation.

$$\therefore \qquad y = 1.0736 \times 6 + 1.7954$$
$$y = 8.237$$

Regression line of X on Y :

$$x - \bar{x} = b_{xy}(y - \bar{y})$$
$$x - 7.875 = 0.8718(y - 10.25)$$
$$x = 0.8718y - 10.06095$$

(ii) Estimate of x can be obtained by substituting y = 20 in the above equation.

$$\therefore \qquad x = 16.37505$$

Note : For estimation of x and estimation of y separate equations are to be used.

5.15 Properties of Regression Coefficient

1. Correlation coefficient and regression coefficients have same algebraic signs.

Proof : Note that $\qquad b_{xy} = \dfrac{\text{Cov}(x, y)}{\sigma_y^2}, \quad b_{yx} = \dfrac{\text{Cov}(x, y)}{\sigma_x^2}$

and $\qquad\qquad r = \dfrac{\text{Cov}(x, y)}{\sigma_x \sigma_y}$

Clearly, numerator of each coefficient is same and denominator of each coefficient is positive. Hence, numerator decides algebraic sign. Thus, all coefficients have same algebraic sign. Hence, if r > 0, then $b_{yx} > 0$ and $b_{xy} > 0$. If r = 0, $b_{yx} = b_{xy} = 0$. If r < 0 then, $b_{xy} < 0$ and $b_{yx} < 0$.

2. Correlation coefficient is a square root of product of regression coefficients.

$\left(\text{i.e. } r = \sqrt{b_{yx} \cdot b_{xy}}\right)$ or correlation coefficient is geometric mean of regression coefficients.

Proof : $\qquad b_{yx} \cdot b_{xy} = \dfrac{\text{Cov}(x, y)}{\sigma_x^2} \times \dfrac{\text{Cov}(x, y)}{\sigma_y^2} = \left(\dfrac{\text{Cov}(x, y)}{\sigma_x \sigma_y}\right)^2 = r^2$

$\therefore \qquad\qquad r = \sqrt{b_{yx} b_{xy}}$

Note : Choose positive square root if regression coefficients are positive, otherwise, negative.

3. Both regression coefficients cannot exceed unity simultaneously.

Proof : If possible let us assume $\quad b_{yx} > 1$ and $b_{xy} > 1$.

Hence, $\qquad\qquad b_{xy} \cdot b_{yx} > 1$

$\therefore \qquad\qquad r^2 > 1$

which is impossible ($\because r < 1$). Thus our assumption is incorrect.

We state few more properties without proof.

4. Regression coefficient can be expressed in terms of correlation coefficient as follows :

$$b_{yx} = r \cdot \frac{\sigma_y}{\sigma_x} \text{ and } b_{xy} = r \cdot \frac{\sigma_x}{\sigma_y}$$

5. Correlation coefficient lies between two regression coefficients.

6. Regression coefficients remain unchanged due to change of origin. In otherwords if a constant is substracted or added from each observation, regression coefficients remain same.

7. Regression coefficients are affected by change of scale as follows

If
$$u = \frac{x-a}{h} \text{ and } v = \frac{y-b}{k}$$

then
$$b_{uv} = \frac{k}{h} b_{xy} \text{ and } b_{vu} = \frac{h}{k} b_{yx}$$

8. If $r = \pm 1$ then, regression coefficients are reciprocals of each other.

9. Regression coefficients are equal if $\sigma_x = \sigma_y$.

5.16 Properties of Regression Lines

(1) Regression lines coincide if $r = \pm 1$. Thus if there exists perfect correlation, points in scatter diagram lie on the same straight line.

(2) Regression lines are perpendicular to each other, if $r = 0$. Thus if the variables are uncorrelated, points on scatter diagram will exhibit maximum spread.

(3) The point of intersection of regression lines is $(\bar{x}, \bar{y})$.

(4) Larger the value of correlation coefficient smaller is the acute angle between regression lines.

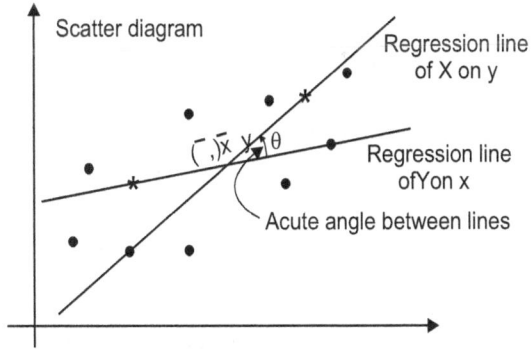

Fig. 5.15

5.17 Standard Error of Regression Estimate

With usual notation r as correlation coefficient σ_x and σ_y as standard deviations of x and y respectively; we state standard error of regression estimate.

(1) Standard error of regression estimate of y on x is $\sigma_y \sqrt{1-r^2}/\sqrt{n-2}$.

(2) Standard error of regression estimate of x on y is $\sigma_x \sqrt{1 - r^2} / \sqrt{n - 2}$.

Hence estimates are reliable for larger value of r^2.

Note : The above discussion leads to conclusion that rather than r we should consider r^2 for testing reliability of regression estimates. Therefore, regression analysis claims validity if r^2 is sufficiently large. The quantity r^2 is called as the coefficient of determination.

5.18 Correlation and Regression Analysis

Correlation coefficient gives the extent of linear relationship between two variables. Whereas regression analysis establishes the functional relationship between two correlated variables. Regression analysis helps in estimation, prediction etc. however correlation coefficient is an indicator of linear relationship.

Correlation coefficient is symmetric i.e. Corr (x, y) = Corr (y, x), however regression coefficients are not symmetric i.e. $b_{xy} \neq b_{yx}$.

Correlation coefficient is unitless quantity, however regression coefficients posses units of measurement.

Computation of regression coefficients by deviation method : Note that by one of the property of regression coefficients we can subtract a suitable constant and make computations easy.

Procedure :

(1) Substract a constant 'a' from x values and constant 'b' from y values.

Denote $u = x - a$ and $v = y - b$.

(2) Prepare table containing columns u, v, u^2, v^2 and uv.

(3) Use the following formulae and compute regression coefficients.

$$b_{xy} = b_{uv} = \frac{\dfrac{\sum uv}{n} - \bar{u}\,\bar{v}}{\sigma_v^2}$$

and

$$b_{yx} = b_{vu} = \frac{\dfrac{\sum uv}{n} - \bar{u}\,\bar{v}}{\sigma_u^2}$$

where,

$$\bar{u} = \frac{\sum u}{n} \qquad \bar{v} = \frac{\sum v}{n}$$

$$\sigma_u^2 = \frac{\sum u^2}{n} - \bar{u}^2 \qquad \text{and} \quad \sigma_v^2 = \frac{\sum v^2}{n} - \bar{v}^2$$

Illustration 12 : *The table below gives the respective heights x and y of a sample of 10 fathers and their sons :*

(i)   *Find regression line of y on x.*

(ii) *Find regression line of x on y.*

(iii) *Estimate son's height if father's height is 65 inches.*

(iv) *Estimate father's height if son's height is 60 inches.*

(v)   *Compute correlation coefficient between x and y.*

Height of father x (inches)	65	63	67	64	68	62	70	66	68	67
Height of son y (inches)	68	66	68	65	69	66	68	65	71	67

Solution : Let $u = x - 62$, $v = y - 65$. We prepare the table to simplify the computations.

x	y	u	v	u^2	v^2	uv
65	68	3	3	9	9	9
63	66	1	1	1	1	1
67	68	5	3	25	9	15
64	65	2	0	4	0	0
68	69	6	4	36	16	24
62	66	0	1	0	1	0
70	68	8	3	64	9	24
66	65	4	0	16	0	0
68	71	6	6	36	36	36
67	67	5	2	25	4	10
Total		40	23	216	85	119

$$n = \text{number of pairs} = 10$$

$$\bar{u} = \frac{40}{10} = 4, \quad \sigma_u^2 = \frac{216}{10} - 4^2 = 5.6$$

$$\bar{v} = \frac{23}{10} = 2.3 \quad \sigma_v^2 = \frac{85}{10} - (2.3)^2 = 3.21$$

$$\text{Cov}(u, v) = \frac{119}{10} - 4 \times 2.3 = 2.7$$

∴
$$b_{xy} = b_{uv} = \frac{2.7}{3.21} = 0.8411, \quad \text{and } b_{yx} = b_{vu} = \frac{2.7}{5.6} = 0.4821$$

$$\bar{x} = \bar{u} + 62 = 66, \quad \bar{y} = \bar{v} + 65 = 67.3$$

(i)   Regression line of Y on X is $y - \bar{y} = b_{yx}(x - \bar{x})$

∴ $y - 67.3 = 0.4821(x - 66)$

∴ $y = 0.4821x + 35.4814$

(ii)   Regression line of X on Y is $x - \bar{x} = b_{xy}(y - \bar{y})$

∴ $x - 66 = 0.8411(y - 67.3)$

∴ $x = 0.8411y + 9.3940$

(iii) Estimate of son's height y for x = 65

$$y = 0.4821 \times 65 + 35.4814 = 66.8179 \text{ inches}$$

(iv) Estimate of father's height x for y = 60

$$x = 0.8411 \times 60 + 9.394 = 59.86 \text{ inches}$$

(v) Correlation coefficient,

$$r = \sqrt{b_{xy} \cdot b_{yx}} = \sqrt{0.8411 \times 0.4821} = 0.63678$$

We choose positive square root because regression coefficients are positive.

Illustration 13 : *Revenue department is trying to estimate the monthly amount of unpaid taxes. Suppose x denote field audit labour hours and y denote unpaid taxes. Using last 10 months data the following summary is obtained.*

$$\Sigma x = 441, \ \Sigma y = 272, \ \Sigma x^2 = 19461, \ \Sigma y^2 = 7428, \ \Sigma xy = 12,005.$$

Determine regression line of y on x. Also obtain standard error of regression estimate.

Solution : Here we require to find b_{yx}.

$$\bar{x} = \frac{441}{10} = 44.1 \qquad \bar{y} = \frac{272}{10} = 27.2$$

$$\sigma_x^2 = \frac{19461}{10} - (44.1)^2 = 1.29$$

$$\sigma_y^2 = \frac{7428}{10} - (27.2)^2 = 2.96$$

$$\text{Cov (x, y)} = \frac{12005}{10} - 44.1 \times 27.2 = 0.98$$

$$b_{yx} = \frac{\text{Cov (x, y)}}{\sigma_x^2} = \frac{0.98}{1.29} = 0.7597$$

Regression line of y on x is :

$$y - \bar{y} = b_{yx} (x - \bar{x})$$

$$y - 27.2 = 0.7597 (x - 44.1)$$

$$y = 0.7597 x - 6.3023$$

S.E. of regression estimate of y on x = $\sigma_y = \sqrt{1 - r^2} / \sqrt{n - 2}$.

Note that :

$$r^2 = \frac{\text{Cov (x, y)}}{\sigma_x^2 \sigma_y^2}$$

$$= \frac{0.98}{1.29 \times 2.96} = 0.256652$$

∴

$$\text{S.E.} = \sqrt{2.96 \times (1 - 0.256652)} / \sqrt{8}$$

$$= \frac{1.4833}{2.8284} = 0.5244$$

Illustration 14 : *Determine regression line for price given the supply, hence estimate price when supply is 180 units, from the following information.*

$x = Supply, \quad y = Price\ in\ ₹per\ unit, \quad n = 7$

$\sum(x - 150) = 119, \qquad \sum(y - 160) = 84$

$\sum(x - 150)^2 = 2835, \qquad \sum(y - 160)^2 = 2387$

$\sum(x - 150)(y - 160) = 525.$

Also find correlation coefficient between price and supply.

Solution : Let, $u = x - 150, \quad v = y - 160$

$$\therefore \qquad \bar{u} = \frac{119}{7} = 17, \quad \bar{v} = \frac{84}{7} = 12$$

$$\sigma_u^2 = \frac{2835}{7} - (17)^2 = 405 - 289 = 116$$

$$\sigma_v^2 = \frac{2387}{7} - (12)^2 = 341 - 144 = 197$$

$$Cov(x, y) = Cov(u, v) = \frac{525}{7} - 17 \times 12 = -129$$

$$\bar{x} = 150 + \bar{u} = 167 \quad and \quad \bar{y} = 160 + \bar{v} = 172$$

$$b_{yx} = b_{vu} = \frac{Cov(u, v)}{\sigma_u^2} = \frac{-129}{116} = -1.1121$$

Equation of regression line of y on x is,

$$y - \bar{y} = b_{yx}(x - \bar{x})$$

$$y - 172 = -1.1121(x - 167)$$

$$y = -1.1121x + 357.7207$$

Estimate of y for x = 180

$$y = -1.1121 \times 180 + 357.7207$$

$$= 157.54$$

$$r = Corr(x, y) = \frac{Cov(u, v)}{\sigma_u \sigma_v}$$

$$= \frac{-129}{\sqrt{116 \times 197}} = -0.8534$$

Illustration 15 : *Compute regression coefficients and hence verify that correlation coefficient lies between them.*

$n = 100, \quad \bar{x} = 60, \quad \bar{y} = 50, \quad \sigma_x = 10, \quad \sigma_y = 12, \quad \sum(x - \bar{x})(y - \bar{y}) = 8400.$

Solution : $\quad Cov(x, y) = \dfrac{\sum(x - \bar{x}) - (y - \bar{y})}{n}$

$$= \frac{8400}{100} = 84$$

$$\therefore \qquad b_{xy} = \frac{\text{Cov}(x, y)}{\sigma_y^2}$$

$$= \frac{84}{144} = 0.5833$$

$$b_{yx} = \frac{\text{Cov}(x, y)}{\sigma_x^2}$$

$$= \frac{84}{100} = 0.84$$

$$r = \frac{\text{Cov}(x, y)}{\sigma_x \sigma_y} = \frac{84}{120} = 0.7$$

Clearly r lies between the two regression coefficients.

Illustration 16 : *A study of wheat prices at Mumbai and Kanpur yield the following data :*

	Mumbai	Kanpur
Arithmetic mean	₹20	₹21
Standard deviation	₹0.326	₹0.207

Correlation coefficient between the prices at Mumbai and Kanpur is 0.774. Estimate the price at Kanpur if the price at Mumbai is ₹25 using the above data.

Solution : Let y : Price of wheat at Kanpur, x : Price of wheat at Mumbai.

We obtain regression line of y on x from estimation of price at Kanpur.

$$y - \bar{y} = r \cdot \frac{\sigma_y}{\sigma_x} (x - \bar{x}) \qquad \left(\because b_{yx} = r \frac{\sigma_y}{\sigma_x} \right)$$

$$y - 21 = 0.774 \times \frac{0.207}{0.326} (25 - 20)$$

$$y - 21 = 2.457$$

$$y = 23.46₹$$

Therefore price at Kanpur is ₹ 23.46.

Illustration 17 : *Given x – 4y = 5 and x – 16y = – 64 are the regression lines, find (i) regression coefficient of x on y, (ii) regression coefficient of y on x, (iii) Corr (x, y), (iv) $\bar{x}, \bar{y}$, (v) σ_y if $\sigma_x = 8$.*

Solution : Here by looking at the equations we cannot decide which of the equation is regression equation of x on y and which is of y on x. We arbitrarily decide one of the line as regression line of y on x, and find regression coefficients. Then we verify whether these values are admissible.

Suppose the equation x – 16y = – 64 represent regression line of x on y. We write it in usual form as

$$x - \bar{x} = b_{xy} (y - \bar{y}) \qquad \qquad \dots (1)$$

Therefore the equation can be reformed as

$$x = 16y - 64. \qquad \ldots (2)$$

Comparing coefficients of y in equations (1) and (2) we get $b_{xy} = 16$.

On the other hand, $x - 4y = 5$ will be regression line of y on x. Writing it in usual form we get $4y = x - 5$.

$$\therefore \qquad y = \frac{1}{4}x - \frac{5}{4} \qquad \ldots (3)$$

Theoretically, equation of y on x is

$$y - \bar{y} = b_{yx}(x - \bar{x}) \qquad \ldots (4)$$

Comparing coefficients of x in equations (3) and (4) we get, $b_{yx} = \frac{1}{4}$

We know that, $\quad b_{yx} \cdot b_{xy} \le 1$

However here, $\quad b_{xy} \cdot b_{yx} = 16 \times \frac{1}{4} = 4 < 1$

Hence, our choice of regression lines is incorrect. Exchanging the choice we get $x - 16y = -64$ as regression line of y on x. Writing it in usual manner we get :

$$y = \frac{1}{16}x + 4 \qquad \ldots (5)$$

Comparing equations (4) and (5) we get, $b_{yx} = \frac{1}{16}$. Similarly, $x - 4y = 5$ will be the regression line of x on y. Writing it in usual form we get,

$$x = 4y + 5 \qquad \ldots (6)$$

Comparing equations (1) and (6) we get, $b_{xy} = 4$.

$$\therefore \quad \text{Correlation coefficient} = r^2 = b_{yx} \cdot b_{xy} = \frac{1}{16} \times 4 = \frac{1}{4}$$

$$\therefore \qquad r = \sqrt{\frac{1}{4}} = \frac{1}{2}$$

(We choose positive square root because regression coefficients are positive).

(iv) Note that $(\bar{x}, \bar{y})$ is the point of intersection of regression lines. Thus $(\bar{x}, \bar{y})$ will satisfy both the equations.

Therefore, we get,

$$\bar{x} - 4\bar{y} = 5 \qquad \ldots (7)$$

and $\qquad\qquad \bar{x} - 16\bar{y} = -64 \qquad \ldots (8)$

Solving equations (7) and (8), we get,

$$\bar{x} = 28, \ \bar{y} = \frac{23}{4}$$

(v)   To find σ_y we use $b_{xy} = r \dfrac{\sigma_x}{\sigma_y} = 4$.

$$\frac{1}{2} \times \frac{\sigma_x}{\sigma_y} = 4 \qquad \sigma_y = \frac{\sigma_x}{8} = 1$$

Illustration 18 : *Obtain Rank Correlation Coefficient for the ranks given by two judges in a contest.*

Ranks by Judge 'A'	Ranks by Judge 'B'
2	2
3	3
8	7
6	6
4	5
5	4
1	1
7	8

Solution :

R_A	R_B	$d = R_A - R_B$	$d^2 = (R_A - R_B)^2$
2	2	0	0
3	3	0	0
8	7	1	1
6	6	0	0
4	5	–1	1
5	4	1	1
1	1	0	0
7	8	–1	1
–	–	**Total**	**4**

Rank correlation (R) $= 1 - \dfrac{6 \sum d^2}{n \, (n^2 - 1)}$

$\sum d^2 = 4, \quad n = 8$

$\therefore \qquad R = 1 - \dfrac{6 \times 4}{8 \times (64 - 1)} = 1 - \dfrac{6 \times 4}{8 \times 63}$

$$= 1 - \frac{1}{21} = \frac{20}{21} = 0.9524$$

Illustration 19 : *Find correlation coefficient between heights of fathers and their sons from the following data : (heights in inches).*

Height of Fathers	65	66	67	68	69	70	72	67
Height of Sons	67	68	66	68	72	72	69	70

Solution : Let Father's height (X), Son's height (Y). $U = X - 65$, $V = Y - 65$

X	Y	U	V	U²	V²	UV
65	67	0	2	0	4	0
66	68	1	3	1	9	3
67	66	2	1	4	1	2
68	68	3	3	9	9	9
69	72	4	7	16	49	28
70	72	5	7	25	49	35
72	69	7	4	49	16	28
67	70	2	5	4	25	10
Total	–	**24**	**32**	**108**	**162**	**115**

$$n = 8, \quad \bar{U} = \frac{\sum U}{n} = \frac{24}{8} = 3, \quad \bar{V} = \frac{\sum V}{n} = \frac{32}{8} = 4$$

$$\sigma_u = \sqrt{\frac{\sum U^2}{n} - \bar{U}^2} = \sqrt{\frac{108}{8} - 3^2} = \sqrt{4.5} = 2.1213$$

$$\sigma_v = \sqrt{\frac{\sum V^2}{n} - \bar{V}^2} = \sqrt{\frac{162}{8} - 4^2} = \sqrt{4.25} = 2.0616$$

$$\text{Corr} = \frac{\frac{\sum UV}{n} - \bar{U}\,\bar{V}}{\sigma_u\,\sigma_v} = \frac{\frac{115}{8} - 3 \times 4}{2.1213 \times 2.0616} = 0.5431$$

Illustration 20 : *The correlation coefficient between two variables X and Y is 0.6. If the means of two series are 13 and 27 respectively and standard deviations are 1.5 and 2 respectively, find the regression line of Y on X.*

Solution : Given : $\bar{X} = 13$, $\bar{Y} = 27$, $\sigma_x = 1.5$, $\sigma_y = 2$, $r = 0.6$.

Regression line of Y on X

$$Y - \bar{Y} = b_{yx}(X - \bar{X})$$

$$Y - 27 = 0.6 \times \frac{2}{1.5} \times (X - 13)$$

$$Y = 0.8 \, (X - 13) + 27$$

$$Y = 0.8 \, X + 16.6$$

Case Study :

Alto Pharmaceuticals Ltd. is a company in manufacturing various life saving drugs. It has a manufacturing unit in Anand (Gujrat) and India wide distribution network. Many sales executives, sales representatives and medical representatives are working throughout the country.

It has been observed by the company that since last six months sales have gone down and had a adverse effect on the company's profit.

Senior market executives had a meeting to discuss the problem and concluded that a incentive scheme is to be introduced to promote the sale. Company collected the data for last six months regarding actual incentive given the sales representative and the sales. Suggest the appropriate statistical tools to know whether the incentive scheme has a effect on the company's sale.

Points to Remember

1. Correlation coefficient (r) lies between – 1 and 1.

2. $r = \dfrac{\dfrac{1}{n} \Sigma \, (x - \bar{x}) \, (y - \bar{y})}{\sigma_x \, \sigma_y} = \dfrac{\dfrac{1}{n} \Sigma \, xy - \bar{x} \, \bar{y}}{\sigma_x \, \sigma_y}.$

3. Corr (ax + b, cy + d) = Corr (x, y), if a and b have same signs
   $\qquad\qquad\qquad = -$ Corr (x, y), if a and b have opposite signs

4. Regression coefficient of y and x $= b_{yx} = r \dfrac{\sigma_y}{\sigma_x} = \dfrac{\dfrac{1}{n} \Sigma \, xy - \bar{x} \, \bar{y}}{\sigma_x^2}.$

   Regression coefficient of x on y $= b_{xy} = r \dfrac{\sigma_x}{\sigma_y} = \dfrac{\dfrac{1}{n} \Sigma \, xy - \bar{x} \, \bar{y}}{\sigma_y^2}.$

5. $r = \sqrt{b_{xy} \, b_{yx}}$.

6. r, b_{xy}, b_{yx} have same signs.

7. If r = ± 1 regression lines coinside.

8. If r = ± 1 and $\sigma_x = \sigma_y$ then $b_{xy} = b_{yx}$.

9. The two regression lines intersect at $(\bar{x} \, \bar{y})$.

10. Regression line of y on x is $y - \bar{y} = b_{yx} \, (x - \bar{x})$. It is used to predict y.

   Regression line of x on y is $x - \bar{x} = b_{xy} \, (y - \bar{y})$. It is used to predict x.

Exercise 5.1

A. Theory Questions :

1. Explain the terms : Bivariate data, covariance, correlation, regression.

2. State the different measures of correlation and describe each of the measures in detail.

3. Describe scatter diagram and explain how it is used to measure correlation.

4. State merits and limitations of scatter diagram as a measure of correlation.

5. Define Karl Pearson's coefficient of correlation or product moment correlation coefficient 'r'. State its merits and demerits. How will you interpret the cases
(i) $r = +1$, (ii) $r = -1$, (iii) $r = 0$?

6. State the properties of Karl Person's correlation coefficient.

7. State the limitations of Karl Pearson's coefficient of correlation.

8. State the merits and demerits of Karl Pearson's correlation coefficient.

9. Explain the term 'regression analysis'.

10. Explain what is spearman's rank correlation and state formula. Also state its limitations.

11. State the equations for regression lines of (i) y on x, (ii) x on y. Discuss the nature of the regression equations in case of $r = -1$, $r = \pm 1$, $r = 0$.

12. Why there are two regression lines ?

13. State utility of regression lines.

14. Explain the least square principle for obtaining regression lines.

15. Define regression coefficients and state the properties.

16. Distinguish between regression coefficients and correlation coefficient.

17. Can any two lines be regression lines ? Give reasons in support of your answer.

18. How would you interpret regression coefficients ?

19. State the situations where regression analysis is used.

20. State the properties of regression (i) lines, (ii) coefficients.

21. With usual notation, prove that

22. $b_{yx} \cdot b_{xy} = r^2$, (b) b_{yx} and b_{xy} cannot exceed unity simultaneously.

23. Define coefficient of determination and state its utility.

24. Show that r, b_{yx} and b_{xy} have same algebraic sign.

25. Define rank correlation, state the formula for Spearman's rank correlation coefficient.

26. How the rank correlation coefficient is computed in case of ties ?

Exercise 5.2

B. Karl Pearson's Coefficient of Correlation from Raw Data :

1. Find the Karl Pearson's correlation coefficient between sales (X) and expenses (Y) from the following data and interpret your results :

Firms	1	2	3	4	5	6	7	8	9	10
Sales (X) (Lakhs ₹)	50	50	56	60	64	65	65	60	60	50
Expenses (Y) (Lakhs ₹)	11	13	14	15	14	15	15	14	16	13

2. Calculate the Karl-Pearson's coefficient of correlation from following data :

Price	22	24	26	28	30	32	34	36	38	40
Demand	60	58	58	50	48	48	48	42	36	32

3. Calculate the Karl-Pearson's coefficient of correlation from the following data :

Demand in Tonnes	9	11	13	15	17	19	21	23
Supply in Tonnes	6	8	10	12	14	16	18	20

4. Compute product moment correlation coefficient between income and expenditure from the following data.

Year	1981	1982	1983	1884	1885	1886	1887	1888
Daily income (₹)	100	110	115	120	125	130	132	140
Average daily expenditure (₹)	85	90	92	100	110	125	125	130

5. From the following data of marks in Mathematics and Statistics, calculate product moment correlation coefficient and interpret the result.

Marks in Statistics	60	70	80	90	10	20	30	40	50
Marks in Mathematics	65	70	80	75	45	40	50	60	55

6. Daily income and savings in ₹ for 10 employees in a certain company are given below :

Income	250	750	820	900	780	360	980	390	650	620
Savings	60	68	62	86	84	51	91	47	53	58

Compute the Karl Pearson's coefficient of correlation between income and savings.

7. Calculate the Karl Pearson's correlation coefficient between advertisement cost and sales from the following data :

Advertisement cost (in thousand ₹)	41	67	65	92	84	77	27	100	38	80
Sales in lakh ₹	46	52	57	85	61	67	59	90	50	83

8. Obtain correlation coefficient between population density (per square miles) and death rate (per thousand persons) from data related to 5 cities.

Population density	200	500	400	700	300
Death rate	12	18	16	21	10

9. The following table gives frequency distribution of 50 clerks in a certain office according to age and pay. Find Karl Pearson's correlation, if any, between age and pay.

Age (in years)	20-30	30-40	40-50	50-60	60-70
Pay (in ₹)	4000	6000	5500	5000	4500

Hint : Take x = the age in years with values as mid-points of class interval.

10. Find the Karl-Pearson's coefficient of correlation between population and pollution.

Population in lakhs (X)	11	12	13	14	15
Pollution in suitable units (Y)	50	52	60	68	80

C. Karl Pearson's Coefficient of Correlation (Summarised Data) :

11. Given that : $r = 0.4$, $\sum (x - \bar{x})(y - \bar{y}) = 108$, $\sigma_y = 3$ and $\sum (x - \bar{x})^2 = 900$. Find number of pairs of observations viz. n.

12. Find number of pairs of observations from the following data.

   $r = -0.4$, $\sum x = 100$, $\sum x^2 = 2250$, $\sum y = 100$, $\sum y^2 = 2250$, $\sum xy = 1900$.

13. Find correlation coefficient between x and y given that : $n = 8$,

   $$\sum \left(x - \bar{x}\right)^2 = 36, \left(y - \bar{y}\right)^2 = 44, \sum \left(x - \bar{x}\right)\left(y - \bar{y}\right) = 24.$$

14. Find coefficient of correlation from the following information.

   $n = 10$, $\sum (x - 30) = 11$, $\sum (y - 25) = 7$, $\sum (x - 30)^2 = 215$, $\sum (y - 25)^2 = 163$,

   $$\sum \left(x - \bar{x}\right)\left(y - \bar{y}\right) = 186.$$

15. Given : $n = 6$, $\sum (x - 18.5) = -3$, $\sum (y - 50) = 20$, $\sum (x - 18.5)^2 = 19$,

   $\sum (y - 50)^2 = 850$, $\sum (x - 18.5)(y - 50) = -120$. Calculate coefficient of correlation.

16. Calculate coefficient of correlation from the following information.

   $n = 5$, $\sum x = 20$, $\sum x^2 = 90$, $\sum y = 20$, $\sum y^2 = 90$, $\sum xy = 73$.

17. Given :

Number of pairs of X and Y series	=	15
Arithmetic mean of X	=	25
Arithmetic mean of Y	=	18
Standard deviation of X	=	3
Standard deviation of Y	=	3
Sum of products of X and Y ($\sum XY$)	=	6870

   Find correlation coefficient between X and Y.

18. From the following data compute the coefficient of correlation :

    Number of pairs of observations   = 10
    Sum of X series   = 9
    Sum of Y series   = 5
    Sum of squares of X series   = 653
    Sum of squares of Y series   = 595
    Sum of product of X and Y series   = 534

19. From the following data compute the coefficient of correlation between X and Y.

    Number of pairs of observations   = 10
    Sum of deviations of X series   = – 170
    Sum of deviations of Y series   = – 20
    Sum of squares of deviations of X series   = 8000
    Sum of squares of deviations of Y series   = 2000
    Sum of products of deviations of X and Y series = 2500

20. Coefficient of correlation between variables X and Y is 0.3 and their covariance is 12. The variance of X is 9, find the standard deviation of Y.

21. If correlation coefficient between X and Y is 0.8 find that between :

    (i)   X and – Y   (ii)   2X and 3Y

    (iii) X – 10 and Y + 15   (iv) $\dfrac{X}{2}$ and $\dfrac{Y}{5}$

    (v) $\dfrac{X-10}{3}$ and $\dfrac{10-Y}{5}$

D. Spearman's Rank Correlation Coefficient :

22. Obtain 'Rank Correlation Coefficient' for the results of beauty contest :

Ranks by Judge A	1	5	6	7	8	2	4	3
Ranks by Judge B	1	7	6	2	8	4	5	3

23. Eight contestants in a musical contest were ranked by two judges A and B, in the following manner :

Sr. No.	1	2	3	4	5	6	7	8
Ranks by Judge A	7	6	2	4	5	3	1	8
Ranks by Judge B	5	4	6	3	8	2	1	7

Compute rank correlation coefficient between the two judges and comment on it.

24. Ranks obtained by 6 students in Statistics and Accountancy are given below :

Ranks in Statistics	5	6	4	3	2	1
Ranks in Accountancy	6	2	1	4	3	5

Compute Spearman's Rank Correlation Coefficient.

25. Obtain the Rank Correlation Coefficient for the ranks given by two judges in a contest :

Rank by Judge 'A'	3	6	2	4	5	1
Rank by Judge 'B'	4	5	2	3	6	1

26. The following data relates to the ranks given by judges in a contest :

Sr. No. of Candidate	1	2	3	4	5	6	7	8	9	10
Rank by Judge A	1	5	6	1	2	3	4	7	9	8
Rank by Judge B	5	6	9	2	8	7	3	4	10	1

Compute the rank correlation between the ranks given by judge A and that of judge B. Interprete.

27. The scores obtained by 6 candidates in drawing (X) and in music (Y) are given below :

Candidate	1	2	3	4	5	6
X	24	29	19	14	30	19
Y	37	35	16	26	23	27

Allot the ranks to X and Y and compute Spearman's rank correlation coefficient.

E. Regression (Raw Data) :

28. Obtain line of regression of y on x for the data given below :

x	06	02	10	04	08
y	09	11	05	08	07

Also estimate y when x = 5.

29. The following data given the sales and expenses of 10 firms.

Firm No.	1	2	3	4	5	6	7	8	9	10
Sales (in '000 ₹)	45	70	65	30	90	40	50	75	85	60
Expenses (in '000 ₹)	35	90	70	40	95	40	60	80	80	50

Obtain the least square regression line of expenses on sales. Estimate expenses if sales are ₹ 75000.

30. A panel of examiners A and B assessed 7 candidates independently and awarded the following marks.

Candidate	1	2	3	4	5	6	7
Marks By A	40	34	28	30	44	38	31
Marks by B	32	39	26	30	38	34	28

Eighth candidate was awarded 36 marks by examiner A. Using appropriate regression line, estimate the marks awarded by the examiner B.

31. The failure of a certain electronic device is suspected to increase linearly with its temperature. Fit a least square regression line through the following data to predict failure rate.

Temperature °F	55	65	75	85	95	105
Failure rate	0	3	7	10	11	11

Also predict the failure rate at 70°C.

32. Samples of soils are collected from various depths below ground level and tested in the laboratory to determine their shear strength. The collected field data are given below :

Depth (m)	2	3	4	5	6	7
Shear strength	14	20	32	39	42	56

Find the Karl Pearson's coefficient of correlation between depth and shear strength. Interpret the result. Also predict shear strength at depth 10 m.

33. A departmental store gives in-service training to its salesmen followed by a test to consider whether it should terminate the services of any of the salesman who does not qualify in the test. The following data give the test scores and sales made by ten salesmen during a certain period.

Test score	14	19	24	21	28	22	15	20	19	20
Sales ('00 ₹)	31	36	48	37	50	45	33	41	39	40

Calculate the coefficient of correlation between the test scores and sales. Does it indicate that the termination of services of the low test scores is justified ? If the firm wants a minimum sales volume of ₹ 3000, what is the minimum test score that will ensure continuation of the services ? Also obtain the standard error of regression estimate.

34. Suppose x is rainfall in suitable units and y is level of rusting of iron material used for construction measured in suitable units ?

x	43	45	59	21	80
y	6	7	8	1	10

Estimate y if x = 30 using regression analysis.

F. Regression (Summarized Data) :

35. Given the regression equations : $3x + 2y - 26 = 0$ and $6x + y - 31 = 0$.

    find : (i) means of x and y. (ii) correlation between x and y.

36. If the regression equation of Y on X is $2X + 3Y = 1$, obtain the regression coefficient of Y on X.

37. Given : $\bar{X} = 80$, $\bar{Y} = 50$, $\sigma_x = 15$, $\sigma_y = 10$ and $r = -0.4$. Find line of regression of X on Y. Also estimate X when Y = 60.

38. The correlation coefficient between two variables X and Y is 0.6. If the means of two series and 13 and 27 respectively and standard deviations are 1.5 and 2 respectively, find the regression line of Y on X.

39. Given the following data :

	Rainfall (in inches)	Yield (in quintals)
Mean	27	40
Standard Deviation	3	6

Correlation coefficient = 0.8. Estimate the yield when rainfall is 29 inches.

40. Following is the information about the bivariate frequency distribution :
$n = 20, \ \sum x = 80, \ \sum y = 40, \ \sum x^2 = 1680, \ \sum y^2 = 320, \ \sum xy = 480.$
(i) Obtain the regression lines.
(ii) Estimate y for x = 3 and estimate x for y = 3.

41. You are given the following information about two variables x and y.

$n = 10, \ \sum x^2 = 385, \ \sum y^2 = 192, \ \overline{x} = 5.5, \ \overline{y} = 4, \ \sum xy = 185.$
Find (i) Regression line of y on x. (ii) regression line of x on y.
(iii) Standard error of regression estimate of y on x.

42. Compute regression coefficients from the following data :
$n = 8, \ \sum(x - 45) = -40, \ \sum(x - 45)^2 = 4400, \ \sum(y - 150) = 280,$
$\sum(y - 150)^2 = 167432, \ \sum(x - 45)(y - 150) = 21680.$

43. For a bivariate data we have $\overline{X} = 53, \ \overline{Y} = 28, \ b_{yx} = -1.5, \ b_{xy} = -0.2.$

Find (i) correlation coefficient between X and Y.

(ii) estimate of y for x = 60.

(iii) estimate of x for y = 30.

44. The regression equations are $3x - y - 5 = 0$ and $4x - 3y = 0$. Find

(i) Arithmetic mean of x and y.

(ii) Coefficient variations of x and y, if $\sigma_x = 2$.

(iii) Correlation coefficient between x and y.

45. The following results were obtained from records of age (X) and systolic blood pressure (Y), of a group of 10 men :

	X	Y
Mean	53	142
Variance	130	165

$\sum(x - \overline{x})(y - \overline{y}) = 1220$

Find the appropriate regression equation and use it to estimate the blood pressure of a man with age 45 years.

46. The two regression equations of variables x and y are $x = 19.13 - 0.87 \ y$ and $y = 11.64 - 0.5 \ x$. Find $\overline{x}, \overline{y}$ and Corr (x, y).

47. The regression equations are given by $8x - 10y + 66 = 0$ and $40x - 18y - 214 = 0$. Find $\bar{x}, \bar{y}$, Corr (x, y). Also find σ_y given that $\sigma_x = 3$.

48. Given the following data :

	Marks in Mathematics	Marks in English
Mean	80	50
Standard Deviation	15	10

The correlation coefficient between marks in Mathematics and English is – 0.4. Estimate the marks in Mathematics obtained by student who scored 60 marks in English.

Answers 5.2

1. 0.7647	2. – 0.9673	3. 1
4. 0.9593	5. 0.95	6. 0.7804
7. 0.7784	8. 0.9207	9. 0
10. 0.9747	11. 9	12. 5
13. 0.6030	14. 0.9955	15. – 0.9395
16. – 0.7	17. 0.8888	18. 0.8566
19. 0.6825	20. 13.3333	

21. (i) and (iv) – 0.8, (ii), (iii), (iv) 0.8

22. 0.5952	23. 0.5714	24. – 0.2571
25. 0.8857	26. 0.1030	27. 0.1857

28. $y = - 0.65x + 11.9$, Estimate of $y = 8.65$

29. $y = 1.01289x + 2.2135$, Estimated expenses = ₹ 78180

30. 33

31. $y = 0.2343x - 11.7423$, Estimated failure rate = 4.6571

32. $r = 0.9863$, $y = 8.2286x - 3.0286$, Estimated shear strength = 79.2571

33. $r = 0.9425$, Justified, $x = 0.6156 - 4.4241$, Estimate of score = 14.04
    Standard error of estimate = 0.454.

34. $y = 0.1471x - 0.8966$, $\hat{y} = 3.5167$

35. $\bar{x} = 4, \bar{y} = 7, r = - 0.5$

36. – 2/3

37. $x = - 0.6y + 110$, Estimate of $x = 74$

38. $y = 0.8x + 16.6$

39. 43.2 quintals

40. (i) $3x = 4y + 4$, $17y = 4x + 18$, (ii) $x = 5.3333$, $y = 1.7647$

41. (i) $y = - 0.4242x + 6.3331$, (ii) $x = - 1.09375y + 9.875$, (iii) 0.4630.

42. $b_{yx} = 5.4952$, $b_{xy} = 0.1484$.

43. $r = -0.5477$, $x = 52.6$, $y = 17.5$.

44. (i) $\bar{x} = 3$, $\bar{y} = 4$, (ii) C.V. (X) = 66.6667%, C.V. (Y) = 100%, (iii) r = 0.6667.

45. $y = 0.833x + 97.851$, 135.336.

46. $\bar{x} = 15.9335$, $\bar{y} = 3.6726$, $r = -0.6593$

47. $\bar{x} = 13$, $\bar{y} = 17$, $\rho = 0.6$, $\sigma_y = 2$.

48. 74

Objective Questions

1. If $X + Y$ = constant then state the Corr (X, Y) giving reasons.

2. If $X \propto Y$ state the Corr (X, Y) giving reasons.

3. If $X \propto \dfrac{1}{Y}$ state the Corr (X, Y) giving reasons.

4. If Corr (X, Y) ± 1 state the nature of regression lines.

5. If Corr (X, Y) = 0 state the nature of regression lines.

6. If Corr (X, Y) = 0.8 then find the Corr (2X, 2Y), Corr (X, –Y), Corr (X/2, Y/3).

7. State the Corr (X, X).

8. State the Corr (X, – X).

9. If $\sigma_x = \sigma_y = 2$, Cov (X, Y) = 0.8, find Corr (X, Y).

10. Give examples of :

    (i)   uncorrelated variables

    (ii) positively correlated variables

    (iii) negatively correlated variables.

11. If Corr (X, Y) = 0 the find regression coefficients.

12. If Corr (X, Y) = 1, $b_{yx} = 2$ find b_{xy}.

13. If Corr (X, Y) = 1, $\sigma_x = \sigma_y$ then show that $b_{yx} = b_{xy}$.

14. Explain why regression coefficients have same algebraic signs.

15. State the point of intersection of regression lines.

16. Find the rank correlation if :

Rank X	1	2	3	4	5
Rank Y	1	2	3	4	5

17. Find the rank correlation if :

Rank X	1	2	3	4	5
Rank Y	5	4	3	2	1

Answers

1. Corr $(X, Y) = -1$ 2. Cor $(X, Y) = \pm 1$ 3. Corr $(X, Y) = 0$

4. Lines will coincide   5. Lines will be parallel

6. Corr $(2X, 2Y) = 0.8$, Corr $(X, -Y) = -0.8$, Corr $(X/2, Y/3) = 0.8$

7. Corr $(X, X) = 1$ 8. Corr $(X, -X) = -1$ 9. Corr $(X, Y) = 0.4$

10. $b_{yx} = b_{xy} = 0$ 12. $b_{xy} = \dfrac{1}{2}$ 15. $(\bar{X}, \bar{Y})$

16. $R = 1$ 17. $R = -1$

Instructions :
1. All questions are compulsory.
2. Figures to the right indicate full marks.
3. Use of statistical tables, logarithmic tables and calculator is allowed.
4. Symbols have their usual meanings.
5. Graph papers will be supplied on requires.

1. **Choose the correct alternative for the following :**   (1 × 10 = 10)

   (i)   The type of sampling approach where each person in the population has an equal chance of being selected is best described as :
      (a) Census   (b) Stratified random sampling
      (c) Simple random sampling   (d) Purposive Sampling.

   (ii) Box plot helps to judge the
      (a) Spread   (b) Symmetry
      (c) Central value   (d) All the above

   (iii) Which of the following is not a central value ?
      (a) Arithmetic mean   (b) Median
      (c) Mode   (d) Standard deviation

   (iv) Karl Pearson's coefficient of correlation lies between
      (a) 0 to 1   (b) – 1 to 1
      (c) 0 to ∞   (d) – ∞ to ∞

   (v)   The standard deviation of 5, 5, 5, 5, 5 is
      (a) 0   (b) 5
      (c) $\sqrt{5}$ (d) 1

   (vii) If $\sum (X - 5) = 20$ for 10 observations, then the arithmetic mean is
      (a) 2   (b) 5
      (c) 7   (d) 0

   (viii) Which one of the following is a drawback of mean ?
      (a) It is rigidly defined
      (b) It cannot be obtained graphically
      (c) It is capable of manipulations
      (d) It is most stable average

   (ix) Median of discrete series is
      (a) middle most value   (b) most frequent value
      (c) lest frequency value   (d) largest value

   (x)   Suppose the cricket players are ranked on the performance in test series. The average performance of players will be given by ...... as average.
      (a) arithmetic mean   (b) median
      (c) mode   (d) quartiles

2. **Attempt any two of the following :**   (5 × 2 = 10)
   (a) Explain the terms will illustration : (i) Regression (ii) Correlation.
   (b) Calculate the mean and median for the following series of observations :
   52, 45, 60, 53, 48, 65, 42, 45, 60.
   (c) Calculate the standard deviation of the following data :
   25, 40, 10, 05, 30, 95, 15, 25, 80.

3. **Attempt any two of the following :**   (5 × 2 = 10)
   (a) Describe advantages of sampling method over census method.
   (b) Following is the frequency distribution of number of students according to marks scored in a certain examination :

Marks	0-19	20-39	40-59	60-79	80-99
No. of Students	18	36	34	22	15

   (i)   State the type of classification.
   (ii) Obtain the class boundaries of the second class.
   (iii) Obtain the class width of the third class.
   (iv) Obtain the class mark of the fourth class.
   (v) How many students are getting the marks less than 59 ?
   (c) Calculate coefficient of variation (C.V.) for the following data :

Class	0-10	10-20	20-30	30-40	40-50	50-60
Frequency	5	9	15	21	6	4

4. **Attempt any one of the following :**   (10 × 1 = 10)
   (a) (i) Describe what is tabulation. Draw rough sketch of table and explain the parts of table.
   (ii) The means of two samples of sizes 50 and 100 are 40 and 25 respectively and standard deviations are 10 and 8 respectively. Obtain the combined standard deviation.
   (b) (i) Define Spearman's rank correlation coefficient. State its merits and demerits.
   (ii) The following data relates to ranks given by two judges in a contest.

Sr. No. of Candidate	1	2	3	4	5	6	7	8	9	10
Rank by Judge A	10	5	6	1	2	3	4	7	9	8
Rank of Judge B	5	6	9	2	8	7	3	4	10	1

   Calculate rank correlation coefficient from the above data and comment on it.

5. **Attempt any one of the following :**   (10 × 1 = 10)
   (a) Following are the values of import and export of finished goods in suitable units.

Export	10	11	14	14	20	22	16	12	18	13
Import	12	14	15	16	21	16	21	15	16	14

   Calculate Karl Pearsons correlation coefficient between export and import values.
   (b) Calculate Median and mean deviation about median. Also find the coefficient of mean deviation about median for the following frequency distribution :

Class	5-15	15-25	25-35	35-45	45-55
Frequency	5	15	20	15	5